Hot in Magnolia

Cupcakes & Kisses

Hot in Magnolia
Cupcakes & Kisses

Minette Lauren

Published Internationally by Minette Lauren
Magnolia, TX USA
minettelauren.com

PRINT ISBN 978-1-7340968-1-1
EBOOK ISBN 978-1-7340968-0-4

This is a work of fiction. Names, characters, places and incidents are either the prod-
uct of the author's imagination or are used fictitiously, and any resemblance to
any person or persons, living or dead, events or locales is entirely coincidental.

Acknowledgments

I would like to thank:

Amy Sharp, Grammar Queen, for her editing guidance
and helping to make this story shine.

Joanna D'Angelo, Cheer Team Captain, for editing, polishing
and coaching me through the publishing process.

Cristina Donoso, Website Designer Extraordinaire,
all your nights at Bubbles are on me.

April Stevens, most talented BFF, thanks for
your shaping opinions of this novel.

The real town of Magnolia, Texas and the surrounding area, for
its beauty, hospitality and kind inspiration. (I hope no one minds
that I elaborated on shops and restaurants that don't yet exist).

My very real Mr. Perfect who continues to
encourage and inspire me to write.

In memory of my mother and best friend.
Thank you for giving me a life full of love and inspiration.
Your strength, intelligence and compassion for others, lives on.

Chapter 1

Melvina Banks was put down by vanity—literally.

She'd flipped her hair down, then up, while blow-drying herself into a heated frenzy. As a result, she lay on the cold tile of her bathroom, moaning in pain. That last toss and swish was her back's final undoing. Tucked into flesh-colored Spanks, she lay on the teal-and-white-checked floor. Small bullets of sweat beaded on her freshly painted face.

Hell, there goes my makeup.

Patting her hands on the floor around her, she searched for her cell phone. Hoping she'd knocked it from the corner of the sink in her fall from grace, she winced as another spasm shot through her lower back. Then she remembered it was in her bedroom on the bed. Probably lost beneath the mound of clothes she'd plucked from her closet while trying to decide what to wear.

If I die here, they'll eventually discover my lifeless form gripping my roller brush for all eternity.

She wished she'd accepted Mona's invitation to set her up on a blind date. At least the poor fellow, whoever he was, would be able to hear her scream from outside and call for help.

Instead, she had shaken her head, saying she didn't need the additional complication in her life. Besides, sitting across from a stranger, making awkward small talk while he silently judged if she were worthy enough for him to pay for her dinner, was not Melvina's idea of a romantic night out.

She'd had enough of those dates in her twenties and thirties to know they never turned out great. She usually ended up paying for her own meal and sometimes her date's dinner as well. She was embarrassed to admit she was left with the check more than once.

Melvina tried to push herself up from the cool floor and gasped as a lightning bolt of pain shot along her spine and down to her hip. She was due at the Magnolia Ladies dinner in twenty minutes, and it took fifteen minutes to drive to town. It wouldn't be the worst thing in the world to miss a Magnolia Blossom Ladies League dinner, but she had a role in the actual event. She was meant to introduce Cecilia Lockwood, reigning president, so that Cecilia could then introduce their esteemed guest for the annual fundraiser.

This year's proceeds were allocated to the construction of another fire station in the growing community of Magnolia, a blossoming suburb of Houston. The guest speaker would be none other than Riley James Nash, renowned chef and area native, recently making his big splash on the Food Network. He was the owner and head chef of Braised, the hottest new restaurant in Houston, and there were rumors two other locations were opening in New York and San Francisco.

Ah, to be a Food Network star....

If that happened, she would be able to open her dream cupcake shop, maybe even expand to other places. On many occasions, she'd imagined building a cupcake mini-empire, including big cities like San Francisco. She'd flown there once for a cupcake convention and had fallen in love with the small town of Half Moon Bay. With a population of only ten thousand residents, Half Moon Bay was more her speed than San Francisco proper. But the folks who visited the small coastal town on the weekends would provide plenty of business for her booming imaginary bakery.

Unfortunately, she would never own her own business if she couldn't make the right connections and get someone to back her dream. A dream that wouldn't materialize if she didn't get off the floor and make it to that dinner. Riley Nash could very well be her lucky lotto ticket to owning her own bakery.

She placed her hand on the white cabinet door and slid herself across the tiles, squeaking again with pain. Putting both of her heels as close to her buttocks as possible, she pushed hard with a heaving grunt and then repeated the motion several times until she'd slid herself into the bedroom to the foot of her bed. Reaching up, she fumbled her hand around on the mattress and tugged. A mound of clothes showered her, and a button on one of the dresses tangled in her freshly brushed, long blonde hair. She tried to swim free of the many layers of fabric, blowing out her breath hard when a scarf floated over her face.

"Ow," she complained, finding the loop in her hair to release the oversized button. The sultry beat of the old but catchy *Junk in the Trunk*, by The

Black Eyed Peas, blared from above, taunting her rather curvy rump, currently stuck on the bedroom floor. Melvina had chuckled when her friend, Mona Calhoun, had downloaded the tune onto her cellphone the last time they had cocktails at Bubbles.

Melvina imagined her skinny, small-bottomed friend wiggling around on her own front porch, centered in the middle of High Valley Estates Golf Community. Mona was a trust fund baby who was still spoiled rotten at the age of forty-one and was one of the first people who'd bought in the elite new housing community.

Some of the stauncher neighbors had complained about Mona's lively paint choices for her mini-mansion and the amount of time she sipped margaritas while watching Louis, the lawn guy, trim the hedges. More than likely, the residents were upset about the laughter coming from inside Mona's house after the lawn work was finished. Louis was a twenty-something attractive Latino and Mona was almost twenty years his senior…but age never stopped Mona.

She often bragged about her cougar status, telling anyone who'd listen, "As long as they're of legal age, handsome is handsome." Right along with, "What's good for the goose…."

Magnolia, Texas, had seen a lot of recent growth. Houston's high-flying oil tycoons had bought up land and built new housing developments for the increased population. New immigrants and people around the country were flocking to the beautiful area daily. The sudden growth was the reason Melvina wanted to open her own bakery. This was the time, and it was now or never.

"Damn it." Melvina swiped at the mattress, pulling the quilt and its entire contents down on her head. Her cat yowled as it flew through the air, landing on Melvina's tummy. Melvina's answering yowl echoed around the room as Leo dug his claws into her soft flesh, using it as a springboard to skedaddle to safety. Wincing with pain from the scratch marks she knew she would sport for a week, Melvina sifted through the pile of discarded dresses until she found her smart phone. Of course, it was Mona trying to video chat with her. She groaned and slid her finger over the glass screen. They had been friends since the first grade, so fortunately or *unfortunately*, Mona had seen much worse when it came to Melvina.

"What are you doing?" Mona's lips made a wide oh, resembling the goldfish in Melvina's turtle tank. The heavy red lip liner accentuated the minimal flesh, making her lips appear puffier than they were, but she wasn't fooling anyone. Mona had been dubbed Skinny Lips in high school by Martin Holley, the captain of the basketball team, and she had been self-conscious of their minimal contours ever since.

"What does it look like I'm doing?" Melvina huffed out, frustrated at her incapacitated state.

Mona's brows twitched, but her forehead remained smooth thanks to her regular trips to her cosmetic surgeon for Botox injections. "Do you know what time it is? The dinner is in fifteen minutes."

"I know, I know—" Melvina took a deep breath and tried to sit up. Groaning again, she slumped back to the floor. "I need your help."

"What's wrong?" Mona fretted.

"My back!" Melvina moaned again.

"Okay, okay, I'm on my way."

The phone screen danced around, flashing images of jangling car keys, doors opening and closing, Louis's bronzed, shirtless figure as he trimmed the hedges, Mrs. Parker's disapproving stance from across the street, the sunset over the golf course, and Mona's fancy, hot pink pumps.

"Wait!" Melvina called out. "I need you to go to the dinner without me and introduce Celia. I'll be there eventually, but I won't be there in time." Melvina paused while Mona started her tirade of why this wouldn't do and insisted on coming to help.

"I'm going to call Pop," Melvina said. "He'll send Eli over to help me up."

"Are you sure?" Mona asked. "I can be there in five minutes."

"Yes. Don't worry, I'll be there," Melvina assured her friend. "My back is a little tweaked, but once I get up and take an ibuprofen, it will all be okay."

I hope.

"Alright, but if you don't show up in thirty minutes, I'm sending out the fire department, and you know I will. Most of them will be at the dinner and Manny would just love to help you, I'm sure."

"Don't you say anything, Mona or I'll dig out the yearbook!"

Mona gasped. "You wouldn't dare!"

"I would!" Melvina declared. The eighth-grade yearbook featured a thirteen-year-old Mona with a mouth full of metal braces and an acne breakout that rivaled Mount Vesuvius. "I swear to God, I will print it in the 'Ladies Journal' next month," she warned.

Manny Owens was Melvina's secret crush for just about most of her life. He was now the chief of the Magnolia Fire Department and a widower since his wife died two years ago. Melvina knew she didn't stand a chance with the hottest bachelor in town, and everyone knew Cecilia had dibs on him anyway. They weren't an item yet, but Celia had earmarked him for her personal use, and every woman in the county who wanted to keep her hair knew it.

"You don't fight fair," was all Melvina heard before Mona hung up. She sighed with relief and blew at a stray lock of hair that lapped across her forehead.

Thank God I can at least stand up to Mona.

Chapter 2

"Pop, I need help. Can you send Eli over?"

"Is Humphrey tied up to the neighbor's Chihuahua again?" he asked.

"No, Pop. It's my back."

"I'm on my way."

"No way. Your back is worse than mine! Look, I'm okay, but I tweaked it and it—oh, I'll save you the details, but long story short, I'm fine. I just need Eli to come help. Door's open, just tell him to come on in."

After a few more minutes of assuring her father that she was fine, and that all she needed was a hand, she hung up. It took ten minutes for Eli to make it from her father's café to her home. In that time, she wiggled a tank dress over her head and shimmied it down her sausage-wrapped figure so that her brother couldn't poke fun at her Spanks when he arrived.

Eli was five years her junior and still acted twelve sometimes. He'd applauded and cheered her when she'd lost the bulk of the weight she'd battled all her life. Melvina wanted to be thin, like the pictures of her mother, who she resembled.

Images of Rayna Louise Banks were sprinkled within the many photo frames of her father's house. Her mother had been a Miss Magnolia Blossom in 1976, the year she married Salvatore Elijah Banks. Melvina's memories of her mother consisted mostly of her waving goodbye as Rayna Louise drove away to an audition—plays, TV commercials, even the ballet once, though Rayna had had no formal training in dance.

Meanwhile, it was Mona's mom who'd helped Melvina learn to print her name, make a construction paper turkey at Thanksgiving, and introduced her to the world of baking cupcakes. The sugary treats made them all happier after the sticky glue of Rayna's empty promises washed away.

She'd made her exit just a few years after Eli's birth. Not happy in the role of a housewife, Rayna was bored. The shimmer of first love wore off after Melvina's birth, and from what others said, Eli was an attempt to patch up the marriage. Pop was too busy trying to make ends meet to notice Rayna's depression pooling into movie star aspirations. He'd worked under the café's previous owner for many years before buying the greasy spoon.

Without a job, Rayna watched too many soap operas and read too many romance novels to be happy breast feeding and changing dirty diapers. As soon as she'd lost the baby weight and had squirreled away enough grocery money to buy a one-way ticket out of there, Rayna was on the first Greyhound to California, or at least that's what the scribbled note had said.

For a long time after her mother's departure, they were a sad bunch. To make her father happy, Melvina perfected the art of baking. Her love of cookies and cakes helped pack on the pounds during puberty. Unfortunately, it also made her a wallflower at every dance and awkward with boys. No one ever asked her to Homecoming or Prom. On the other hand, no one ever picked on Melvina, because she baked cupcakes for the class on a regular basis. Her gift for baking, coupled with her being the smartest and funniest girl in school, helped her through those difficult teenage years.

But it was hard to be overweight when your mother was an infamous beauty. In the absence of Rayna, Mona and her mother had always been there. Melvina had learned to cope with life through mixing, baking, icing and putting sprinkles on top.

After two years at Jen's Jazzercise with dual enrollment at Jim's Gym, located in a souped-up, air-conditioned metal building next to the Cowboy Baptist Church, Melvina had shed enough pounds to gain a few open-mouthed stares and whistles of appreciation, but she mostly equated the stares to shock. She had shed half her body weight and transformed her plus-size frame into a curvy, hourglass shape of a more confident woman.

The extra pounds had been hard to lose and harder still to keep off. Along the way, close friends were always quick to remind her what a beautiful face she had. Mona had even sent Melvina's picture to a modeling agency for large ladies without telling her. Melvina didn't talk to her best friend for a month after the very awkward phone call from the agency. She didn't need affirmation that she was pretty enough to grace the pages of a magazine like her mother, she just wanted to be a healthy weight.

Owning her own bakery was the real catalyst for getting her life together. All the sweat she'd poured out on the elliptical machine, all the grunting she'd emitted during sessions with her trainer, and all the sighs she breathed out over the delectable desserts she'd resisted were all for her benefit and not to impress others.

As for relationships—her ideal man would appreciate her no matter what size she wore, and support her dream no matter how challenging.

At forty, she was tired of running Pop's Café and wanted a legacy of her own. Her inspiration for her recent weight loss had been kick-started by a series of videos she'd watched over and over again. The narrator in "Take Charge of Your Future" and "Become a Better You" convinced her that she first had to control her body before she could control her success. She was still in charge of all the baked goods at Pop's, but she had learned to control her impulse to sample every batch. The recipes she used were ingrained in her memory, and she assured herself that her loaves of pumpernickel, wheat, and rye tasted exquisite whether she sampled them or not. The customers coming in daily were testimony to that. Her new view on dieting had led to an abundance of sugar-free, gluten-free, and other healthy treats that were making Pop's Café eternally busy.

"What in the world?" Eli's usually smooth Texas drawl came out an octave higher with unsuppressed surprise. "Melvina Rayanne Banks, what have you done to your room?"

She hated when her brother used her full name. It was bad enough to be named after her Grandpa Melvin, but the Rayanne was just a sore reminder of the mother who used to call her by her middle name.

"Dang, Mel, don't you ever clean around here?"

She lifted her arm from the pile of clothes like a red mailbox flag. "Don't even get me started, Eli," she snorted with a mixture of laughter and agitation. "If I tinkle myself after all I've been through this afternoon, I will not make your favorite gluten-free brownies for a month."

She doubted her brother was gluten intolerant, but as she had packed on the pounds after her mother's abandonment, Eli had become an exercise and health food junky. His fit body was drooled over by most of the Magnolia ladies. This year gluten was evil, and she could already see that sugar was soon to be on the chopping block when he could convince himself to actually live without it. Melvina had survived the fat-free craze, the calorie-counting phase, and now the gluten-free world of Eli. Her talent for whipping up delicious treats that were low calorie, low fat, and low carb was what made her everyone's favorite baked-goods gal.

"Geez, Mel, looks like your closet exploded. Are you havin' trouble deciding what to wear?" The earnest concern in her brother's voice melted her heart. He had been her personal cheerleader her entire life, and certainly through her battle of the bulge. Eli never missed an opportunity to tell her she was beautiful, even before she'd lost the weight. He was a peach and she could never stay mad at him for long. Bending down, he wrapped his arms around her from behind and gently helped her to her feet, dusting off a piece of lint from her shoulder when he set her from him.

Melvina sighed with relief, placing her manicured nails on her lower back for added support. "I gained back five pounds after bake sale week," she said with a sigh. "Maybe I should have gotten all my workouts in and I wouldn't have had this unfortunate incident." She gave a stalwart nod, more to comfort herself than Eli. "It's just a minor setback, and I will lose these pesky five pounds this month."

He nodded, reassuringly. "You'll do it, Mel. I have faith in you."

"At least I figured out what to wear while I was sprawled on the floor." She smiled.

"You're beautiful Mel. Please don't wear that gunnysack you reserve for special occasions. It's time you let the Magnolia Blossoms see the real you."

"Eli, that is the only thing that looks good on me right now and I'm already late," she said as she stepped around him and hurried to the bathroom to grab the ibuprofen from the medicine cabinet. She winced as she walked, keeping her hands firmly on her lower back.

When she returned, Eli held up an emerald green evening gown. Its silky material and simple cut whispered elegance.

"That's not mine." She paused, fingering the silk strap. "It's Rayna's." They hadn't called their mother "Mom" since she'd walked out on them all those years ago.

"It doesn't matter who it belonged to. It would look beautiful on you."

"It's not my size."

"Then why do you have it?" Eli arched a brow.

"I don't know. It was in my closet when I left home, and I suppose I packed it up by mistake. Look, I don't have time for this trip down memory lane, and I'm not in the mood for a therapy session either. Not tonight."

Eli shook his head in disbelief as he sifted through the pile of clothes on the floor. "Well, how about this one?" He held up a burgundy cocktail dress. It had a tight bodice and mermaid cut skirt.

Melvina's cheeks heated.

He had to go and find that one at the bottom of the pile.

10

She'd bought it last week for the dinner and it'd thrilled her when she'd tried it on. Sparkle Babble had the best choices for eveningwear in the county, and Mona had talked her into buying the slinky designer dress. But when she'd tried it on again last night, she just couldn't muster the guts to wear the body-hugging dress. It was meant for some swank actress hitting the red carpet, not her and her extra five pounds.

Not with all those eyes staring at me.

"Melvina, if you don't wear this pretty dress, I will personally follow you to the dinner and tell the fire chief he has started a fire in your pants."

Melvina grabbed the dress and glared at him. "Ha, ha. Do you know just how corny you are?" Without another protest, she went back into the bathroom and slammed the door. She didn't have time to reason. She was late and if she didn't hurry, she would miss seeing Riley Nash.

Chapter 3

The four ibuprofen she'd gulped down with a Diet Coke didn't do much to help the pinched nerve in her back. Grandma Edna had warned her that once she turned forty, everything would go kaput. Melvina now had to wear glasses to drive and to read. She could see great as long as nothing was too close or too far away. She had managed to jump the weight hurdle to land on the ladies-who-wear-glasses train, and now she was on the back-out-of-whack bus for the second time this year. Her chiropractor said it was all the time she spent hunched over a bowl of muffin batter, kneading bread, and hauling heavy racks of baked goods.

She wanted her own bakery, so the over-the-hill ailments would have to wait. Maybe Mona would have something in her medicine bag to get her through the night.

Melvina parked her car under the awning over the circular drive. All the guests would have arrived by now, so it wasn't like she was blocking the way. She wobbled on the strappy silver heels that sparkled in the chandelier lights of the hotel lobby. She might look snazzy in her new designer dress, but if she walked any stiffer, someone would check her rear to see if a stick was protruding.

As she made the turn down the last corridor, she spotted Mona walking swiftly toward her. She heard a round of applause as Mona gave her the hurry-up wave.

"He's just gone up. You haven't missed anything except Celia's boring accolade about her cake-bake ribbon." Mona rolled her eyes. "Everyone knows your red velvet was way better, and besides, her daddy was one of the judges. Celia left that jellybean in the center of her carrot cake on purpose. Everyone in Magnolia knows her affinity for green jellybeans."

Celia's boasting was the least of Melvina's concerns at the moment. She tottered behind Mona into the grand ballroom and skirted her way around the white cloth-covered tables.

Damn, I missed dinner.

Her empty stomach growled in protest. The tables boasted what looked like a chocolate mousse cheesecake with whipped cream and raspberries dotting the side. The fire chief nodded at Melvina, and she smiled in return. Mona elbowed her and Melvina winced, biting her lip.

"That bad?" Mona's stage whisper earned her a glare from Celia, who was seated at the next table. Mona made an ugly face after the strawberry-blonde woman turned her attention back to the stage.

Melvina groaned softly and murmured, "And then some. Got anything in your bag stronger than Advil?"

Mona groped beneath her seat, grabbing a silver sequined bag. Pulling out a Pez dispenser with a piglet head, she popped out a pink pill and set it next to Melvina's wine glass. A moment later, a waiter came out of nowhere and filled their glasses to the rim with white wine.

Picking up the pill, Melvina thought about the time Mona's mother took them to a Pez store at the mall. She had bought them each a dispenser and a package of candy refills. Melvina made a Pez-filled cupcake that admittedly looked fun but tasted terrible. Heck, she'd had many a failed recipe along the way before she'd learned to perfect her baking style. She popped the pill into her mouth—the bitter taste on her tongue warned her the pill wasn't Pez candy. Melvina grabbed the wine glass and took several large gulps. Droplets of wine escaped the corners of her mouth, and she dabbed at them with a napkin, trying to avoid splashing the liquid onto the maroon satin of her gown.

Melvina tried to focus on the handsome chef speaking at the podium.

"…and I also would like to thank the firefighting men and women of this wonderful community for putting their lives on the line every day to ensure the safety of others," he went on. "It is because of you that we are gathered here to raise funds for the much-needed new firehouse. Magnolia is a growing community, and with growth comes responsibility. I am honored to have helped oversee the preparation of tonight's dinner. I hope you will enjoy my contribution to this occasion, and I appreciate each and every one of you who donated here tonight. The plates weren't cheap," Riley Nash said in a sexy, southern drawl. He grinned, as laughter filled the ballroom over his quip.

It was a one-thousand-dollar-a-plate event. Luckily, Melvina had received a deep-discount rate because she'd coordinated the engagement and baked cupcake baskets to donate for the silent auction. Mona had been eligible for the discount rate as well, since she was technically Melvina's "plus one."

Melvina had paid for their dinners with the second-place prize money she'd won last month at the cake auction. She wanted to contribute more, but her finances were tight at the moment. Not to mention she'd donated a lot of time planning the event along with all the other volunteer work she did. As treasurer of the Blossoms, Melvina was considered Celia's "right-hand man."

She brushed off her guilty feelings over the discounted tickets.

You deserve to be here as much as anyone else.

Riley put his hand up to quiet the crowd. "Also, I want to acknowledge the little lady responsible for planning this dinner tonight and innocently telling my brother she didn't know what she was going to do to entertain you people."

Celia started to stand when Riley announced, "Let's give a warm round of applause to Miss Melvina Banks. My brother swears she makes the best cupcakes in all of Texas, so make sure you bid high tonight on those delicious baskets."

Celia sat back down and stared daggers in Melvina's direction. The president of the Magnolia Blossoms offered a light golf clap and a stiff smile.

Melvina blinked in confusion as Mona elbowed her. "Get up," Mona hissed.

Whatever Mona had given her had made Melvina's back feel better, but her legs were like noodles. She gripped the table and stood nodding politely at the other guests in the ballroom. Smiling in the general direction of the super-hot man-chef who called her cupcakes the best in Texas, she gave a little wave, not knowing what else to do. She knew her baked treats were good, but praise and affirmation were always the sweetest reward.

"And what a lovely lady she is," Riley said with a wink before turning to address the attendees. "Everyone enjoy the rest of your dessert. My brother Ran Nash and the Tomball Cats are going to start the night off with a little music. It would be my honor if Miss Banks would join me for the first dance of the evening."

Melvina felt Mona pop her on her derriere with her dinner napkin. "You go, girl." Mona pulled her chair away and gave her a gentle shove in the direction of the handsome man in the black tux.

Riley placed the microphone in the stand and walked toward Melvina with a beaming smile that exuded confidence. A warm feeling of ease washed over her, and she was surprised at how light she felt—like she was floating on a cloud.

"May I?" It was a redundant question but seemed appropriate nevertheless as Riley extended his hand to the woman standing before him in the middle of the dance floor. Melvina Banks gave him a glorious smile.

His brother Raphe had told him about the lady at the café who was the sweetest thing he'd met this side of Louisiana, but he hadn't mentioned how beautiful she was. Melvina's long blonde hair shone in the candescent light of the chandeliers sparkling overhead—someone took it upon themselves to dim the light before he could determine the exact shade of her green eyes. Her skin was smooth, and she wore a gown that pushed her breasts together, distracting him for a moment as his eyes slid down to his feet.

He wasn't the world's best dancer, but he could cut a rug when the time called for it. His mother had insisted on dance classes a few years back when one of the country club hens decided to throw an annual family gala.

He was in high school and had protested at first until he met the private instructor his mother had hired. Leena had taught him more than how to dance, and for that, he was grateful. She had taught him about sex, love, and the difference between the two. He thought he had loved Leena. The dance instructor was gentle with him, and he didn't have any scars from their parting, just sweet memories from his seventeenth summer.

Melvina's eyes glinted and she lifted her chin in a slight challenge. "I'm a big girl," she said simply.

Riley tried not to let his jaw drop. He cleared his throat. "I'm sorry—" he began, wanting to apologize. Had he been that obvious in his admiring appraisal?

"It's okay," she interrupted him, holding up her hand. "I'm sure you're used to skinny model types like Celia. I won't hold you to it if you don't want to dance." She glanced around the room, clearly looking for an escape even though every eyeball in the room was focused on them.

Shoot! His face flushed with heat. Melvina had it all wrong! Yes, her breasts were voluptuous, but he was staring because she was a knockout.

"Are you crazy? And miss out on dancing with the prettiest lady at the ball?" Riley knew he was laying the charm on thick, but she really was the loveliest woman he'd ever seen. He loved the way her dress hugged her curves, and if it wasn't politically incorrect to say so, he'd tell her he never trusted women who only ate salad.

He also knew all about Celia and her type. He'd done some digging and found out she usually took full credit for all the Magnolia Ladies' fundraisers and events. Riley's younger brother Raphe, who was a firefighter in Houston, had made the initial connection with Melvina. Riley had gotten some of his best recipes from the brotherhood of firemen. Those hardworking men graced his kitchen the first Sunday of every month for the barbecue he hosted. Firemen really knew how to cook. And, they appreciated good food.

A friend had stopped by Raphe's firehouse with a pink box full of cupcakes. Raphe asked about the lady who'd baked the delicious sweet treats, and his friend told him about Melvina baking for her father's café, and how much she did for the community as a whole. When visiting their brother Ran in nearby Tomball, Raphe stopped by the café to buy cupcakes to take back to the station—he also got a chance to meet the cupcake lady herself. He overheard her chatting with a customer at the lunch counter about needing entertainment for the fundraiser. Raphe told Ran, who volunteered his band that same day.

Riley had been looking forward to meeting Melvina after his brother told him all about her. Evidently, Melvina was an event dynamo, and was always organizing charity dinners for firefighters, bake sales for the elementary school, and promoting literacy at the local library. Not only was she kind, but she made the most scrumptious cupcakes in Texas. Pastry and desserts weren't his forte, but Riley made a pretty good red velvet fluff cupcake, a special recipe he'd invented himself. He had a hankering to challenge her to a bake-off just to watch her in action heating up his kitchen. Right now, she was heating up the ballroom in her wine-colored gown.

No way would he let her get out of dancing with him. As she began to step away, he took her by the hand and pulled her into his arms. Coaxing her around the dance floor, he felt her body relax against his. Smiling as other couples soon joined in, he silently thanked Ran for starting the music with a slow, soulful bass. They moved around the floor at an easy pace.

Riley's eyes met Melvina's and her smile almost made him forget the steps to the waltz. The kind of smile that told him she knew something he didn't. A dimple graced one of her rounded cheeks. Damn! Melvina was sexy, but not like the kind of gal you might see shopping in Gucci at the Galleria. She was beautiful and wholesome, like the leading ladies on Lifetime. Not that he watched the channel, but his mother and sister were suckers for romance, so he usually found himself absorbing the innumerable movies that played non-stop over the holidays.

Right now, Riley was having a hard time concentrating on the waltz as he stared at Melvina's sparkling green eyes. She winced as he missed the step and accidentally clipped one of her toes with his black, hand-tooled leather cowboy boots. "Oh no, sorry. I'm usually much better at this."

"Don't worry," she said, a pretty blush highlighting her cheeks.

Trying to redeem himself, he righted his step and twirled her around. Unfortunately, he'd caught her off balance and Melvina gasped as she stumbled back. Too late! Her curvy backside bumped the mayor and his wife, who then stumbled into the new doctor and her new husband, who then crashed into Celia, who grabbed a hold for dear life to the fire chief before falling into the trio of chocolate fountains.

The domino effect sent the elaborate fountains spinning as Celia's spiky heels caught the corner of the tablecloth. Chocolate flung in all directions like a literal shit-storm hitting the fan. Dancers spattered in milk, dark and white chocolate stood in varying displays of shock, anger and disbelief. The Tomball Cats fumbled a few notes but played on, switching quickly to a line dance that was directed to pick up at the front of the stage. It drew a greater portion of the guests away from the mess and helped to curtail the waves of laughter that rippled around the ballroom.

Riley had tightened his hold around Melvina's waist to ensure she didn't fall. "Are you okay?"

"Oh my god, I can't believe what I've done." Melvina moaned with sheer embarrassment.

"That wasn't all you, sweetheart. I think my momma would be covering her eyes if she saw what I just did. After all, it was my toe stepping on your toe that started the whole affair." He had to take credit for the mishap, since he was staring at her cleavage when he missed a step and sent their balance off kilter.

Riley spotted Raphe wiping chocolate off his dance partner. When his brother's gaze locked with his, Raphe tossed the dirty napkin on top of the chocolate fiasco and made his way over to Riley. "Hey Bro, what up?" Raphe sounded like a country rapper, hip-hop, thug wanna-be. Riley smiled at the outdated meant-to-be-amusing slang. Raphe's catlike smile revealed his barely disguised amusement.

"Glad you made it. I see you missed my speech." Riley had seen his younger brother enter through the side door sometime after Melvina's belated entrance. He was in the company of a hot date and had a smudge of red lipstick on his collar, so Riley understood the where and why for the delay. The dinner was paid for, so it didn't matter that Raphe was tardy. "Can you escort this lovely lady to our table and get her a glass of champagne? I need to help clean up this situation." Raphe nodded and took Melvina by the arm. She darted a glance over her shoulder as she was led away to Riley's table. He noticed her cheeks were still stained pink in embarrassment from the accident.

He was such a klutz. Blowing out a breath, he strode to the group wiping chocolate from their evening attire.

"Sorry, folks. Not sure what happened there, but it might have just been my fancy two-steppin'. I'd like to pay for the dry-cleaning of everyone who got dipped or dabbed, and champagne is on the house for anyone who wants it, plus a room at the hotel is on me to use tonight or any other future night if you already have plans. Just tell Lonnie at the front desk that Riley Nash sent you."

The expressions on the faces of the guests transformed from annoyed to appeased in a manner of seconds. A few folks told him it wasn't necessary, but still pinched the proffered business cards and headed toward the lobby. In his experience, it was rare that anyone turned down *free* when he was the one offering. His celebrity chef credentials carried a lot of weight, and the swank new hotel that just opened in the Galleria of Magnolia was nothing to snub your nose at. The elegant outdoor shopping, apartments and dining mixed developments were making a hit all over Texas, and Magnolia was one of the wealthy areas of Houston's overflowing housing markets. The Woodlands was nearby, and the Texans' famous quarterback frequented the hotel on several occasions.

A milk-chocolate-spattered Celia approached him but waved away his apology and offer. "I know it wasn't you. Melvina is a bull in a china shop. She might be good at baking and making a couple reservations, but she can't handle the attention of a man like you, Riley Nash." Her eyes darted over the length of his tux and back again. The calculating gleam in her eye spelled trouble.

Celia would be considered quite a beauty by most, but he didn't like her style. She wore her sleek strawberry-blonde hair in a tight chignon at the base of her neck, and her ivory skin was flawless. Her lips were a perfect shade of pink, but her words angered him. He hated her casual dismissal of Melvina's hard work, and how she instantly blamed Melvina for the chocola-tastrophe. By all rights, he knew the mess was his own doing. He couldn't believe he had accepted Celia's invitation to dinner next week. Damn! She'd cornered him before the event had begun. Before he'd met Melvina in person.

Now what?

He thought of a million things he wanted to say, but then thought about the contract he had just signed with his publicity agency. Reaching out, he wiped a dab of chocolate off Celia's cheek. "Trust me, the mistake was all mine." He tasted the chocolate on his finger, sizing her up with a cool stare…. He tried not to laugh at her bedraggled appearance. "Yum, I think there is a little Amaretto in here." Winking at her pinched expression, he turned and walked away.

Lord have mercy, I'm on a roll tonight!

Melvina's hand shook a little as she downed the champagne that Riley Nash's brother had handed her. She scanned the room for Mona, who was currently in Jorden McBride's arms being whirled around the room. They'd known Jorden since they were kids before his parents shipped him off to his relatives in New Hampshire. He'd returned recently for his work in the oil patch. They had seen him a few times at Pop's Café, but he seemed to be in Houston most of the time. Melvina suspected Mona was head over heels, but their old schoolmate had grown up to be a quiet sort of man—hard to read.

Riley's brother cleared his throat. "I'm Raphe. You probably don't remember me, but I bought a couple dozen cupcakes from you a while back." He grinned.

"Oh, wonderful! I hope you liked them. You must be the brother who told Riley about my cupcakes."

"Yes'm. I heard you telling someone you needed entertainment, and so I told Ran."

"Well bless your heart. I really owe you one. We have a set budget for this charity dinner, and I have to be a wizard sometimes to make the balance sheet work out for the treasury." Melvina was happy that she got to meet the nice brother who helped her complete the event, but he was wearing at least three Hershey bars worth of chocolate on his lapels as she spoke with him, and his date was currently marching back from the ladies' room looking none too happy with the stains on her white silk gown.

"Well now, darlin', don't you look good enough to eat." Raphe's smile was devilish as he snaked his arm around the model-thin redhead. The corners of her mouth were tilted down, and her lips pressed together so hard that she could have been Mona's younger sister.

Trying to apologize, Melvina set her champagne flute down and stood up from the table, but the room began to spin. She grabbed onto the table and knocked Raphe's champagne flute over, splashing it onto his date's dress. The redhead squealed, and Raphe tried to blot her down with a napkin until she stamped her foot and spun around in disgust.

"I am so—so—sorry," Melvina wasn't sure why her words were coming out slurred. This was only her second drink of the night and she never even finished her first.

Raphe's voice rang with good-humored laughter. "She'll get over it. I bought the dress for her anyway and I'll buy her another. It's not a big deal. If you ask me, I thought the whole scene was a hoot! All that chocolate flying and those uptight people squawking like a bunch of chickens with a fox in the henhouse."

Melvina clutched her spinning head. What was in Mona's Pez dispenser?

There was no glimpse of her cheeky friend anywhere. She would have to call Eli to drive her home. Even though she'd done her part as treasurer, coming to the event had been a disaster. Outside of the chocolate fiasco and her own clumsiness, the fire department should benefit nicely from the event. Melvina reminded herself that getting a new fire station was more important than her own problems.

She searched for her small evening bag but couldn't find it. Then she remembered she was at Mr. Nash's table, not hers, way in the back. A wave of self-consciousness assailed her as she thought about walking the long distance between their tables to find her handbag. Raphe must have read her look.

"I can walk you back to your table if you left something there, but I think my brother, Riley, wants to see you again."

Melvina's eyes widened. She certainly didn't want to be stumbling around in front of Riley Nash. "I'll be okay. You have your date to attend to.

Tell your brother I'm sorry, but I'm not feeling very well." She didn't wait for Raphe's response and was saved by the return of his date. The handsome younger brother was too caught up soothing the redhead's ruffled feathers to stop Melvina's retreat.

Uh oh! Here comes trouble.

Melvina spotted Celia making a bee-line toward her as she reached her table.

"That was not funny! I hope you learn something from all this." The stick-thin woman waved her arms, encompassing the chocolate-covered mess on her dress.

Melvina gaped at the usually aloof ice princess with her daggers out. Of course, she'd never seen Celia drenched in chocolate, either.

"Yes indeed, I have." Melvina tried to bite back the thousand retorts crawling up the back of her throat like soldiers storming the beaches of Normandy.

Uh-oh! Those aren't words.

Before she could make a move to the bathroom, she projectile-vomited all over Celia Lockwood's shoes, the only part of the Blossom President not covered in chocolate. Celia's screeches echoed around the room, but Melvina couldn't be bothered by the woman's antics. The night had turned into a fiasco.

Melvina's skin felt hot and her head was spinning. She wiped her mouth with a random napkin and turned to leave.

Mona found Melvina before she reached the lobby, cackling about the whole event, but Melvina couldn't focus. Her friend's voice was disturbing her inner peace, of which she had very little right now. She needed to get to the parking lot before she soiled another part of the hotel.

"Mona, I have to get outside quick. I'm going to be sick again, and I don't think I have anything left to throw up. I didn't have much to drink, and I haven't eaten since noon. What was in that Pez dispenser?"

"Just a little Xanax—" Mona took in a whoosh of breath. "You aren't preggers, are you?"

"Geez Louise, Mona," Melvina muttered, pressing her hand to her stomach. "You know all about my love life. It would have to be an immaculate conception if I were. Now get out of my way so I can get out of here."

Mona tittered but took Melvina's arm in a supportive grip and led her out the door. Melvina's car was parked in the circular drive a few feet from the entrance.

"Wow, the valet must be psychic," Mona marveled.

"I left it here." Melvina rolled her eyes at her friend's outrageous remark.

"There wasn't any valet when I arrived. Must have been on break, so I left the keys under the mat. Look, I hate to ask this, but since you're the one who roofied me, you can drive me home."

Mona slapped her leg. "Melvina Rayanne, I never did such a thing! You asked me for a painkiller, and I gave you one."

Melvina's voice found clarity as she opened the passenger side of the car and threw the keys to Mona. "You gave me a sedative, not a pain reliever."

Mona got in the driver's seat, glancing back wistfully at the twinkling lights of the hotel lobby, probably looking for Jorden. "When I got divorced, I took them all the time for pain."

Melvina winced and rolled down the window, hanging her head out like a terrier. "You took them for emotional pain, not back pain. You can't mix Xanax with alcohol! It makes you sick, or worse."

Mona stepped on the gas, speeding toward the 249 freeway. "I don't know what you are talking about. I took those with three martinis every night before bed and it did me a world of good."

Chapter 4

Melvina woke the next morning with a massive Xanax hangover. Not the pounding headache and upset stomach brought on by too much alcohol, but the sluggish, listless, can't-wake-up feeling that only a strong drug can trigger. She didn't feel hungover from the alcohol because in truth, she hadn't imbibed that much. The sedative, on the other hand, had hit her hard, and she had to hit the snooze five times that morning before finally making herself roll out of bed. Pop's Café wasn't going to open itself. She'd taken over the early shift for her father twenty years ago while attending the local college.

She'd had little interest in any other career besides baking, but she loved to read, so she got a Bachelor of Arts in English and then continued working for her father. No one else in the family had ever attended University. Afterward, she thought the degree was pointless, but it motivated her to volunteer at the library and start a literacy campaign in their community.

Houston was the fourth largest city in America, and Magnolia was near enough to draw the overflow of multicultural residents. It was best for everyone in the small town if the citizens could communicate. She tried to stay out of the politics of residency. People were people no matter what color or where they came from. Everyone had the same basic needs—a roof over their heads, food for their families, acceptance and support from others. She found, in her experience, that if people were treated well, they acted well in return, and that made the community stronger.

The phone alarm went off again as she stood in the shower, letting the hot water run over her groggy body. "For the love of God," she grumbled, shutting off the water and grabbing her towel from the rack. Melvina moved slowly for fear of repeating yesterday's fiasco. Amazed, she acknowledged that her back felt much better than last night. Maybe Mona was right. Who would have thought Xanax for an injury? Could stress be the real cause for hurting her back?

I need a vacation.

She would talk to Pop about it over brunch on Sunday. Eli would be there and maybe he wouldn't mind helping out for a week. Melvina had seen a spa retreat advertisement in a magazine at the library. She desperately needed a massage. She'd search Groupon and find a good price within her budget.

Turning the alarm off, she stared at the disaster she'd made of her room. Piles of clothes littered the floor, shoes spilled from the closet, and undergarments lay scattered over the dresser. She needed a maid. It wasn't usually this bad, but housework wasn't her forte. Spotting her purse on the floor, she winced. It was bad luck to leave your purse on the floor—a sure thing her money would be running away from her this week.

Hm, maybe that's a good thing.

Hadn't she thought about going on vacation? Spas cost money and so did fancy beach resorts with fruity cocktails—okay, vodka martinis or something with fewer calories. Melvina shook herself out of her daydream.

You don't have fancy resort money, Melvina, so stop thinking about it.

Keys, keys, where did she put her keys?

After searching the whole house twice, she remembered Mona had driven her home, so she called Mona.

A husky male voice answered, "Hello? Oh, sorry, I think this is your phone. Mine's over there. Here sweetheart." Blurry images flashed across the screen as the man set the phone down. Then another kind of flash—of the man's naked behind as he got up out of bed and walked away. It wasn't her preference to video chat, but since Mona always video-called her, Melvina hit the redial button from the last time they spoke. Suddenly Mona's face filled the screen.

Mascara smeared the area beneath Mona's eyes and her lips looked like she had swiped her lipstick off with a sander. "Melvina?"

"Uh-yeah. Who was that?"

Mona's face went from guilt to excitement in two seconds flat. "You didn't recognize that perfect behind?" Peals of laughter exploded from Mona's smeared lips. She tried to cover her mouth to suppress the outburst.

"It's Jorden!" she whisper-squealed.

The male voice responded to Mona's statement. "I'll be out in just a minute."

Melvina gasped with shock, covering her own mouth, then shaking her head. "You go, girl."

"Melvina, sweetie, I gotta go. I'll come by the café later so we can gossip," Mona stage-whispered before clicking off the phone.

Melvina gave a little whistle at her friend's fast moves. Mona had most likely driven Melvina's car back to the hotel to pick up her own vehicle. That's probably when Mona ran into Jorden again—or scouted him out like an eight-point buck during hunting season.

Melvina called Eli, promising him extra gluten-free crunchies for his salads this week if he could get her to work on time.

Regaling Eli with the comedy of errors of the previous evening, Melvina couldn't help but chuckle as he guffawed, slapping the steering wheel of his Jeep as they pulled up to the café.

"It's not funny," she snorted, and they both fell into giggles.

"Oh, it most certainly is." He shook his head as tears of laughter filled his eyes.

"I screwed up my meeting with one of the most renowned chefs that I really wanted to impress. He already knew about my cupcakes. Pitching my business plan could have been a no-brainer and he might have even helped back me, or at the very least, given me some pointers on how he became such a success. Instead, I made a fool of myself in front of the entire town and Celia." She blew out a breath. "I don't even want to think of what I'll say to her."

Eli wrapped his arm around Melvina and pulled her in for a side hug. "It'll be okay, Mel. Don't hang your head. Just smile and tell the world that you make the best baked goods in the South. Not many people can boast that they do all the good things that you do."

Melvina touched her head to his. "Thanks Eli." Her little brother was her rock in times like these and supported her even when she made of muck of things. She got out of the car and waved as Eli drove out of the parking lot.

Putting herself in baking mode was just what she needed. It would help her forget the calamity and concentrate on better things, like the upcoming literacy class she would be teaching. Maurice Salas was making progress and that made her feel good. If she could help him finish the sixth grade, she could work with him over the summer to prepare him for the seventh.

One day at a time.

She always told her students to focus on the moment and to be patient for things to come. Well, now she would take her own advice and focus on muffins instead of mayhem.

Melvina tried to keep a low profile, hiding in the kitchen for most of the breakfast rush. She escaped Celia's morning dash for an Americano and a no-fat cran-orange muffin. Melvina had secretly fantasized about stuffing it with one of Mona's Pez dispenser pills. Maybe that would let Celia's sphincter relax enough so that stick would fall out. Melvina giggled to herself as she took out the latest batch of cakes from the oven to cool on wire racks. It was Darcey's turn for a lunch break and there was no getting around manning the cash register. Dutifully calling out to the young waitress, Melvina reminded her to put her order in and take a break.

"I don't know what I want today, Melvina. Just whip up something good without too many calories." Darcey weighed about a hundred and ten pounds wet and lived off pizza and nachos as far as Melvina knew. She mentally rolled her eyes when the slim waitress complained about being too heavy while sipping Pepsi Cola and snacking on buttered bread.

"There ain't no such thing," Melvina wagged her finger at her. "Now get your skinny butt on break before I come sit on you."

Darcey bobbed up on her red patent leather pumps, leaning low over the counter in front of the fire chief. "I know you're just playin' Mel. You aren't fat no more." Darcey spun around, twirling her long, honey-blonde braid as she popped her bubble gum. "You're lookin' downright hot! Watch out Chief, this woman might just steal your heart."

Melvina tried to hold onto a smile as the heat crept up her face. She was used to the twenty-year-old's nonsensical talk and lack of manners or boundaries, but of all people, why did it have to be Manny that she went loose-tongued on? The look Melvina gave Darcey must have said it all. "Okay, okay. I'm going to punch out. I'll just snag a burger off the line. There's always extra fries." The slender blonde sashayed to the back, swinging her hips for the chief and the two firefighters who accompanied him.

"Sorry boys, she'll be back in thirty minutes. Anybody want fresh pie? I made apple and cherry this morning, and the cupcakes just came out of the oven half an hour ago." They all nodded eagerly and Melvina relaxed. She didn't know how Manny fared after the chocola-tastrophe, or if he saw her toss her cookies on Celia, but she'd bet her Jimmy Choo shoes that he'd found out about her mishaps. She pushed her shoulders back as she poured them another round of coffee, and then went to fix their desserts. She boxed up an extra dozen cupcakes for the men back at the station, showing her appreciation for the dedication to their job in baked treats and smiles.

As she rang up their checks, discounting their meals fifty percent and taking off the desserts and coffee completely, Manny fussed at her generosity. "Melvina, we have been over this before. This is a small town, and you feed us well all the time. You need to charge us for at least the lunches that we get most every day. We don't want you going out of business on account of eating you out of house and home."

"Don't you worry about business at Pop's," she said, with a flick of her hand. "We have it all under control. Besides, the boys tip generously and I appreciate it. Maybe Darcey will be able to afford…a new car soon." She had wanted to say etiquette classes, but the bright yellow car with the orange bumpers jumped to mind, saving her from sounding sore.

Manny smiled, taking the change she offered with the extra box of cakes. "I know Celia was in a huff last night, but don't mind her. Everyone has accidents." He winked as he turned to follow his men, then looked back as he closed the distance to the door. "But Darcey's right, you are looking hot." And with that, he let the door swing closed, the bell dinging hard against the glass.

Melvina tried not to melt into a puddle at the register. She already knew she looked like a gaping fool as the large man in overalls who wore a Texans hat stared at her holding his tab, then waved a ten-dollar bill in her face. She felt an elbow in her side as Darcey slid in front of her, taking the man's check and punching the keys on the old-time register. Melvina stepped back, mopping at her forehead with a napkin.

"I see you still haven't recovered from last night's fiasco, Melvina, or is that a hot flash you're having?" Melvina looked up to see Celia towering over the counter, hearing her tap her four-inch stilettos.

"Well there does seem to be a lot of hot air in here."

Celia dodged the dig, sliding into the nearest seat at the counter. "That's the heat rolling off the fire chief and his men," she tittered and glanced around as though waiting for others to join in. Darcey was oddly silent, filling sugar dispensers and clanging salt and pepper shakers around on the half-moon bar. The saucy twenty-year-old went up a notch in Melvina's book.

In spite of Celia's attempt at humor, Melvina could tell that she had something more on her mind. She hoped it wouldn't spill out on her as Celia pulled a thick a ream of papers from her tote. She pushed them toward Melvina. "We have a lot of work to do. The Magnolia Blossoms got a letter from the IRS informing us that the balance sheet for last year is off, so I need you to recheck these figures before the meeting with them tomorrow at noon.

"What? I don't think that's even possible, and I'm not getting out of here until after five. Pop is doing inventory until then." Melvina tried not to let her head spin. When Celia got something on her mind, she wanted it done as soon as possible, but it didn't always mean that it was needed right away. The chocola-tastrophe must have her digging for rare and cruel forms of punishment. "Celia, I doubt that the IRS would only give you one day to have these figures re-tallied."

"Oh, you are right about that, but remember that day you asked me to donate the paper for the literacy thing?"

Melvina nodded. "That was last month."

"Well I accidently laid the letter from the IRS in the stack that I donated, and your librarian friend delivered it back to me this morning. It's due back today actually, but I set an appointment with their auditor tomorrow, explaining you were busy today. Since you are the treasurer, it's *your* job." Celia paused with a cat-like smile, "Oh honey, I did you a big favor. At least you don't have to meet with them until tomorrow."

"Me?" Melvina gaped.

Celia stood, her purse knocking over the creamer that Darcey had just filled. "Oh, don't cry over spilled milk." She laughed. "It's not like the Magnolia Blossoms have any real wealth for them to find error with. We are a charitable women's club. Everything we do is a tax write-off. I'm sure you'll figure out where you messed up—eventually."

Melvina could feel the heat rolling off in waves. She was gripping the end of her apron with both hands to prevent giving Celia a middle-finger salute as the Blossom president made her way to the exit.

"Why do you let that old biddy get to you?" Darcey smacked her gum and blew a large pink bubble from candy-colored lips.

"She's younger than me, darlin'. And as much as I hate to admit it, I am the treasurer and somehow, something must have gone wrong." Melvina hadn't prepared the tax reports for the Magnolia Blossoms but had taken them to the accountant they had used for the last couple of decades. He had never made a mistake before, so Melvina couldn't imagine what could have happened this time. It was her job to find out. She plucked the cell phone out of her apron pocket and dialed Stanley Goldstein to see if he could meet with her that evening.

The clang of the bell over the door made Melvina look up just in time to see Riley Nash enter the café. He looked around, surveying the diner counter and the other seating options. Darcey took that moment to disappear. Melvina grabbed a menu and smiled at Riley while listening to Stan on the phone. She couldn't help wondering how much the handsome chef knew of the disaster she'd made of the rest of the evening. It was everything she could do *not* to relive the events over and over in her head.

"Coffee?" She held up the pot while continuing to talk with Stan. "Yes, that'll be great, yeah. Okay, awesome possum." Melvina put the phone in her pocket and looked at Riley, wondering why he hadn't answered. Raising one eyebrow, she tilted her head at the coffeepot she was holding and turned over a cup with her free hand.

He smiled, nodding his head. "I thought you asked and answered. Not sure if there was any other choice."

Melvina retraced her side of the conversation with Stan, agreeing to meet him at the café in a couple of hours. "Sorry, I was just on the phone with the tax man."

Riley's whiskey colored eyes bulged in horror. "By all means, you are forgiven. I get chills just hearing that three-letter word."

"IRS or tax?" Melvina quipped.

"Both! Please stop, you're making my skin crawl." He rubbed his arms for effect.

Melvina laughed, "I don't think we're in all that much trouble, but you just missed Celia Lockwood strolling in here to dump the Women's League tax problems on me with less than twenty-four hours to decipher the issue," she groaned.

He pushed the cup forward, reminding Melvina to pour. "That bad, huh? I saw her getting into her little red Beamer as I pulled in, but I waited until she cleared the parking lot before I got out." He grinned.

"Smart man," Darcey tossed out as she whizzed by carrying a tray laden with piping hot burgers and fries to a table of men in construction vests.

"I sure like the looks of that. Hook me up."

Melvina's heart twisted. Riley was closer to her age than Darcey's, but men of all ages liked twenty-something twigs with long legs and long blonde hair. Melvina at least had the blonde thing going for her. "I think she will be happier if you make your play for a date in person."

Riley gaped at her for a moment. "What? No, not her! I meant the double bacon hamburger with what looked like a mound of cheese, avocado, and was that a charred jalapeno I saw cresting the edge of the plate?"

A sizzle of heat zapped through her body—similar to the reaction she'd had when he'd taken her in his arms at the ball. His sexy smile and gorgeous body didn't give him away as a chef. He looked more like one of the firemen from the station—a very fit, hot fireman. But she loved that he appreciated a good meal. "It's our Smokin' Hot Jalapeno Firehouse Burger. The firefighters love it, and most everyone else around here does too. If you want it totally Texas style, we can throw a slab of brisket on top."

His white teeth flashed a sultry smile. "I just love Texas. Let's do it!" Riley winked.

Melvina's face warmed with pleasure as she went into the kitchen to prepare his order. When it came to all things culinary, baking was at the top of her list, but she'd come up with the burger when she was back in high school. She'd tested her recipe out on Eli, and he'd been a willing guinea pig. Turns out, he couldn't get enough of the specialty burger. Eli played on the high school football team and brought the guys in to Pop's Café after every game. It became a regular menu item. The home-cut waffle fries were nice and crispy, and everyone raved about her homemade Jalapeno ketchup.

When Melvina brought Riley's order out, Darcey was chatting with him. Seated next to Riley was his brother, who played in the band. Melvina liked their sound, at least what she heard of it before she got sick and had to leave. She regretted not being able to enjoy the music for even a short while.

Melvina nodded a polite hello, set Riley's plate down, and slipped away before he could engage her in conversation. With Darcey chatting, no one seemed to notice her coming or going. It appeared the sexy chef did indeed like the eye candy that Darcey supplied.

Melvina walked back to the employees' restroom and shut the door to lean back on its cold metal surface. She would let Darcey take over and get Ran's order. She remembered the name because she had written the check for the band yesterday afternoon from the Magnolia Blossoms' account. At least she wouldn't have to double-check that until next year's return.

She stood in front of the mirror studying her reflection with a critical glare. Sure, she had lost the weight and yes, she had good hair, but the crow's-feet at the corners of her eyes and the lines around the sides of her mouth were visible from all the years of smiling for customers and laughing at Eli's jokes. Her breasts were full and her hips a little too wide, but her waist had downsized enough to make her curvy. With the right dress, makeup, and lighting, she could be Rayna Louise Banks. Men had always drooled over Rayna....

Why don't I have that same effect?

She turned from side to side, pushing a wayward lock of hair back into the ponytail she was sporting. Pulling a tube of lipstick from her apron, she dabbed a bit on her lips, taking care not to make it look too fresh. She wanted to look nice, but not like she was trying too hard. This was her chance to talk to one of the country's hottest chefs.

Get your bum out there and network.

She had dreams, and she needed backing, advice and inspiration. So what if he wasn't attracted to her? You didn't have to be attracted to a person to speak to them. They were kindred cooking spirits and shared the same love of food. The way he had salivated over the sight of the plates coming out of the kitchen gave her the gumption to go back. Those dishes were *her* creations. Striding through the double kitchen doors and out into the diner, Melvina made a bee-line to the counter. Only Ran was there.

Staring down at him with a blank look, Melvina asked, "Everything okay?"

Wiping his mouth with a well-used napkin, he shook his head and moaned. "That was the best burger I have ever had."

Ran was better looking than his brother, but too pretty for her taste. It was still hard to be in the presence of such a perfect-looking man while he was praising her food. Hiding her disappointment, she began to clear away plates and wipe down the counter.

Ran must have noticed her discomfort. "Riley had to run," he said as he caught her eye. "He got a phone call from Braised. Apparently, there was a kitchen fire at the restaurant, but Raphe's on the scene, so it should all be fine."

"Is that the fireman brother?"

"Yep." Taking his napkin and wiping his mouth one last time, he stood. He laid two twenties on the table and returned his Monte Blanc polished leather wallet to his pocket.

"That's too much. Let me get you some change," Melvina insisted.

"Keep the change for you and Darcey. You both deserve it. We'll be back. I promise."

"Thank you." Melvina watched him leave through the double glass door with a single hand in the air. The backward wave was as casual as the man. Ran took the helmet from his bike and threw one leg over before revving the engine. Darcey made a false swoon and moaned just behind her as Melvina wiped down a table.

"What I would do for a man like that." Darcey fanned herself.

Melvina laughed good-naturedly. "It's Friday night, young lady. You better start thinking about rolling silverware and getting off before five to go home and get ready for your date with Lance."

Darcey lingered at the counter a beat longer before spinning on her heel and disappearing into the kitchen.

Chapter 5

It was after six when Melvina finally had a chance to sit in a booth reviewing order slips for the day and tallying the tip share. She always gave Darcey the largest cut because the firemen and most of the male patrons around town came to the diner to see her. The rest was split among the kitchen staff, bus boy and dishwasher.

Stan, the accountant, hadn't shown up yet, but Melvina knew he was doing her a favor, so she decided not to be perturbed.

A familiar voice vibrated over her shoulder and she looked up to find Manny Owens standing by her booth. "Hi Manny. Did Roberta see you come in? I'm sure she'll be back to wait on you in a minute. I can get you some coffee if you like." As she began to rise from her seat, Manny put his hand on her shoulder and gently pushed her back down.

"I can wait for Roberta. Mind if I join you?" His voice was friendly, and she appreciated seeing a kind face right now. "How did your day go?"

Melvina thought about it for a moment. "Well besides the busy break-fast and lunch crowd, it was mostly quiet after three o'clock. I admit that I am beat, though. Plus, after Celia's visit, I have to meet with the accountant and then hustle to the library to see if I still have time to tutor my student."

Melvina thought about Maurice and his lack of direction. If she could only find more people to show him a positive path. Maybe this was an opportunity to enlist a role model. "He could really use a male mentor in his life. His mom, Maria, has been separated from his dad, Jose, for some time now, and I think he suffers not having a man's presence around. You know how junior high can be."

Manny snorted an affirmative.

Melvina chuckled. She was too stressed about the IRS audit to worry about lipstick or how her hair must look. Besides, the hot fire chief was way out of her league anyway. Not to mention there was Celia, who claimed first dibs when it came to available hot bachelors in town. "How about you?" she asked. "Rough day?"

"Naw, just a couple of car crashes off the two-forty-nine. No one hurt, just fender benders, but we have to respond to all calls. And Celia Lockwood came by the station with another fundraiser proposal. She must really love raising money for the fire department." He smiled.

Melvina wondered if he knew about Celia's plans to become Mrs. Manny Owens. "Mm, that she does." Melvina bit the tip of her pen as she stared at the last total for the day. Pop's was going to have to open a second location if they stayed this productive. Or, maybe she could do it. Magnolia didn't have enough places to eat to accommodate the sudden growth of oil patch residents. They really could use a high-end restaurant for swanky dinners and martini lunches but getting a liquor license took time and setting up a place like that took money.

"What's she putting you and the boys up to now? Better give me a heads up so I'll know what I'm getting roped into."

"Just a calendar of the younger guys in their skivvies, holding water hoses and covering their boxers with their hats."

Melvina's head rose from re-tallying numbers, her eyes wide. "You're kidding."

He laughed, leaning back in his seat as Roberta approached and he ordered a coffee.

Roberta twirled a pencil along the edge of her lip. Melvina wasn't sure if she was trying to be seductive or merely daydreaming. The night waitress was only eighteen and didn't have a lot upstairs. Melvina was hoping to groom her into a life at the diner. At least she would have enough pay to afford a simple life and not have to depend on marrying to get by. "You don't want anything else?"

Manny glanced at Melvina. "Thanks Roberta, I'm all good. I just came by to see Melvina."

That piqued Melvina's curiosity. "So, a firemen's calendar?"

"Yes, and apparently, the less the guys are wearing, the better. Celia assures us it will equal lots of profit to benefit the fire station." Manny chuckled with ease, reminding her of one of those smooth cowboys portrayed in the old westerns she used to watch on Sundays with Eli. She was a sucker for Sam Elliot, and although Manny was younger and handsomer, there was something about the rugged, raspy-voiced older actor that turned her on.

"Interesting," Melvina supplied. "I wonder what Celia will try to rope me into on this fundraising project?"

"Yes, indeed. In fact, we actually requested you be in charge of the whole thing. See, the boys at the firehouse think it's a good idea and all. The community is growing faster than the taxes can come into the city. We could use a boost, but we don't want it to be—" Manny shifted uncomfortably in the booth.

"Tawdry, cheesy, tacky?" Melvina inserted.

"Yeah, all of the above. Look, the boys trust you. They know that Celia might be the president of the Magnolia Blossoms and that she has helped direct a lot of energy toward helping our cause, but she—" Manny looked like he was having a hard time explaining.

Melvina took over, "Doesn't make the best cupcakes in town and feed them more jalapeno burgers than the station can handle?"

Manny smiled, nodding with relief. "Exactly. See, you understand."

Melvina looked at him with a cheeky grin. "Well, I would be a fool to turn down a job that lets me see every fireman in Magnolia in their skivvies."

"Would that include a picture of the fire chief himself?" Roberta stood gaping at them with a glassy look of excitement and a mouth hanging open in question. Her bowed lips were painted fire engine red, and lavender eyeshadow graced the top lids of her eyes, making her look like a purple Siamese.

"Roberta, Mr. Simms looks like he could use a refill." Melvina pointed to the circular counter. As the waitress walked away with the coffeepot, Manny looked disheartened at his empty cup.

Melvina stifled a laugh as she rose to get another pot for the chief. When she returned to fill his cup, she saw the accountant enter the café and wave. She guessed her time with the chief was over, just when things were starting to warm up.

"Nice chatting with you Manny. My date's here, so I guess I have to go."

Manny took a sip of his coffee then looked up in surprise, "Date?"

Melvina didn't know whether to laugh or be offended. It had been a while since she'd been on a date, but there was no reason to disbelieve that she could have one. "Yeah, Celia set me up with Stan The Man. You know him?" She motioned to the elderly gentleman wearing khakis and a pastel colored, button-down, short-sleeve shirt.

Manny nodded at Stanley as Stan waved back. "Ah, must be a business thing."

Melvina quirked a brow at the chief, "Is that a slight against Stan or me?" Putting one hand on her hip with the other still holding the coffeepot, she supposed she looked like Flo from the old seventies show, "Alice." Eli and Melvina had watched countless reruns when they were really little. It was one of Pop's favorites. She tried not to follow it up with a, "Kiss my grits!"

Manny looked down at his coffee and then back up at Melvina with an awkward stare. "I—I just didn't think you and Stan could be an item. I mean, he's gay, right?" The last statement was whispered. The chief looked very uncomfortable now that he had said the G word.

Melvina took pity on him. She wasn't sure why she bothered to stand up for her old-maid status. Maybe it was to see if he had any interest in her. It was a silly thing to say, and she liked Manny as a friend first, so there was no reason for her to get terse with him. "I was just teasing. It's no secret that the only love in my life is baking. I've got better things to do." Gathering up her books so she could go get a cup for Stan, she said her goodbyes to Manny as he stood to leave.

"Melvina," Manny called out to her, then stopped. He stood there as if he was searching for something else to say.

Melvina paused, setting her files down on the counter. Her heart skipped a beat and she held her breath.

"It was nice talking to you," he finally said. "Great coffee."

Melvina watched him leave, letting her breath out slowly as her heart returned to its normal cadence.

Chapter 6

Melvina hit the alarm on her phone for the third time, but it wouldn't quit. It was Mona calling her to video chat. She swiped her finger across the screen, answering the call.

"Melvina Banks! I hear you were cozied up with the chief last night. Do tell." Before Melvina could utter a word, Mona pressed on. "I can't believe that I have to hear the details of your love life through the likes of Jill Baker."

"What does Jill Baker know about my love life? What are you talking about, Mona?" Melvina wiped a finger under her left eye, thinking to herself that no one over thirty should ever video chat. She looked like a truck had rolled over her, leaving track marks on her face. By the time she'd gotten home from her meeting with Stan, she was so pooped she'd just fallen into bed. She'd forgotten to take her makeup off and the crusted mascara made her look like one of Eli's football buddies after a rough quarter.

"She knows you were with Manny last night, cozied up in a booth at the café."

"We were not. Manny came in around six o'clock for a cup of coffee and to talk about the newest fundraiser that Celia has roped the Blossoms into, though I think this particular event might have every woman in town trying to become a Blossom."

Mona's lips were painted an Easter pink today with a fuchsia line around the outside, creating pointy peeks. "Well, rumor has it that he all but proposed to you in the café."

"Oh, for the love of—Manny isn't interested in me. We're just friends. He stops into the café all the time. I don't know why you listen to Jill, anyway. Didn't she start that rumor about Alex's wife, Kara, and had them in couple's therapy for a year, even though Kara never once talked to Mac Green?"

"I guess you're right," Mona conceded, chewing her bottom lip.

"Where's the eye candy this morning?" Melvina asked, changing the subject. "Hey, you were supposed to come tell me all about it at the café yesterday. What happened with you and Jorden?"

Mona began giggling and dove off screen for a moment. "Well, Jorden called in sick yesterday, so we spent the whole day in bed and well, you know—we never got out of the house." Peals of laughter burst from the speaker and Melvina clicked the volume down a few notches.

"Well good for you, Mona. He's got a nice behind." What else could she say? "Look, Mona, I need to get up and get ready to go to the library. I missed last night's literacy meeting and I promised Celia I would drop off some accounting figures to the Blossoms."

"Why do you let that woman dump all that stuff on you?"

"Because I'm the treasurer, remember? I like the things that the ladies' league does for the community, and though Celia isn't my favorite person in Magnolia, she *is* the president and I want to do my part to help out."

"You do enough parts for three people, Melvina. There aren't many good-hearted people like you around, and Celia Lockwood wouldn't be president if she hadn't climbed up on your back to get it. It just ain't right."

Melvina had heard that a thousand times, but what could she do? She believed in the cause, so she let it go without fussing. "Let's meet later for lunch or dinner. I gotta go."

"Lunch. I've got plans tonight with Jorden." Mona bit her lip and rolled her eyes heavenward.

Melvina laughed, "Lunch it is. I'll text you after the library."

Melvina parked the catering van in the library lot. She really needed to get up to the hotel and pick up her little convertible before it got towed. She had talked to a manager at the hotel the day after the fundraiser dinner, and he said he would keep an eye on it, but he warned her that they usually towed the ones they didn't have on their roster after three nights.

Her 1967 Shelby was a gift from Pop on her sixteenth birthday, and she had kept it running ever since. It was about time for the engine to be rebuilt again. Mac would be happy to get his hands on it whenever she could find the time to be carless. Maybe now was the perfect time. Pop said she could use the van until the Drew-Thompson wedding party next month. He hadn't booked any other catering events because the café was too busy. The idea of driving around all her errands in what she referred to as the *Grocery Getter* did not appeal, but the timing would be convenient for everyone. Maybe she would stop by the shop and leave Mac the keys after lunch with Mona, then ask if one of his boys could pick it up. Harlan and Larry would have a fight over which one got to drive it. Being a small town, her muscle car was somewhat of a celebrity piece.

"Miss Banks, are you coming in?" Maurice opened the door to the library for her as Melvina approached.

"Why yes, Maurice. I'm coming in to make up for missing last night." She gave him her biggest smile and gave his shoulder a reassuring squeeze.

"I really missed you, Miss Melvina. I have a project to do this weekend and I don't know where to start, plus I have an English test on Monday." Maurice's eyes were thickly veiled with sooty black lashes that he'd inherited from his pretty young mother. He had a habit of looking down when he was sad about something. Was he upset by the amount of homework he had to do?

"It's okay Maurice, I'll help you. I have time today, and I can come back later this evening if your mom can drop you off. The library is open until nine."

Despite her reassurance, Maurice continued to study his shoelaces as they approached an open table where she set her purse and he removed his book bag. "Anything else wrong?"

He shook his head, but she wasn't convinced. She would distract him with math homework first and as they delved into whatever project he'd been assigned, she would see if Maurice would tell her what was really going on.

Soon they were making an outline of the solar system and thinking up ways to display the planets for his science project. Melvina told Maurice how Pop had been too busy to help her when she was in school, and that her friend's mom had helped her with projects and costumes for plays.

"My dad can't help us, either. My sister wants to see him, but I don't think he's coming back." Shrugging one shoulder, he leaned on the wood table, stretching his elbow out farther as he rested the side of his face in one hand.

Melvina blew out a breath and started carefully. "I'm sorry to hear that, Maurice. I know it must be tough for you and your family. I'm sure you miss him."

Maurice shrugged again and looked uncomfortably back at the door.

"You might think grown-ups have all the answers, but not all of us do. Maybe your dad had to go find some answers for himself." She watched as Maurice picked up a marker and started scribbling on one of the work-sheets they had used. What was she supposed to say? She couldn't promise that everything would be okay. Maurice was too smart for empty promises and he'd suffered his share already.

"You know, I had a mom that left when I was just a little younger than you. I know how it feels to miss a parent. Would you like to hang out with another adult who might have more time for you right now?" Melvina studied him as she waited patiently for an answer. He chewed on the marker cap as he continued to draw the sun. She could tell he was turning the suggestion over in his head.

His voice was tentative. "Like you?"

"Yes, like me, but maybe a big brother type. Someone you can do fun things with. I know a few nice guys at the fire department who could use some help washing their trucks, and maybe they would even give you a ride when you're done." She didn't want to spell out mentor program because Maurice was sensitive about accepting charity. He hadn't wanted to accept free lunches when the principal tried to sign him up. He brought a sandwich and a piece of fruit every day in a plastic grocery store bag. If he craved a hot meal, no one would ever know.

After several moments of deliberation, he made eye contact, "Okay."

Melvina picked up the markers and stacked the books they'd used. "I'll set something up at the station and I'll let you know when we can set up a time, maybe next weekend. Until then, I think we have worked hard enough for today. I'll pick up some Styrofoam balls, glue and tissue paper we can use for the project and we can meet back here tonight. Deal?"

His broad smile melted her heart. He was a good kid. She nodded, squeezing his shoulder once more before picking up her purse and texting Mona.

Chapter 7

It was after one and she was starving. She stopped by the Blossom office to drop off the tax papers and did a mental happy dance when the receptionist told her Celia had gone out for lunch.

She took the catering van back to Pop's and parked it in the reserved spot around back, then rushed to the front to meet Mona. They drove Mona's sporty new Lexus the short distance to Bubbles and were lucky to find parking on the street near the entrance.

Sliding into the booth opposite her best friend, Melvina sighed. "It feels so good to see the inside of any other restaurant besides Pop's. Don't get me wrong, I love the café, but I get sick of eating my own cooking every day. Besides, it's my day off and I deserve a change of scenery."

The swanky new lounge opened early for appetizers and drinks from Thursday to Sunday. It wasn't a place to fill up, but it was a great place to gossip with friends while enjoying a cold, crisp glass of champagne and a cheese tray or a small salad. Today, Melvina opted for the grilled chicken skewers and a glass of Prosecco. Mona ordered the cheeseburger sliders with country brie and mango-jalapeno jelly. She batted her eyes with innocence in the bartender's direction as she asked the waitress for a stiff dirty martini.

"Speaking of change in scenery," Mona purred with a twitch of her Botox brows.

Melvina looked over her shoulder to see Riley Nash headed their way. She pasted a calm smile on her face, hoping she didn't show her panic as she took in his medium-blue colored denim with a stonewashed front. The snug jeans hugged his powerful thighs and Melvina wondered if he had ever been a bull rider. Images of Riley strapped into the stirrups with one hand snugged into the horn of his saddle, rocking back and forth as a large bull bucked furiously beneath him, danced across her vision.

She must have been gaping as he approached, because he gave her a curious look, arching a thick, sexy eyebrow.

Mona gave her a kick under the table, snapping Melvina out of her fantasy.

For God's sake! Get it together, Mel.

"Hi, Melvina. What a pleasant surprise. I was just looking for my brother, Raphe, but I think I must have gotten here before him. Raphe's notoriously twenty minutes late for everything. That's why I'm ten minutes late myself," he grinned sheepishly. "Mind if I join you ladies until he gets here? I hate being the lone guy at the bar."

Mona kicked Melvina under the table again as she craned her neck, motioning Melvina to scoot over. Melvina cleared her throat and nudged her purse to the side to make room. "Of course not. Please, have a seat."

Riley eased into the booth, filling the table like the infamous but muscular and drop-dead gorgeous elephant in the room. Mona, who was never at a loss for words, sat silently smiling at the hunk, not offering a bit of help. Melvina struggled for small talk but couldn't muster a coherent thought. The man smelled as delicious as a cinnamon roll. Was that Bulgari soap? It was her favorite. Finally, she looked at her drink and thought refreshments might be a good start. "You thirsty?"

"Yes, and I am starving too. Your salad looks good, but I think I could use something more substantial. Do you think they have a bigger cheeseburger than that?" He motioned to Mona's petite sliders.

"It's more of a cocktail place than a restaurant, but I'm sure the chef can fix you up. He caters to a tapas sort of crowd, but I've been to one of his barbecues before, and I know he can put together a mega-mean brisket burger. I'll get the waitress to ask." Melvina waved down the young brunette who was serving their section and made the request. Riley ordered a whiskey with one cube of ice and then turned to ask them if they would care for a bottle of champagne.

Mona lit up in anticipation, then her eyes went flat, showing her disappointment. "Oh damn, I can't. I gotta hot date tonight. I don't wanna go home sloppy. I guess I'll hold off, but thanks for the offer."

Riley looked at Melvina. "What about you? Raphe will be here soon. He'll finish a glass or two."

Melvina felt a surge of mixed emotions. He was just being friendly, but why offer to spend money and time on someone you weren't into? He'd said she was pretty when they danced the other night. Maybe he *was* interested, and hell, it was her day off and she wasn't driving. "Well, if you don't leave me stuck drinking the whole bottle, I can have a glass or two," she smiled.

The waitress brought the wine list on a tablet and Riley made a selection, seeming to enjoy playing with the electronic toy. "This sort of technology is what I need at Braised. It's just the right touch of class that upscale Houstonians will appreciate with their rack of lamb or Chateaubriand." Handing the tablet back to the waitress, they settled casually into conversation. Riley talked about his new restaurant in the city, and they found themselves comparing industry stories in no time.

After an hour slipped by and still no Raphe, Melvina had more than just a glass. "Hey, where's your brother?" she asked. "I think I'm a bit tipsy." She suppressed a small giggle as she put a hand to her mouth.

Riley fished his cell phone out of his pocket, looking at his messages. "Whoops, I think I'm at the wrong place. Raphe said The Vine, not Bubbles. I guess I remembered passing this place the other night and thought, it would be fun to check out. I better call him. He's probably mad I stood him up."

Melvina watched Riley as he rose from the booth and strolled outdoors to call his brother. It was polite that he didn't try to call from the table and yell over the growing crowd. The place had filled up in the time they'd spent chatting. Now people were milling around the bar and standing at the cocktail tables, scouting out booths.

"Melvina, he is HOT!" Mona trilled. "You had better bag and tag this one and have some fun. I don't want to hear anything else from you tomorrow except that you were on your bathroom floor for a good reason, like falling out of the shower having super kinky inferno sex." Mona's curls bobbed as she whipped her head in the direction Riley had gone and back to Melvina.

"Shush! For God's sake, Mona, people can hear you, and I'm sure he will be back any minute." Melvina hoped the other patrons hadn't heard her stage whisper, too.

Riley appeared a few minutes later and slid back into the booth. His leg now rested easily against hers.

Melvina looked at him in question. "Is he upset?"

"Who, my brother? Naw, he's left me hangin' so many times over a hot hookup, he owes me a little slack. Raphe said he'd make his way over in a bit. Seems he met someone at the bar while he was waiting for me, so it's likely I may not see him tonight. Glad I ran into you ladies." His smile was genuine as he topped off their glasses and frowned at the empty bottle. "I guess we didn't need Raphe's help after all."

"Oh geez, I'll probably feel that tomorrow." Melvina rubbed one temple as though the hangover had already started, but in truth, she would love one more glass. The splash that was left would be plenty, and she should ask Mona to drive her back to Pop's soon.

As if on cue, Mona looked at her cell phone and started to rise. "Oh geez, Melvina, I hate to be a party pooper, but I need to go home and get ready for my date. If I'm giving you a ride back, we better skedaddle." Melvina felt disappointment wash over her tingling senses as she realized it was time to say goodbye. Reaching for her purse, she nodded.

Riley looked as crestfallen as she felt. "I hate to see you ladies rush off and leave me to the vultures." Scanning the room, it was evident that half the bar was single ladies or groups of ladies, and several were making their attentions obvious. She could count at least three sitting with their arms crossed in such a way that pushed their cleavage up higher and pointed in his direction. "If you need a lift home, I can take you later. Let's have another round," Riley suggested with a crooked grin. It was impossible for any woman to resist that smile. Melvina wanted to pour champagne over him and lick it off. She didn't want to be an inconvenience when his brother arrived, and she didn't want to stay just to keep the cougars at bay.

Before Melvina could protest, Mona stood and said her goodbyes, throwing a meaningful look at Melvina, then waltzing out of the lounge without a second glance. Was the champagne making her slow or was she hesitant to leave the warmth of his side? When Mona left, he didn't move to the other side of the table. Instead, he waved down the waitress for another bottle.

"Whoa, who will drive us?" Melvina was a stickler for not drinking and driving, and though Riley didn't seem the least bit buzzed, he had already had two glasses of champagne and the whiskey from earlier.

"The champagne is for you, lovely lady. I'm going to have a water and if I do decide to have another sip, we'll call a cab and I'll see you home safely," he promised.

Melvina wanted to protest, but she didn't have a valid excuse. The only thing hot about the evening ahead of her was the hunk sitting right next to her. It was her night off, and the only thing she had lined up at home was a bubble bath and a stack of novels on her bedside table. Humphrey, her seven-year-old basset hound, had a doggy door and a free feeder. Her big yellow tomcat, Leo, had a clean litterbox and would likely dine with Humphrey. They would miss her, but the few extra hours she might spend

away from home wouldn't destroy their pawsome world. They were probably asleep in her bed right now.

Oh God! It's sheet day!

If she somehow snagged an intimate night with Riley, he would see her
dog-rumpled sheets and very disorganized bedroom—

Not to mention my Spanks!

On second thought, she hoped he did get too drunk to drive, then they'd
have to take a cab and maybe he wouldn't notice.

They spent two hours after Mona left swapping stories of best meals
ever and sharing recipes.

"Caramel drizzled over white-chocolate-covered pretzels with praline
sprinkles is one of my favorite Christmastime treats," he said, licking his
lips with anticipation.

Melvina was impressed that his handsome cowboy exterior was accompanied by a molten warm center, filled with an artistic desire to create
delectable dishes and share them with the people he loved. She couldn't
suppress a culinary moan as he described his special holiday menu, and how
he was planning to create dishes for the new restaurant, inspired by the box
of old recipes his grandma had left him after she passed away.

*Gorgeous, successful, family oriented, yet he looks like he could tame a wild
steer. Yummy.*

Melvina smiled up at Riley, wondering again why he hadn't moved to
the other side of the table. Raphe was obviously caught up elsewhere. Not
that she minded the warmth of his shoulder and thigh radiating through her
thin cotton blouse and jeans. "You must have been special for your grandma
to write down all her recipes and leave them for you."

He leaned over, lifting the bottle of boutique champagne out of the ice
bucket, removing the linen towel. She wanted to remember to look up the
vintage later. Its crisp flavor with just a hint of lemon and orange intrigued
her senses. Money was tight while she was saving up for her cupcake shop,
but on special occasions, there was no harm in splurging.

He nodded as the golden liquid splashed into her glass, and she reclined
into the soft cream leather of their booth. She was relaxed now and comforted by the love of food they shared. The stories he recounted of Ran and
Raphe reminded her of growing up with Eli. Riley was a blessed man to have
such a loving family. Her mother's absence stormed through her thoughts,
and like a jagged streak of lightning, it zigzagged to Maurice and his sister,
who'd been abandoned by their father.

"Wait a minute. I can't have another drink." She slapped a hand to her forehead, remembering Maurice and the homework help he would be returning to the library for. "I promised Maurice I would meet him." Looking at her cell phone, she was dismayed to see it was already six-thirty. She was supposed to meet him at seven and she still needed to get to the store to buy the supplies for his project. She stammered a thanks and tried to leave.

"Hold on now. You don't have a car, do you?" Riley looked a bit flustered. He made a sign to the waitress to bring the check.

Thwacking her forehead again, "Oh God, you're right. I left the van at Pop's." A groan of frustration trailed from her words.

"It's okay. I can take you wherever you need to go." Riley signed the check, leaving a big tip for the happy waitress. Shocked by his generosity, since it was almost as much as the bill, Melvina tried unsuccessfully to look away.

"I appreciate that, but it isn't necessary. You've done enough, really." She glanced back at the overturned champagne bottle. Like Cinderella after the ball, Melvina was aware that the clock was ticking. Her time with the prince was about to end. "Well, on second thought, I could really use a lift to the library."

Riley couldn't believe his luck. He'd walked into the wrong lounge to meet his brother, then ran into the one person he hadn't been able to get off his mind since the moment he took her into his arms and waltzed with her at the gala. He'd hoped to get to know her better by dropping by the café, but she'd been so busy and then he had to leave too soon.

Here in this casual atmosphere with the right mix of conversation and champagne, they were connecting. It had been years since he'd had such a good time with someone he was interested in. Hell, the time he'd spent with Melvina was like talking to the perfect woman. Her love for family and food rivaled his own. She loved her dad and practically ran his café, and she adored her younger brother, who seemed to be a great guy and always had her back. But, the thing about Melvina that touched him the most was how much she cared about the people around her and more pointedly, the community. Everything was going great until she remembered her date with that guy Maurice.

He hadn't noticed a ring on her finger, and there hadn't been talk of a fiancé or boyfriend. He had a distinct feeling from Mona's quick exit that she was trying to set him up with Melvina. Maybe Mona didn't know about Maurice or didn't like him. Maybe it was a first date for Melvina and this Maurice guy. He couldn't fault her for that. She was beautiful and deserved a fun night out.

I just wish it was with me.

The library sounded a little bookish. Maybe she liked the nerdy type. Riley wasn't dumb by any means—he'd played football in high school and college, but he'd always had big dreams of building a chain of restaurants and then expanding into other markets. He'd financed his first restaurant with the backing of some of his mother's connections, but they'd all benefited from their investments and then some. Reading was a pleasure he indulged in on a lazy Sunday afternoon lying in his backyard hammock. But, the idea of hanging around the stacks discussing the wonders of the Dewey Decimal System didn't exactly top his list of hot dates.

She asked him to stop by a Walgreens and he patiently waited inside his car. He skirted around asking if he could help. Drugstores were filled with womanly items and he was polite enough not to ask what she needed. She waved him off, saying she'd be back in a jiffy. When she returned, Riley stepped out and opened the door for her, and received a smile for his efforts. His heart sank a little as they approached the small-town library next to the railroad tracks and old train depot.

"Here we are. Only five minutes late. I'm sure your boyfriend won't mind—"

Damn! Way to sound sophisticated.

Melvina's head spun back toward Riley. Her eyebrows raised. "You thought Maurice was—" She flung her head back and whooped with laughter. Heat flashed through Riley. He understood his mistake immediately, but the heat wasn't from his embarrassment. He loved watching her laugh. She was the girl next door, the girl everyone loved to talk to in high school, the woman he would like to have on his arm at any party and someone he was already thinking to introduce to his family. Melvina's cheeks bloomed with color and her eyes glittered with mirth. Her long blond hair hung loose over her shoulders and he suppressed the desire to brush it back. Her complexion was smooth and just a tad golden from the sun. He wanted to slide his fingers down her cheek and brush his lips across hers.

Just then, a boy knocked at the car window. Riley pushed a button and the glass glided down.

Melvina offered the youngster one of her enchanting, warm smiles. "Well, howdy. What are you doing out here?" she said in a soft voice.

"I was worried you'd forgotten—" His big brown eyes were wide and shining with unshed tears. "Or you were in an accident or something." The young Hispanic kid clearly mooned over Melvina, but Riley bet she didn't have a clue about the crush. She opened the door as she soothed the boy, patting him on the shoulder and handing him one of the bags. The boy grinned and scampered up the steps of the library.

Turning to Riley, she leaned in through the open window. Her top gaped and the heart-shaped charm that floated on the silver chain winked at him from her gorgeous cleavage.

Lord help me maintain eye contact.

"Thanks so much for the ride." She gave him a smile that promised warmth and intrigue, the kind that most women attempted to look fascinating, but Melvina was authentic. He'd traveled the world learning from the best culinary experts and spent time in the company of exotic, gorgeous women. They couldn't hold a candle to Melvina's genuine beauty. It emanated from her core and its sincerity reached her eyes when she smiled, leaving him with no doubt of her interest. "I really enjoyed the conversation and the champagne."

"The pleasure was all mine." He smiled back, wishing he was the one meeting her in the library after all. "I hope we can do it again sometime." Riley glanced behind her at the boy, who was waiting by the door. The kid didn't look happy about Riley delaying Melvina. Maybe his father was waiting inside. Had he been wrong about her available status? "Do you need a ride? I can come back for you later."

She tapped the car twice and waved. "Naw, I'm all good, but thanks again."

Riley adjusted himself, making room for the added excitement of her derriere swaying as she ascended the steps of the library and disappeared inside. Through the old building's window, he spotted her hugging the boy as they walked past the front desk.

It's not like we were on a date or anything.

So why did he feel so deflated? He' had a great time with her, and from the way she was so open about her family, he could tell she was enjoying herself too.

She doesn't owe you any explanations, man.

But he wanted to take her out on a date. He wanted more. True, he was physically attracted to her—

Those curves, that hair, that smile—

But his instincts told him to go slow. Melvina wasn't that kind of woman. He drove out of the round-a-about and turned back onto the main road as he pondered his bachelor status. Women threw themselves at him often enough and Riley hated to admit he'd had his share of one-night stands, but over the past couple of years, he'd been avoiding those sorts of fast-and-loose encounters. His restaurant was thriving and continual growth in his business kept him too busy for barhopping. The thing about one-night stands was that they only lasted for one night, and lately he recognized the stirrings of a need to share his successes with someone who got what he was all about.

His mind skipped back to his business, and he pointed the Infiniti toward the city. He needed to check on things at the restaurant. When the cat's away, and all that.

Riley tried to tamp down on his growing feelings for the curvaceous cupcake lady, but he couldn't heed his own warning.

There's just something about Melvina.

Melvina worked with Maurice on the solar system layout on a sketch-pad with colored pencils. They took the plastic balls she had bought from Walgreens and covered them in strips of plaster, leaving them in the back room to dry. The librarians allowed art projects to be constructed in their study room and didn't mind the planets drying overnight.

Maurice would come back and paint them tomorrow and then they would string them all together around the large sun. The blow-up beach ball had been a mite bigger than the other smaller balls she had found in the toy section, but it was the best she could do for the pickings. Maurice was very creative and seemed to enjoy the homework. Two hours later, when his mother came to pick him up, Maurice was practically hopping up and down, telling his smiling mother all about his project.

Melvina waved as they exited the building, then pulled out her phone to call her brother for a ride. The lights flicked on and off twice, signaling the library was closing in ten minutes.

"Hey, Melvina."

Looking up from her phone, she was surprised to see Manny staring at her.

"Hey, Chief, what are you doing here?"

He held up a book and smiled. "I've been having a little insomnia, and I thought it might be a good idea to give my computer games a rest and do a little reading. I read an article about how computers activate your brain and interfere with REM sleep."

Melvina read the well-worn spine, "'The Silver Chalice.'" She let out a low whistle. "That's a long one."

Manny held the old book up and studied its size. "Yeah, it might take me a while to get through it, but it's one of the classics I missed reading. It's been on my list for a while. Have you read it?"

"Yes, I have, but I don't remember much about it. I read it in high school and all I can remember is thinking I would never get through it to finish my book report in time." They both laughed.

"I guess I'm sure to get some sleep."

"And then some. I know I sure did." Melvina ran her finger over the returns cart and pulled out a book in an emerald-green jacket. "How about this one?"

Manny studied the title on the cracked binding, a smile spread across his face. "'The Last of the Mohicans,' now that's a good book."

She sighed. "Oh, you've read it. I love to help people find the right book, but I think we're out of time." Nina, the librarian, was staring at them from the counter, waiting for Manny to move through the empty checkout line. They were the last people in the building.

"No, I like the Mohicans. I've probably forgotten most of it, and it will be all new again after so many years. I'll get them both. Thanks." Manny seemed to hesitate before nodding and entering the roped-off section leading to the counter.

Melvina stepped out into the dusk and gazed at the streetlight that blinked on overhead. Spring was bringing more hours of light every day and Melvina was ready for summer to come. The sound of cicadas moved in waves around her, and a mosquito landed on her bare arm. It was time to shed the jeans and put on shorts soon. She would have to spend a few days in her garden to get her legs ready for summer clothes. The diner wasn't far away, so Melvina decided to walk to Pop's. The exercise would do her good.

"You need a ride?" Manny's truck pulled up slowly beside her.

She shrugged her shoulders and lifted her hands. "I was trying to get some exercise. I left my car at the hotel the other night, and I've been too busy to go pick it up."

"Hop in, I'll take you to it."

If it had been anyone else but Manny, she would have said a flat no, but he was kind and she had liked him for so long. She really did need to get her car back since she'd never made it by the auto shop. The twenty minutes would be out of the fire chief's way, but he didn't seem to be in a rush to get home. "Okay, but only if you let me drop off a few pies tomorrow at the firehouse."

He laughed. "I never say no to pie."

Leaning over, he opened the door and gave it a push. A car made a wide berth around them, honking for the inconvenience. Manny made a polite salute, even though the driver never glanced back.

"So, life's been busy?"

Melvina turned in her seat as she clicked the seatbelt in place. "Huh?"

"You haven't had time to go get your car," he reminded her.

"Oh yeah, right. I've been helping Maurice with his school studies and I'm swamped with tasks for the ladies' club. Plus, the diner and the usual life chores. Actually, I've kind of ignored those. My house is a complete mess." So was her life. She had put a lot of things on the back burner lately.

"I can send Janie over if you like. She's been a great help to me. I even have her do the station once a week just to keep things nice and clean. The boys aren't all bad, but men just don't seem to have the same touch."

"I would say I understand, but my brother is much neater than I am. He was the one with the organized room, and I could never seem to keep my stuff off the floor."

Manny nodded. "Maurice, is that the kid you were helping in the library?"

"Yeah, he's sweet and smart too. His dad took off and left the family, so no surprise he's struggling with school. I've been trying to get him to spend time with someone who might be a good influence. I was going to ask you if maybe he could help wash fire trucks one day. I'll hang nearby to watch out for him, but I think he could really use a positive male role model. The guys might show him the importance of work and commitment to service, and he would probably love to see the inside of a fire truck."

"No problem. It would be good for the guys, too. I haven't been paying enough attention to see if the men are keeping up with maintenance. It would be a good excuse to get everything squeaky clean. Poor little guy. Is his momma okay? Does she need any groceries or anything?"

"They are pretty proud. I already tried to help in that department, but she's stubbornly holding it together alone. I've made sure to bring baked cookies and such whenever I see Maurice. He thinks it's just a reward for doing his homework, but at least this way I know he has had something to eat. I always make a loaf of bread for him to take home."

"You're a good soul, Melvina."

"I try, Chief, but if I think too long about all the needy children out there, it gets overwhelming. I just do what I can."

"Maybe we can put some of that money from the calendar toward a mentor program here in Magnolia. There seems to be a demand, and I know a special lady who seems to have an interest in advocating for those kids in need."

"Talk to Celia. I bet she has that money earmarked for the fire department and something else for the Magnolia Blossoms, but if she would part with the funds for anyone, Chief, it would be you."

As they rolled up to the awning that covered the circular drive for hotel guests, Melvina hopped out. "Thanks again for the ride."

"You're welcome." Manny smiled and reached a hand toward her as if he wanted to say something else. Melvina paused with one hand still on the door.

"You-uh, busy tomorrow night?"

"I have a late shift at the diner, but I don't go in until noon. Do you need something?"

Manny paused. His eyes shone with interest. "I—I was just wondering if you might have time to swing by and talk about the calendar."

"Of course. I'll come by with the baked goods in the morning and we can go over whatever we'll need to get ready. I'll talk with Celia first. She probably has her own plans on what she wants."

"Melvina?"

"Yes, Chief?"

"Call me, Manny, please. Maybe we could sketch out the plans first, without Celia?"

"All right, Ch—Manny. See you tomorrow."

Chapter 8

Melvina hit the alarm clock twice before realizing the wretched noise was coming from her cell phone. It was Mona again.

"Mona, why is it you insist on video chatting with me every morning? Don't you know that no one over thirty should ever hold a phone at this angle?" Melvina tried to straighten her neck in her groggy state, blinking at the unsightly reflection of her double chin in the screen. Even skinny people had double chins when the back of a head was propped up on a mound of pillows. It annoyed her that her skin's elasticity was failing, and her new slimmer size was accompanied with a slight sag that she wished she could will away.

Mona pursed her over-drawn lips, making her after-forty smile lines look like they had sprouted roots up the crest of her upper lip. "I don't call every morning." She paused waiting for Melvina, who declined to argue.

"Listen—Lisa Andrews heard from Tanya Freeman who talked to Lucy Mason that Georgia Messing was in the library last night and saw you talking to Manny. And Jody Watson told Trisha Harper that Lonnie Jones saw you get in Manny's truck down the road from the library—real suspicious like. Now why is it I have to hear about the mysterious and apparently active love life of my bestest friend through the Magnolia grapevine?" Mona's eyes were narrowed with unsuppressed annoyance.

Melvina groaned. She would have laughed at the absurdity of it, but nothing was sacred or stayed secret in Magnolia, Texas. "Look, Mona. I don't know why I have to explain every non-incident that ever occurs in my life, but Manny said hello in the library, and I decided to walk to the diner and get a ride to the hotel to pick up my car. The fire chief saw me walking and offered a ride. He's a nice man is all."

Mona panned the phone toward the bedroom door where Melvina could see Jorden lying in her bed snoring. All but his most private parts were uncovered.

"Mel, you really should jump that nice man's bones before you shrivel up and die from lack of sex. It's good for the complexion, I tell you."

Melvina waved for Mona to move the phone and mouthed the words, STOP IT, before rolling her eyes. Mona started walking the phone toward the bed, zooming in on the sheet-covered part of Jorden's body.

"I'm hanging up Mona," Melvina called out as Mona's hand moved to lift the sheet. Pressing the END button and tossing her phone to the empty spot on her bed, Melvina sighed. Looking at the vacant half, she silently wondered why she slept on one side.

Mona's complexion did look nice. Maybe Melvina needed to step out of her shell and meet someone willing to take her up on a one-night stand. It wasn't that she didn't want a relationship, it's that she had no luck with men. She'd been heavy most of her adult years, which made her feel like she wasn't what men were looking for, and now that she was shaping up, she couldn't imagine where to start. No matter how much weight she'd lost, she still felt awkward when it came to matters of the heart. The few dates she had tried never worked out well. She just didn't connect. She was forever known as the cupcake lady, a Magnolia ladies' club member, volunteer at the library—good ol' Melvina Banks.

Pop had tried to set her up with a few men over the years, customers who regularly ate at the diner, but she had shied away. She'd crushed on Manny even before he was widowed, and some deep part of her felt guilty for nourishing the crush, even if it was only in her head. His wife's passing made him available, but Manny's interest made Melvina feel ashamed. Maybe her secret fantasy somehow put a vibe out there that she wanted him to be available and now that his wife was gone, Melvina felt awkward. Did she pick unavailable men so she wouldn't actually have to put her heart on the line?

Melvina shook the meandering thoughts away and stepped into the shower. She needed to run by the diner to get a few things to take to the station and she should call Celia and ask about the charity calendar she was supposed to oversee. Not to mention, she still needed to drop off the paperwork for the audit. Celia wouldn't accept the excuse that she hadn't been in the office when Melvina had dropped by yesterday. Manny had asked her not to tell Celia about their preliminary meeting, so she would have to skate around her plans when talking to the Blossom president.

Firetrucks zoomed out as Melvina drove up to the station. The men who recognized her gave her a quick wave as they sped down Nichols Sawmill Road. She noticed the open garage bays and decided to leave the treats for the men for when they returned. They would work up an appetite if there was a real fire, but it was most likely Mrs. Kinder. She was eighty-eight and had a slew of cats. More than likely, Miss Kitty was up in the tree again and couldn't get down. The aging calico was blind and skittish. It was a weekly occurrence that the firemen had dubbed The Miss Kitty drill. The chief thought it was good practice for new volunteer recruits to go, while the experienced firefighters had a good time razzing them on their return. Miss Kitty had a vicious bite.

Melvina entered through the open bay and made her way to the kitchen. Firemen were great cooks and usually took turns churning out meals when they were on shift. She'd swiped Joe Kuntz's recipe for cocktail meatballs. Who would have thought grape jelly and chili sauce would make for such a dynamic concoction?

She set the boxes of individual cherry and apple pies next to the sugar and creamer on the break tables. The place was empty. Glancing around she wondered where *all* the firemen were. It looked like they'd all just raced out of the station. She hoped it wasn't something major.

She opened two large tin containers and carefully lifted out two dozen chocolate cupcakes decorated with a thick swirl of chocolate frosting and red sprinkles, arranging them on the cardboard trays she'd brought with her. Turning to leave, Melvina spied Manny drumming away at his dinosaur of a computer in his office.

"Oh, hey Manny. I thought the house was empty."

Manny looked over the rim of his reading glasses. "Hey, Melvina. I didn't know you were here." He stood, taking his glasses off and stashing them in his desk drawer.

"I didn't know you wore glasses."

He fidgeted with the stapler, several papers, then set a glass paperweight on top of the neat stack. "You weren't supposed to see those." He cleared his throat. "Ever since my last birthday, I have had to wear 'em to read."

Melvina hadn't seen him wear them at the library but decided she would let the topic go, nodding. "Maybe we should use some of that calendar money to buy the station a new computer. Looks like that one is past its expiration date."

Manny laughed. "Yeah, it's old like me, but I like it. It does the job, and truth be told, I can't keep up with technology. It seems like every day they come out with something new and I have to read another manual to understand how to turn the darn thing on."

He shook his head and came around the desk. "Wanna cup of coffee? It's not the best, but it's fresh. I set it on to brew before the boys got the Miss Kitty call."

"Aha, I knew it!" she chuckled.

"It's good for them and better than having everyone laze around here and eat. No offense." He motioned at the cakes and pies.

"None taken. Hopefully they will have earned the calories when they get back." The space in the galley kitchen was small, and Melvina felt awkward as she tried to move past Manny, who was pouring coffee for them. She walked into the dining area, pulled out a chair and took a seat. She plucked an artificial sweetener and a coffee stirrer from the plastic cup in the middle of the table and set them on a napkin. "I haven't talked to Celia yet," Melvina said. "I keep missing her at the office. She must be working on some other project. I'll try calling her later this afternoon. When is this calendar shoot supposed to take place?"

"Celia is ready to start tomorrow, but I don't know how all of this works. I was hoping you might be able to prepare us." The pink stain creeping up his neck was at odds with the chief's usually controlled demeanor.

"I did some thinking on this last night and have a few ideas. I know most of the men at the station are married with kids—and their wives might not approve of this particular charity venture. Maybe we should broaden it into a good-natured competition, and involve all the fire stations in Montgomery and Harris counties? Then they could bring the handsomest of their unit to compete with yours. The top twelve selected will make a great calendar, and the money that will be made on the tickets to attend the pageant will be enough to warrant having the whole affair.

"We can do a semi-final and final pageant and string them a week or two apart. We'll need to advertise to the public and solicit the TV and radio stations. Maybe we can raise a prize amount from the contest so that all the fire stations could benefit as well." Melvina's words picked up speed as she did what she did best—manage an event.

"Wait a minute! Pageant? I don't think—"

Melvina waved both hands at him. "It's just a word Chief, don't get your panties in a wad." She giggled as he shot her a reprimanding glare. "It's not like we're gonna curl their hair or put lipstick on them, but we may need to do some man-scaping before they hit the stage."

"Stage?" he bellowed. Sweat beaded up on the chief's forehead. "I—I don't know about all this. Maybe we should rethink—"

Melvina could no longer hold back her laughter. The alarmed expression on the tough guy's face was priceless. "Don't worry about a thing," Melvina soothed, patting his hand. "It will be tasteful, the guys will love all the attention, but best of all, it will raise money for the fire department, and god willing, start a mentor program for the kids."

He blew out a breath as she spoke. Her pitch was doing the trick. She knew the chief supported the community, especially allocating funds to help underprivileged kids. Manny tipped his chair back and balanced on the back legs as he brought his cup to his lips.

Please, say yes, Manny. Kids like Maurice could use the support.

Melvina hoped the intense expression on his face as he downed the last of his coffee meant he was seriously considering the idea.

Melvina took a final sip of her own, set her empty cup on the table, and stood to leave. "I'd better get back to Pop's. My shift starts at noon, but there's inventory to do today. I'll try to catch Celia one more time on my way to work."

Manny walked her to the open bay where she had entered. His proximity allowed him to reach out and touch a wayward lock of hair that the wind had tossed across her face. Melvina's eyes widened at his tender action. His smile was warm, but his eyes were searching. "Melvina, would you like to go out to dinner sometime?"

All the air whooshed out of her lungs at once. Mona had said he was interested in her, but she hadn't thought it was true. She hadn't prepared herself for the very moment she had spent years longing for.... Yet here she was. *That* moment was actually happening, and all she could do was stand gaping at him like a guppy out of water.

His blue eyes were flecked with ivory around the pupils and framed with thick dark lashes he'd inherited from his Italian father. His mother had been quite a beauty in her day. The crinkles around the corners were warm and expressive. Melvina found it hard to look into those striking eyes at the moment. For a man approaching his mid-fifties, he was in perfect shape and could give the younger firemen a run for their money if he chose to compete in the calendar event. Manny was one of the kindest, sexiest men she knew, and he was asking her to dinner.

"Um, yeah, sure. Anytime," she bumbled.

"How about this weekend? Friday or Saturday?"

"I've got to work this weekend."

"Then next weekend."

"I haven't made the schedule that far out." Melvina wasn't sure why she was stalling. She made the schedule, and she was actually off Saturday, but would now have to work because she was too nervous to go out with Manny.

"Okay. Let's play it by ear. I'll check back with you next week." His smile was warm and knowing. She knew he probably sensed her jitters but wasn't put off by them. Manny wasn't only handsome, he exuded warmth and had a protective nature.

"Great! Looking forward to it," she said as she backed into the flag-pole and stumbled a step. Manny grinned and waved as she got into the catering van. She drove from the firehouse to the lion's den. It was time to face-off with Celia.

Riley didn't know why Celia Lockwood had summoned him to her office, but he didn't plan to stay long. They'd wrapped up the charity event funds, and he didn't like the way Celia had treated Melvina the night of the ball. He nodded at the secretary, who motioned him into the spacious, modern office. Stainless steel, glass and black-lacquered finishes made up the min-imalist decorated room. The only pop of color was a picture of Celia in a red frame that must have dated back a few years.

Riley removed his ball cap as Celia rose from her expansive glass desk, giving him a wide smile. Her thin figure was clad in a tight, pale gray designer suit and sexy red high heels. He hoped she wasn't torturing her-self on his account. He didn't care how she wrapped the package, women like Celia were toxic.

"Mr. Nash, I'm so glad you could come. Please, have a seat." She motioned to the chairs parked in front of her desk. Once he was seated in the soft dark leather, she came around and sat on the desk's edge, leaving very little room between them. It also put her feminine assets in his immediate field of vision. Riley propped one ankle on his opposite knee and leaned back. He hoped the message was clear.

"I wanted to commend you once more on the wonderful dinner arrangements for the charity fund-raiser," she began. "It was our best event to date, and all due to the excellent menu selections."

Riley fidgeted. "I don't think you can credit me with all of the success. Miss Banks did a hell of a job putting it all together. It didn't hurt that the hotel is new, and the ballroom is beautiful." He hated looking down, but he didn't like craning his neck up to look at Celia, and he certainly didn't want to look straight ahead. The stitching on his Lucchese boots was safer territory.

"Melvina?" Celia chuckled. "She's nice to have around to pick up the slack, but she's no wizard when it comes to finances. I won't go into all that. She's not interesting enough to talk about right now, but I will tell her you approve."

Celia was certainly sharpening her claws and out for blood. Riley's own blood began to boil. He stood, coming face to face with the designer beauty. He was six feet tall, and he guessed she was only four inches shorter without the heels. "I think this meeting is over."

She put a hand on his chest. "You can't be serious? Melvina was probably a hundred pounds overweight at the last ball. Are you a chubby chaser, Mr. Nash?"

"I take offense to just about everything you've said today, Miss Lockwood. Now, if you will excuse me." Riley turned and made his way to the door.

Celia followed him at a clipped pace. "Wait! Riley, I'm sorry. I don't know what's gotten into me. I've behaved deplorably. Can you give me just a few more minutes of your time?"

Riley turned back, one hand on the door. Celia's catty expression changed to soft, imploring desperation.

"Okay, but I won't stand for your insults of Miss Banks."

"Agreed. I don't know why I'm downing Melvina. I think I'm just mad she ruined my ball gown. Silly of me, I know. Forgive me. I'll be on my best behavior—I promise." She had both hands on him now, one on each bicep. "I would like to ask you to host another dinner. You will be paid for your time. We're creating a fund-raising calendar for the fire department, and the chief mentioned to me, only moments before you arrived, that he would like to allocate a good portion of the proceeds to fund a mentor program for Magnolia."

Riley blew out a breath. He wanted to be angry and he didn't want to be a pawn in Celia's game, but after hearing her last statement, how could he say no? He'd always had a soft spot for children in need. He would have to put his dislike for Celia aside and try to work something out so that the kids could benefit. Besides, it would possibly put him closer to Melvina, though he remembered working solely with Celia on the last event. Amazed that he could have ever considered going out with the vamp holding onto him like a prize bull, he reminded himself it was before he saw how badly she treated Melvina.

Celia was leaning into him, smiling playfully. Her breasts brushed against the front of his shirt. "What do you say? Do it for the kids?"

Riley waited a beat, blew out another long breath and nodded. Celia made a cooing noise, then planted a kiss on him before he had time to step back. He was still holding onto the door.

When he didn't return the kiss, she stepped back and straightened her blazer. "Well, then, that's settled."

Celia's bright red convertible was parked outside the office, and Melvina sighed with relief. She was ready to drop off the accountant's figures and be done with the whole mess. The numbers checked out correctly, except for a load of receipts that Celia had added to the stack when she handed Melvina the files at the diner.

Apparently, Celia had forgotten to include them in the initial filing and had filed an amendment without telling Melvina or Stan. That was a big no-no for the IRS. There were thousands of dollars in receipts for things that Melvina wasn't sure the Blossoms could deduct. Designer shoes, make-up, and spa days were not charitable tax write-offs. She would let Celia battle that out with the auditing agent when their extension ended next week. She had done her part with Stan and the initial meeting with the auditor. Now it was up to Celia to face the taxman.

Melvina approached the office and saw Riley through the glass door. Celia's secretary looked uncomfortable as she motioned for Melvina to have a seat. Melvina watched as Riley and Celia locked lips.

Laying the thick file of papers on the secretary's desk, Melvina mumbled something about giving it to Celia and turned to leave. She didn't know why she felt like the bottom had just fallen out of her world. Riley Nash wasn't hers to claim. Celia Lockwood was beautiful, slim, and successful. They looked good together. Both polished and posh.

She revved the engine on the van as she backed out of the lot, causing the wheels to peel out on the pavement. She caught a glimpse of Riley in her rearview mirror. He was standing on the sidewalk, feet braced apart, shouting something at her. He slammed his hat against his knee and spiked his fingers through his hair. He looked flustered.

Talking to him was the last thing she wanted.

Right now, she needed to be alone at home, baking in her kitchen, but being at Pop's would be the next best thing.

Chapter 9

Melvina scheduled herself for kitchen duty the rest of the week. Every morning she gathered bags of flour and dumped them into the large bins, then fed the yeast and started the loaves of bread she would bake for the day. Red-velvet cupcakes cooled on wire racks while she whipped up the fresh cream cheese icing, then filled the sprinkle shakers with the many-colored confections she'd use to decorate the frosted tops of the cupcakes.

Methodically, she moved to the cooler to fetch the four dozen eggs she would need for the pecan pies and lemon cakes. She was in her zone when she was alone in the kitchen doing what she loved. Her worries faded into the distance and a wave of calm washed over her as she entered into a blissful creative flow. Baking was an art, and Melvina was a culinary artist. She knew she had a talent, a gift that brought happiness to others.

Thank the heavens that God gave me baking as a coping skill. My addiction to sugar and flour at least make the world a happier place.

She wore a satisfied smile as she whipped, beat, frosted and kneaded her way through the morning. When the hustle of the breakfast rush bled to lunch, then dinner, she finally hung her apron on a hook and walked to the office to say good-bye to Pop. She watched his slim frame bent over the office adding machine, totaling sales for the day. His full head of salt and pepper hair was brushed back from his forehead, and his matching mustache was perfectly combed and oiled to sleek barbershop perfection. Her heart swelled with pride. Pop had always been there for her.

When did his hair turn so gray?

Melvina rapped on the doorframe to the office. "I'm heading out, Pop. Need anything before I go?"

"Melvina darlin', I think you've done enough. You should have checked out hours ago. Is Eli late again?" He looked over the wire-rimmed reading glasses.

"No, he's out front pouring coffee for Mac and Lynn. All's good. I just wanted to fill the pie cabinet and make extra cupcakes for the library's bake sale tomorrow."

Pop nodded and poked at the adding machine. "All right then, doll. See ya tomorrow."

Melvina waved and started toward the back exit. She was trying to avoid the front of the diner since the day she saw Celia and Riley kissing. It was also the day Manny asked her out.

Too much confusion for one day.

She'd thought about Manny's offer more than a few times but wasn't sure what she wanted to do with that situation. She had mooned over Manny for so long, and now Riley had waltzed into her life, turning everything topsy-turvy. Riley had given her signals, but he had a reputation with the ladies. She didn't know why she felt so hurt over seeing him locking lips with Celia.

It's not like we're dating or anything.

Sharing a few drinks and a ride to the library didn't make for a commitment. On the other hand, her life-long crush on the fire chief had finally sparked to life. Manny had actually asked her out. So why did she high-tail it out of there like her tail feathers were on fire? This was all too stressful. She just needed to get home and relax.

The gravel crunched under her feet as she made her way to her car. She fished her keys out of her purse, and when she looked up, Manny was leaning against the driver's side door.

Caught by surprise, she opened her mouth and whipped her head around to the café and back. "Manny, I didn't know you were out here."

"I wasn't. I was in there," he pointed to the café, "but then Eli told me you were sneaking out the back, and I decided to catch you before you could run," he said with a chuckle.

She couldn't resist cracking a smile as she thought of Eli tattling on her. Ever the matchmaker, her little brother was determined to help her find true love. "I wasn't sneaking out—well, maybe I was, but it wasn't from you."

He seemed relieved as his shoulders relaxed and he let his crossed arms fall. His hands casually hooked onto his jean pockets. "That's good to know. How about that dinner?"

"Um—you mean now?" she sputtered, looking down at her flour-dusted work clothes. "I smell like French fries and pancakes." She had spilled half a bottle of syrup down her pant leg while filling the bottles for tomorrow's breakfast.

"Wonderful. I love French fries and pancakes." He flashed her a grin.

"Chief!" she fussed, shaking her head as she laughed. "I'm not going anywhere like this. There's been enough gossip going 'round. I don't want it to be said that I don't shower or wear decent clothes."

"Okay, I'll give you two hours, then I'll come and pick you up. I got a great place to take you. You'll love it."

What could she say? It would be rude to say no, and she liked Manny. She'd liked him forever. "Won't it be too late? Most places in Magnolia close up early on a school night."

The chief threw her a sly grin. "Never mind you that. I know a place."

She was outmaneuvered and wasn't sure why she was resisting. She was hungry and Manny looked good enough to eat. "Okay, how should I dress?"

"It's casual but wear what you want. You look beautiful no matter what you wear, and besides, it's your smile that I like." The crinkles at the corners of his eyes were warm, and Melvina felt heat rush from her head to her toes. It wasn't a proclamation about her looks, so much as a declaration about her as a person. He liked who she was.

Isn't that what I've always been searching for?

"I like your smile too," she blurted.

Pushing himself away from the car, he opened the door for her. As she slid in, he said, "See you in a couple. Drive safe."

Chapter 10

Melvina fussed over her hair, but the humidity had turned it into a big ball of frizz, so in the end, she decided on a thick braid with a long golden strand left to grace one side of her face. She wore the bright red lipstick she had bought at Sephora during her last shopping trip with Mona. The saleslady told her that red gave the perception of bright and friendly. That must be new, because Melvina had always thought red lipstick was all about sex appeal. In any case, the fiery hue complemented her skin tone. She didn't know where Manny was taking her, so she didn't overdress, but she wouldn't rely on jeans.

One time, a blind date had told her to dress casual for dinner, and the guy had taken her to an uptown French restaurant in the city. The hostess sat them in the back corner near the kitchen door. Everyone else was wearing evening attire, but her date was oblivious in his jeans and cowboy boots. Tonight, she chose a plain black cotton maxi dress with a braided belt and silver jewelry to accent its simplicity. Her flat sandals had silver beads as well and laced up each calf with thin leather straps. She looked spring chic with a hint of the golden tan she had from toiling in her garden.

When Manny showed up, she breathed easy. His tan cotton pants were pressed with a sharp crease, and his blue shirt crisp with starch from the dry cleaners. They would fit in anywhere they might go in Magnolia, but also prepared for anything upscale they might find in the city.

Manny let out an appreciative whistle as he strolled up the stairs of her porch. She was enjoying the last sip of her diet soda and lost in her book when he'd pulled into the drive. The weather was balmy, and she was a little sad that she couldn't sit for another hour or two enjoying the story.

"You sure look pretty." Manny's Texas manners were simple but charming.

"Thanks. You too. I may not smell like pancakes anymore, but you might like this new perfume I bought."

She lifted her wrist expecting him to take a sniff, then Manny surprised her when he pulled her up into his arms and waltzed her around the white-painted planks of the covered porch. His nose grazed her neck as he breathed in the slightly sweet jasmine scent. The heat of his breath tickled her sensitive skin as he exhaled.

"Mm," he murmured as he lifted his head, staring into her eyes. "That's nice. I like it."

Melvina flushed under his warm gaze. "Thanks. I'll tell Mona. She made me buy it. I don't usually have a reason to wear perfume." She bit her tongue so she would quit tripping over it. Why she wanted to advertise that she didn't have a life was beyond her, but she needed to stop acting like she didn't deserve to be appreciated.

Hello! Take the advice from those self-improvement DVDs you bought.

"Well, it smells heavenly and matches your beautiful skin." His thumb gently circled the inside of her wrist as he let go of her waist and motioned to his truck.

Melvina was glad she was wearing the loose-fitting dress. It would be easier to get into the passenger side of the tall cab. Especially given how butterflies were dancing in her stomach and her legs felt weak from their impromptu twirl across her porch.

Get a grip on yourself and act like you know how to go out with a man!

They drove through a few country roads and out to the highway. "Where are you takin' us, Manny?"

"It's a surprise. You'll see."

Once they hit the forty-five, Melvina knew they were headed into the city and was glad she'd dressed up some. It was forty-five minutes into Houston from Magnolia, and when they arrived, she was indeed surprised. The valet took the truck and Melvina stared up at the red awning with *Braised* written across it in white, cursive lettering.

Oh, Lordy!

What were the odds? She admitted she'd been curious to try Riley Nash's hot new restaurant, but this wasn't exactly how she imagined it. As Manny took her arm to escort her in, she couldn't find a reasonable excuse not to enter.

They walked across the red-carpeted entrance and admired the modern chandeliers illuminating scarlet walls. The rich wood floor and earthy colored leather booths gave the restaurant a feel of opulence paired with comfort. She imagined a gentleman's smoking room or a library in a wealthy manor home. A glass case filled with expensive cognacs and a multitude of other spirits took up the entire wall behind the Victorian-style mahogany bar. She recognized some of the labels and was amazed by the selection. The place was impressive, and the smell of seasoned, seared meats made her mouth water. Riley's place was a hit. Every barstool was occupied, and it was standing room only throughout.

Manny studied the crowded room. "Don't worry, one of the guys has an in and he set it all up. We have a reservation."

Melvina had heard that Braised was booked months out—she was surprised the chief had managed to snag a table, but then she knew that Riley's brother was a fireman and probably knew a few of the Magnolia firefighters.

The hostess led them to the second level and asked them if they preferred to sit inside or outside. The glass walls were open to the setting sun and a few stars were blinking in the distance. Manny looked at Melvina and she smiled, nodding.

"Outside is where I always like to be, but if you prefer inside, I'm okay with that too."

Smiling at the hostess, he said, "You heard the lady. We'll sit on the patio."

The young woman held the menus against the front of her black, skin-tight mini dress and motioned to a table near the ivy-covered wall of the terrace.

Melvina's nerves settled once they were seated and the Cosmo she'd ordered was half-finished. Multiple scenarios ran through her mind of Riley seeing her there with Manny. Ultimately, she didn't want Riley to think she was here with Manny because she saw him kissing Celia. She reassured herself that Riley wouldn't think anything because he wouldn't think of her in that or any other way. He might have flirted with her a little and given her a ride to the library, but that was it.

Just relax and enjoy your night out with Manny.

He was a nice man, a good-looking man, and up until a few weeks ago, she'd really wanted him to notice her.

Manny leaned back in his chair, sipping the whiskey in his short rocks glass. "Are you ready for next week?"

Melvina was perplexed, "Next week?"

"The contest between Harris County and Montgomery. You're coming, right?"

"Oh, that. I, um—I don't know. I haven't seen Celia and I think she might have another one of the Blossoms working on the whole event. I worked up a schedule and a plan the day I left the firehouse. I left it with her secretary, but I haven't touched base with Celia since. We've been playing phone tag."

It was a white lie. Celia had called her several times, but she hadn't answered. Instead, she'd sent Celia a list of details to forward to another Blossom to arrange. She was pretty sure she would be giving up her seat as treasurer at the end of the year and moving on to other volunteer work. Her relationship with Celia had grown sour since the chocola-tastrophe.

Melvina was also pretty sure Celia was guilty of some sort of tax evasion and was trying to hang her out to dry. Not to mention, after the Riley kissing incident, she just couldn't bring herself to go back there. How Riley could be interested in a woman like that was beyond her, except that Celia looked like one of those glossy magazine ads for women's cosmetics.

"You let her run over you, Melvina. The only reason I agreed to this whole affair is because I knew you would make it fun and community friendly."

Melvina finished her cocktail and Manny motioned to the waitress to bring another. "I am running it, sort of, but from behind the scenes. I don't want to be out front taking all the credit. I chose a nice photographer, Tiana Wanson. She's one of the firemen's wives. You'll like her. She does family photos and prom pictures, so there won't be anything illicit or embarrassing to worry about, and Bubbles is hosting the pageant.

"I asked the hotel to loan us their portable stage for the event. We'll set it up with a few of the lights and equipment from the Tomball Cats, and Raphe Nash's model girlfriend has agreed to emcee. I think that will take care of the publicity as well. The tickets are being sold all around town at every grocery, barbecue place and gas station. The radio stations in Houston are pushing it on the air as part of their donation to the cause, and if we fill up, there's a nice open field next to the bar where we can set up a tent for the event." She was breathless as she finished running down the list of everything that had been set up.

Manny rubbed his chin, "Well, I guess I can't argue with all that. It sounds like you've more than done your bit planning it out. I still wish you would be there."

"We'll see." Melvina caught sight of Riley walking through the open glass doors. He stopped to direct a busboy to a table and then took a rocks glass filled with amber colored liquid off a tray. Melvina remembered he liked expensive whiskey.

As Manny launched into a comical story about a new recruit, Melvina's gaze kept straying to Riley. He moved with a smooth confidence and was obviously a big attraction to the clientele. He was stopped several times in the few moments it took to reach her and the chief.

"Melvina, how nice to see you here." His smile was genuine, and his eyes shimmered with sincere interest.

Melvina's tongue froze in her mouth. All she could manage was a smile and a nod.

Riley turned to Manny. "Hello again," he said in a polite, business-like tone. "We met at the ball the other night. You're the Magnolia fire chief, right? I'm sorry. I'm terrible with names." Riley held out his hand for a firm shake.

"That's okay, Mr. Nash. I got the upper hand on this one, since everyone in the area is clamoring about your restaurant. If it wasn't for your brother, Raphe, I doubt I'd be able to show Miss Banks such a nice time tonight. I'm sure you know Raphe is a big fan of Melvina's—she's forever baking up treats for the firefighters in the area."

Melvina blushed at the compliment and the way both men kept looking at her.

"That I do," Riley replied, glancing at Melvina. "But unfortunately, I haven't been able to pin her down to show me any of her trade secrets." Riley turned back to Manny, a heavy eyebrow raised in question. "You must be the table I saved for Raphe. He told me you were bringing a date. I didn't know it was Melvina."

Melvina's blush turned into a slow burn. Riley had used the "D" word. Manny had been careful to skate around calling it a date and Melvina had half convinced herself it was just a dinner between friends. She opened her mouth and then snapped it shut.

I'm stuck. Well and truly stuck.

If she waved it off as just two friends having dinner, she'd hurt Manny's feelings. She could never do that. That's the kind of thing women like Celia did. But staying quiet would most likely confirm to Riley that she was dating the fire chief.

Does it even matter if Riley thinks I'm dating Manny?

Her chest tightened as she remembered Riley kissing Celia. He was a hot bachelor with a successful restaurant. Judging from all the women ogling him from the surrounding tables, he had his pick of dates.

Manny brought her attention back to the conversation with another compliment. "Melvina makes the best pie in Magnolia and probably all of

Texas," Manny said with a grin. "But I haven't been out of Montgomery County enough to know for sure."

"I think everyone outside of Montgomery County would probably agree with you, Chief. I had a slice of peach pie last time I was at Pop's that was to die for." Riley echoed with a grin of his own.

Melvina let out the breath she'd been holding. Riley's smile had been genuine. Manny was a wizard at putting people at ease. It was the one reason she hadn't said no tonight. She knew if things didn't work out, he would never make it awkward to move in the same circles after. His graceful candor was admirable.

She smiled, putting her hands to her cheeks. "Stop it! You're both making me blush."

"May I propose a toast then," Manny said, lifting his glass. "To Melvina, the best baker in all of Texas and to the continued success of Braised. I hope we visit here again soon."

Melvina's hand shook a little as she lifted her glass. Manny was a laid-back kind of guy, but he was also shrewd. His toast was clearly a declaration of his interest in her. She glanced at Riley and caught the slight stiffening of his jaw before he lifted his own glass to join in the toast.

"Thank you, Chief." Riley turned to an approaching server, who whispered in his ear. He nodded and turned back to them. "If you'll excuse me, duty calls. I wish you both a pleasant evening."

Melvina watched the back side of him as he walked away. Busboys, cocktail waitresses from the lounge and new guests swallowed him up as he ranged farther out of view. When she looked at Manny, he was studying her.

"How long have you known Nash?"

The question was casual enough, but Melvina hesitated before answering. She gave herself a mental shake. Her long-time crush had the potential to go somewhere if she could stop being such a ninny. "We just recently met at the ball. Celia mentioned he might be involved in the catering for the firemen's calendar. She's been dinging me with e-mails to contact him." She shook her head as she toyed with her napkin.

Manny nodded, "But you haven't, I take it?"

"No. I—uh, have been busy juggling everything else." Melvina lifted her glass, realizing it was empty. That made two Cosmos down, and they hadn't even ordered the appetizer. "Um, can we not talk about the Blossoms tonight?" She didn't want to get into the messy details of her emotions, not even by herself. She had been skating around identifying her feelings for the moment.

Manny nodded sagely as the server arrived with a bottle of champagne in a silver bucket with a stand. She placed it at the end of their table and set down two glasses.

Manny cleared his throat. "I'm sorry, I think you're mistaken," he said to the waitress.

She smiled broadly as she removed the foil off the cork and untwisted the wire basket. "Compliments of Mr. Nash. He said to bring you the best in the house. You guys must be special." Her tongue clicked as the cork popped and the champagne fizzed just a bit over the mouth of the bottle. The chief didn't argue, and instead offered his thanks, pushing the first glass toward Melvina. "I should have thought of it myself," he said with a wink.

Awkward didn't begin to describe what Melvina was feeling, but as the mist of bubbles tickled her nose, she couldn't help but smile. There were worse things in life than to have two good-looking men showing an interest in her.

Dinner was an array of seafood appetizers followed by beef and lamb entrees and capped off with a creamy chocolate mousse and cheese tray for dessert. Melvina tried not to overindulge, but she didn't want Manny or Riley to think she didn't like the food. Riley may not know her recent past, but most everyone who came into the diner knew how long it had taken her to lose the weight and how hard she had battled her bad habits until now. Not wanting to fall off the horse completely, she snacked and nibbled with care. She deserved a reward for all her efforts.

And when am I ever going to go out on a date this nice again?

After the two cocktails and what she supposed was half a bottle of champagne, she waved off Manny's offer of port and opted for a strong cup of Earl Grey with a dab of honey. The alcohol had done its job and she was comfortable in the luxurious booth observing the crowd as Manny went to the restroom.

Sipping the tea, she watched Riley through the glass wall, inside the dining area as he directed the bartender toward the back. He then strolled behind the bar to make the next round of drinks himself. His dress shirtsleeves were rolled up, and he was laughing with an older couple seated at the bar.

He was all in.

Melvina admired a man who put everything into what he loved, and it was obvious that Braised was his baby. The proud papa wasn't afraid to bus tables or even polish the glasses.

"They must be understaffed tonight," Manny said as he slid back into the circular booth. He'd sat across from her throughout dinner, but now he'd shifted in closer. He didn't touch her, but she could feel his warmth and smell his sandalwood soap and mild cologne. The waitress smiled at him as she passed by, reminding Melvina that Manny was handsome and available. If he was truly interested in her, she should take this opportunity to see where it went.

So why do I keep staring at Riley?

"I know, I was just watching how Ri—er, everyone here pitches in to help out," she offered as an excuse for watching the bar. "Sorry, it's the restaurant server in me that feels for anyone left in the weeds. I have nightmares about it myself. When I waited tables in high school for Pop, they would drop these big tour buses off for lunch on their way to Houston. By the end of the night I was falling off my feet." She shook her head at the memory. "I still help the girls out when we hit a rush, but I don't like to wait tables anymore. I'm happy to hide out in the back, baking."

Manny sipped the last of his coffee and passed his credit card to the server as she returned with the bill. The simple cowhide wallet was well creased from use. "Well, I'm sure the guests miss your pretty face, but no one can argue you make the best biscuits in town."

Melvina laughed. "Well now, there's that." She waved off his compliment and latched onto something she felt more comfortable with. She knew she was a good cook and though Eli, Pop and Mona continually told her she was pretty, in her heart, she still felt like the chubby cupcake girl from high school.

His rich voice rumbled over her, chastising. "Why do you do that?"

"Do what?" Her defenses went up.

"Brush off every compliment I try to give you outside of baking a pie. I mean what I say, Melvina. You're a beautiful woman, inside and out, and I'd like to take you out again." His words melted her defenses.

She felt a rush of warmth hit her cheeks from his blunt words. "I'm sorry, you're right—thank you for the compliment. I appreciate it and the wonderful dinner. It was quite a treat."

Manny nodded and leaned toward her, brushing her lips with his in a soft caress. Melvina didn't have time to back away and it was over before she had to think about kissing him back.

"Well, now that that's settled." He scooted from the horseshoe-shaped booth, standing up to scrawl a quick signature across the bill. He held out a hand to Melvina and helped her stand. As they took their leave, Melvina darted a glance at the bar, but Riley was gone.

A cool breeze lifted the folds of her dress, twirling the hem around her bare calves. Stray wisps of her hair had come loose from her braid and now tickled her neck. She shivered and Manny wrapped his arms around her, rubbing her arms as they waited for the valet. "Cold?"

Melvina thought about it. "No, it was just the breeze tickling me. My neck is sensitive and my long hair...." she lost her train of thought as he moved her braid and ran his hand over the sensitive skin at the nape of her neck. Goosebumps danced down her spine and rushed over her extremities. The valet arrived with Manny's truck. She heard his audible sigh of regret.

The drive home had been quiet as they listened to a soft jazz station on the satellite radio. Melvina would have pegged Manny as solely a country music fan but was pleasantly surprised by the pre-programmed opera, piano and classical stations he flipped through. When they pulled into her drive, she realized she'd forgotten to leave the porch light on, and the house was inky black. She heard Humphrey's baying as Manny came around to open her door.

Manny looked back at the house, "What's that?"

"Humphrey, my old basset hound. He's harmless, but a great alarm system if you want to know about every jackrabbit, squirrel or possum that enters the yard. Eli must have brought him back from camping. We kind of share Humphrey since his condo doesn't allow pets. It's great for Humphrey. He likes to lay around while Eli fishes. It works out well since I work long hours at Pop's. There's a doggy door, so at least he doesn't have to hold his bladder."

They stepped up on the porch and Melvina turned to Manny, "Would you like to meet him?"

Manny pushed a stray wisp of hair from her face and cupped her chin in his hand. "Maybe later." He bent his head, brushed her lips with his, and waited a beat for her to meet him halfway. Melvina brought her hands to his shoulders to steady herself and let the kiss deepen. Manny's physique was firm. She could tell he didn't just sit behind his desk at the station. His shoulders were strong, and she felt his biceps taut against her as he enfolded her in his embrace. His breath was a mixture of whiskey, coffee, and the after-dinner mints they'd both had on their way out. His tan skin, dark hair, and piercing blue eyes were definite assets, but his masculine presence was the kind you read about in heat-filled romance novels. He was all male. He didn't hide his desire as the kiss pulled them together and she felt the extent of his interest. She pulled back, holding onto the door.

"Manny—" she put a hand on his chest to signal she needed space.

He stood back, but she couldn't decipher his expression in the darkness. "I'm sorry.... I've been wanting to kiss you." His breath caught and he blew it out with a long sigh. "I've been wanting to do that for a long time."

Melvina's eyes widened. "Really?"

The rumble of his chuckle vibrated against her hand, making her realize she still had her hand on his chest. She covered her awkwardness by fishing for her keys in her purse.

"Yes, Melvina. If I haven't made things clear, I like you. I like you a lot." With those final words, he gave her one more quick kiss and made his way down the porch steps and back to his truck. Melvina unlocked the door to greet an eager Humphrey, who thumped his tail against the wood frame. She held up her hand in a parting wave to Manny as the lights of his truck washed over the chipped white paint railing and pink impatiens flower baskets hanging from above.

She turned on the interior light and bent down to scratch Humphrey behind the ears. Her knees cracked from the stiffness of a long day. She stood and stretched to relieve the pressure. She thought about her evening with Manny and how she'd felt when he kissed her. He was handsome. She was attracted to him, and as her knees just reminded her—she wasn't getting any younger. Mona's momma would have told her she needed to get her head out of the clouds and take what was in front of her. As the saying went, one in the hand was better than—but that expression left her thinking of a rather naughty scenario. Somehow, she wasn't sure she felt that way about Manny. He had done everything right and was a gentleman in every capacity, so why did she keep thinking about Riley? It was all getting too complicated.

The phone in her purse vibrated and Melvina thought to ignore it. When it didn't stop after a few continued rings, she was sure it was Mona trying to video chat. Dropping her purse on the counter, she moved to the bath-room to turn on the shower. She needed the hot water to run over her skin, to relax and to think about what she would tell Manny next time he called.

Chapter 11

Things would be difficult to explain the next time he saw Melvina, but the problem was that he hadn't been able to find her. Riley had gone to the café several times, but she had either been swamped in the back baking or out running errands. He went to the library once out of desperation, but with no luck. He couldn't even check out a book because he didn't have a library card. The librarian didn't seem impressed when he handed her his business card, and instead insisted he have something besides a driver's license to prove residency. Montgomery County was apparently strict about people living in the district.

He was getting frustrated, and his baked goods purchases were starting to show around his usually taut middle. Every time he entered the restaurant looking for Melvina, he walked away with a sizable box of treats. He loved her frosted cupcakes and was absolutely addicted to her pecan pie. Riley also wanted to talk to her about adding some of her desserts to Braised's menu in addition to explaining Celia's kiss at the Blossoms' office. He knew Melvina had seen them. But she'd torn out of there like a bat out of hell and he didn't get a chance to explain that it was a one-sided situation.

Seeing Melvina sidled up beside Manny in his restaurant was a punch to the gut. True, they weren't dating, but there was something special about this particular woman. From the moment he'd taken her in his arms on the dance floor, he knew he wanted to get to know her.

She had that girl-next-door beauty and a heart of gold. From the chatter he'd heard around the café, she was single, and for some strange reason, she'd been that way for a long time. And now, suddenly, she was here in Braised with the town fire chief, who was Magnolia's number one bachelor, or so Darcey at the restaurant had said. Raphe had given him that tidbit after chatting up the waitress on a cupcake run for the firehouse.

Riley wanted to take Melvina out. They shared so much in common and he wanted to find out more about her. He couldn't help but feel that she liked him too.

Damn! Now, I've blown my chance.

He wouldn't have put it past Celia to have orchestrated the entire charade, knowing Melvina was on her way. She'd no doubt put on a show just to seal the door shut on any opportunity he might have had with Melvina. Damn Celia Lockwood and her meddling ways.

When he'd first seen Melvina at Braised, he thought maybe she was looking for him. Maybe her brother Eli, Darcey, or Pop had told her how many times he'd stopped by looking for her. But then he noticed Manny, who seemed to only have eyes for Melvina, and something squeezed his heart like a vice.

Riley could admit that Manny wasn't bad to look at, and he had influence in the county, so why wouldn't Melvina fall for him? Most women were impressed by Riley's success in the restaurant biz or his television persona, though he avoided the media thing now. He didn't care for all the hoopla of reality TV. But the only thing Melvina seemed impressed with was his ability to cook, and damned if he didn't like that about her, too.

He'd remembered how much she liked the champagne the afternoon he spent with her at Bubbles, so he'd sent a bottle to the table. He wanted her to enjoy her time in his place, with or without the fire chief. With the laughter he'd heard as he wiped down the bar, Riley figured maybe it was too nice of a time, and he wondered if his generosity had backfired.

After torturing himself through half the evening, he decided to hide out in the back doing paperwork until Melvina and the chief had left.

It was almost closing time now, and Riley sat at the bar watching a cube of ice melt in his whiskey. The TVs were programmed to ESPN, and he watched the highlights of the Rockets game.

"Penny for your thoughts?"

Riley recognized the rich southern tone of his brother, Raphe's, voice before turning to see his smiling face.

"I'm not sure they're worth a penny, but I'm not up for sharin' right now anyway. Have a seat and watch the highlights of the game with me." Riley pulled a stool out, welcoming his younger brother.

"I already saw it. Ran and I were at the game earlier."

Riley looked at him with surprise, "How come I wasn't invited?"

"I only had two tickets, and you were working. Besides, Sheila dumped me, and the game was last-minute." Raphe held a hand up to the bartender, ordering a draft beer. A customer at the other end of the bar made a loud moan at the missed dunk.

Riley nodded at the screen. "Doesn't look like I missed much anyway."

Raphe took a drink of his beer, "Naw, it was a good game, but they lost by four points in the end."

"Sounds like it hasn't been your night. First the model, then the game. What happened?" His words were light, but he cared about his siblings. He didn't think Raphe had too much invested in the waif-thin woman he'd brought to the ball.

"Actually, it's not all that bad. She was just a good time. I was the same to her. She moved on to some producer guy she met, and I moved back to being single. It's a place that feels like home to me," he smiled.

Riley knew his brother went through women like he went through cheeseburgers. Both were delightful while they were being devoured, but sure to be consumed in a short time. "Good, so your heart's still intact?"

Raphe chuckled. "Good as new." He playfully punched Riley in the arm. "What about you? You look like you just lost your best friend."

Riley drained the last of his whiskey and he flagged the bartender for another round. Raphe waved him off. "I gotta drive. I had two at the game earlier."

Riley nodded, pressing his lips together as he swallowed hard. "Ah, smart man."

"So?" Raphe waited.

"It's nothin' really. I've just been trying to connect with Melvina, from the diner, to ask her out and I hadn't had any luck running into her until tonight." Riley studied the remaining amber liquid in his glass.

"So, what's the problem? Did she shut you down?" Raphe looked surprised.

"I didn't get a chance to ask her. She was here with Magnolia's fire chief, Manny, thanks to you."

"Shoot. He called me about getting reservations tonight. I had no idea. Man, sorry about that."

Riley shrugged off the apology.

"The chief is a good guy. I worked with him once when there was a huge disaster out in Conroe. The blaze covered—" Raphe stopped mid-sentence. "I mean, he's the big fish in the little pond thing, you know."

Riley knew all too well. He had grown up in a small town and knew how it felt to be top dog. He wasn't feeling that so much right now, and that was new for him when it came to women.

Raphe clapped him on the back. "Well don't just sit here and cry in your whiskey. Go fight for her."

Riley shot his brother a glare, shaking off the hand that clasped his shoulder. "First of all, I'm not crying in my whiskey. Second of all, what am I supposed to do, swing by the diner every hour on the hour until I see her leavin' work and throw her in my trunk?"

Raphe nodded, thinking. "That's not entirely a bad idea, except it would be rather time-consuming and illegal. Besides, Darcey told me something last night that could be of use. She's the pretty blonde who does the day shift at Pop's diner. Anyway, tomorrow's her day off and we're going to Bubbles in the afternoon for drinks. Melvina usually works the front on Darcey's day off, but she's letting the fill-in waitress work so she can do some baking. Darcey said the early shift ends at 2 p.m., so I bet Melvina will be leaving around that time."

Riley's ears perked up and Raphe's grin revealed he'd done more than just chat with the pretty waitress. "You dog. Doesn't she have a boyfriend?"

"Didn't mention one to me, but then again, we didn't do that much talking."

Riley clapped his brother on the back this time. "Well, whatever the situation, thanks for the info. I'll try going by tomorrow and see if I can run into her. I have an invitation that she can't pass up."

Chapter 12

Melvina was feeling it now. Her back ached and her feet throbbed. She wrapped a rubber band around the thick stack of checks with her own chicken scratch scrawled across the green and white paper. Pam, a morning waitress, called in early to report that her sister's water broke, and she was rushing her sibling to the hospital. The fill-in waitress, Barb, couldn't make it in, so that put Melvina in the waitress seat. Pop came up to help and the busboy took over delivering water and silverware setups during the rush.

She was glad she didn't have to depend on waitressing to make a living. It was a young person's job and usually a thankless one at that. It was a relief that most of the locals knew her and there were few complaints as long as the food was hot and they had enough sweet tea to keep them cool.

All she wanted to do now was go home and soak her feet in Humphrey's baby pool. She would water the garden when the sun set and take a quick nap before figuring out what she would feed them. She usually fed Humphrey whatever she ate, sticking to meat protein and fresh vegetables. It was better for him than just plain dog food, and he was in decent enough shape for his years.

She punched the time clock and rolled up her dirty apron, sticking it in her work tote. Waving to Pop, she opened the back door, sliding her keys from the magnetic holder in her purse.

A sleek black coupe pulled up along the back exit as it started to rain. Melvina bumped her hip against the back door to close it, and she started to make haste for the catering truck Pop had lent her when she took her Shelby in for repairs. The coupe's window slid down and she recognized Riley.

"Wanna hop in? It's pouring just over the hill and I guarantee it's coming this way." He flipped the locks and pushed the passenger side door open.

Melvina glanced up at the darkening sky. "All the more reason for me to hustle home. Thanks anyway," she waved.

"Melvina, wait! I want to show you the garden. The one we use for the restaurant. It's here in Magnolia. One of the reasons I'm out here so much."

That got her attention. A man who gardens couldn't be all that bad. Maybe his reputation had been overblown. Not to mention, she felt compelled to explain that going to Braised last night was a surprise to her. She didn't want Riley to think she was stalking him. The sprinkling turned into hard rain and she didn't have time to dicker. She took the invitation and got into the car.

Suddenly self-conscious as the smell of leather and new car washed over her senses, she apologized. "I'm sorry. I know I smell like fries right now, but I've been waiting tables all day." She shrugged her shoulders and looked down at the stained sleeve of her shirt.

"It's okay. I just left Braised, where I was smoking fifty pounds of brisket for later tonight and I probably smell like our secret whiskey barbecue sauce." He winked at her, then added, "Besides, barbecue and fries go great together, don't you think?"

Melvina smiled. She couldn't argue with that, but she wished she'd had a chance to shower before bumping into him.

The small farm off the narrow, curvy road was about a ten-minute drive from town. The lush greenery reminded her that spring was turning to summer, and the heat of the day was only mildly cooled by the brief rainstorm. As they got out of the car, a gentle breeze blew their way just before the humidity rolled up in a wave off the pavement.

Melvina gazed around her, spying a modest house with a white picket fence sitting on what looked like a hundred acres of land.

"Wow, this looks like my granddaddy's place. We used to spend the summers with him and grandma, chasing garden snakes and catching fireflies." Melvina looked across the green fields with cattle roaming in the distance. Two donkeys were close by the fence and she wandered over to pet them when they stuck their heads between the wooden rails. "Cute, what are their names?"

"Shrek and Donkey," Riley replied, deadpan.

Melvina turned with a smile. "Really?"

"My nephews named them. They'll be home soon. They're probably swimming at my mom's place. When school's out, they can be a handful for my sister, Lexi. This is her place. It used to belong to my grandparents, but my parents didn't want to work the land, so my sister bought it from them for a song, and now she's nice enough to let her big brother use a chunk for Braised."

Riley gestured for Melvina to follow him. They walked through a stand of trees that shaded one side of the house. Riley flipped the latch on the picket fence, and they stepped into an oasis of fresh rosemary, chives, and pots filled with mint, basil and thyme. A bay leaf tree was surrounded with white stones, and dill weed overflowed a box in the window above. Flower baskets with an array of pansies and impatiens dotted the herb garden courtyard, and big tomatoes hung from vines lined along the fence. It was a gardener's dream. Every herb she could think of grew in abundance, and the added flowers made it a beautiful spot for anyone to enjoy.

"Oh my." It was all she could say as she picked a sprig of rosemary and rubbed it between her fingers, then rubbed her hands over her arms. She loved the scent and hoped it would cover up the smell of the diner that lingered in her pores. "It's beautiful. I have a small garden of my own, and I bring herbs to Pop's on occasion, but it's nothing like this. I think I'm jealous." She turned in a circle, then closed her eyes, breathing in deep.

When she opened them, Riley was in front of her, holding a small bouquet of flowering basil. "Anything you want, you can have."

Melvina gulped. "Nice offer, thanks." She could feel her cheeks heating and cursed her fair skin. He was probably laughing at her country innocence. She admitted she hadn't traveled much outside of Texas and her inexperience with men left her blushing a lot.

Riley seemed to sense her insecurity. "I mean it. If you want some herbs to take home or maybe some cuttings to start your own plants, you're welcome to them." He reached for a gardener's box made of wood with a pair of shears and a small shovel and handed the items to her. "I've been wanting to show you this place since we talked that day at Bubbles. You mentioned you liked to garden. I didn't mention the place then because I was already planning to surprise you, but I haven't been able to catch up with you before last night."

Her eyes skittered away at the intensity of his gaze. "Yeah, I've been busy. I hadn't planned on going anywhere last night, but then Manny caught me after work and twisted my arm. He didn't tell me where we were going until—" she looked down at the corrugated brick that made a path through the maze of herbs and flowers.

"Manny, oh yeah, the chief." Riley's smile stiffened. "No worries. I've been busy too, but I did drop by the café a few times to talk to you. I even tried to flag you down outside the Blossoms office. Celia asked me to do this charity thing for the mentoring program they want to start."

Melvina started walking through the garden, picking at jasmine and making a few small cuts from other plants. "Yeah, I had stopped by to drop off some papers. I noticed you guys were—busy, so I just left them with the secretary. Celia and I haven't had much contact since the ball." Her mind flicked from the shock to the emptiness she'd felt over seeing Riley and Celia's embrace to the vision of Celia drenched from the fountains. "I mean, I did paint the lady with chocolate."

The memory gave her a momentary giggle she couldn't suppress. Her giggle grew into laughter as Riley's own chuckle chimed in. When Melvina snorted, they both engaged in peals of squawking that had her leaning against a fence post. As she leaned forward, tears filling her eyes from the infectious laughter, the post gave way along with the panel of fencing it was attached to. Melvina landed flat on her butt in a pile of something she didn't want to name. The smell rolled up in the heat as her hand squished into the soft, oozing surface.

"Ew! What is this?" She held her hand up for inspection.

"Oh, no! Oh my God, Melvina, let me help you up." He rushed toward her but stared at the offending hand for a moment before lifting her up by her armpits. He chuckled a bit, but then tried to press his lips firmly together as he steadied her.

"It's manure. Yuck!" she groaned.

They both burst into laughter again and Riley accidentally stepped on the wooden planks of the broken pickets, tripping past her and landing on his knees in the same mess.

She gasped as he'd tumbled over but wasn't able to catch him in time because of her own sorry state.

Melvina was lucky to have only one jeans pocket and her right hand splattered with the thick brown muck, but Riley had fallen a little farther, was up to his elbows on both sides, and firmly planted on both knees. She yelped, then giggled, and took his hand with her soiled one, laughing so hard she thought she would pee her pants. Riley gave her a tug and she landed next to him, though luckily not in the manure he seemed glued to.

"Yuck is right. I'll have to thank Lexi for all the tender care she's provided my garden and let her know she ruined any chance of me impressing a lady or snagging a kiss." He shook his head as the laughter ceased and they both caught their breath.

Melvina was momentarily silenced. Did he just say he wanted to kiss her? She shook off her surprise and covered it with a joke. "Oh, I'm impressed all right. I can now attest to the fact that Braised uses all, one-hundred percent organic fertilizer." She pushed herself up, wiping her hands on the grass as she did so.

"You're not upset?"

"I was raised around livestock, Riley. We may stink to high heaven, but it won't kill us. However, now I think I could really use that shower. French fries, barbecue, or whatever—nothing in the world pairs with cow manure. There's no way we can get back in your pretty car after this romp through the garden."

She tried unsuccessfully to peek around to see the damage to her derriere as Riley found the garden hose. "We can start with this. I don't have a key to Lexi's place, but I can call my mom, and someone will drive over and let us in."

They made their preliminary cleanup and waited out front on the wooden porch swing. A baby blue minivan rolled up the drive, and as quick as it rolled to a stop, three young boys popped out of the doors and bee-lined it to the porch. All came to a screeching halt as they approached Riley.

"Ew! Gross!" They all chimed in as they sized up the state of the duo's soiled clothes. "You got poop on you, Uncle Riley."

"Yes, sir. We got into some trouble out back in the garden. Boys, this is Melvina. Melvina these are my nephews, Larry, Curly and Mo," he teased.

"Nuh-uh!" They all complained in unison. The two taller boys looked to be seven or eight, but the youngest one was only four or five. He lifted his arms for his uncle to hug.

Riley reached down and picked him up, holding him high so he wouldn't soil the boy's clothes. "Now I see who loves me most." He chuckled as he nuzzled the child, blowing strawberries on his neck. The others teased their youngest brother, "Ew, he stinks and now you will too."

Riley responded by lunging out and grabbing them all. Pulling them onto the grass, he tussled with them just past the hedges.

A pretty blonde walked up, shaking her head at the scene. "You're gonna bathe them all for getting that mess on them, Riley James Nash." She stepped forward and held out her hand to Melvina, "Hi I'm Alexa, Riley's little sis, but you can call me Lexi. Everybody else does."

Melvina looked at her hand, then waved awkwardly. "I'm Melvina. I was just here admiring your garden. Trust me. You don't want to shake my hand." Both women laughed.

"I guess you're right. Let me get the door open so you can get cleaned up. I've got a pair of sweats you can borrow, so don't worry about a thing."

Melvina liked Riley's sister already. She had a warm smile and sincere eyes. She laughed heartily with her brother but didn't give him a hard time about the inconvenience of cutting her day short. She showed Melvina to one of the bedrooms, which also had a bath. The room was surprisingly neat, and all but a few toys were put away. A set of twin beds with matching Disney car comforters and a shelf of model cars complemented the boys' décor.

"Sorry, it's only a three-bedroom house, and the younger boys have to share this room. I would love to have a guest room, but most everyone spends the holidays with Mom and Dad so it's not like it would ever get used anyway—except for now." Lexi grabbed a sailboat and a plastic fish from the bathtub, then pulled a couple of towels from the closet. "I'll go grab my shampoo and conditioner. All I have is baby shampoo in here. Damien, my littlest, always gets it in his eyes, so I don't keep anything stronger in this room." Melvina nodded as Lexi rushed off.

One look at herself in the half wall mirror made her gasp. "Lord have mercy," she said aloud.

And to think he wanted to kiss me. He must be crazy.

Lexi returned with a fresh box of rose-scented soap, warm-up pants, a fresh T-shirt and designer shampoo. "This should be all you need, but if you want anything else at all, don't hesitate to ask." She paused, smiling brightly as her eyes roved over Melvina. "My brother has never shared his garden with anyone besides me. You must be special."

Melvina didn't know what to say to Riley's smiling sister. She nodded, thanking her for the clothes as Lexi politely shut the door.

It was nearing five o'clock as she found her way back into the empty living room at the front of the house. She stood awkwardly, wondering what to do next. The clinking of pots and pans from what must be the kitchen drew her around the corner into a brightly painted yellow breakfast room. Riley was on the other side of the counter, pulling baking sheets from under the kitchen stove. He looked up, suddenly noticing her. "Would it be okay if we stayed for dinner? I feel kind of bad to shower and run." He smiled broadly as Damien entered the kitchen yelling, "Yay!"

Melvina liked seeing him with his nephews. He was such a good uncle to them. "Only if you'll let me help."

Riley nodded, motioning to the oven. "Sure, preheat it to three-seventy-five and I'll get the food out of the fridge." He turned to Damien. "Let's see what your momma's hiding behind the milk, butter and left-over pizza." He tickled Damien until the child giggled and squealed for mercy. Riley turned his attention to the fridge and rummaged around for ingredients. Gus and Bert traipsed in, took their seats on the bar stools, and plopped their chins on their hands, watching Riley and Melvina with interest.

"Whatcha doin', Uncle Riley?"

"I'm gonna make dinner so your momma doesn't have to worry about feeding you rug rats."

Damien again yelled, "Yay!"

Gus, the oldest, rubbed his forehead in an expression beyond his years. "I don't know, Uncle Riley. You aren't gonna make any of the funny stuff you made last week for breakfast, are you?"

Riley chuckled. "What's wrong Gus? You didn't like my mushroom frittata?"

"There wasn't any fruit in your fruit-tada, Uncle Riley." The middle child, Bert, scrunched up his face in a frown. "It was just eggs, green stuff and mushrooms. I hate mushrooms."

Riley pulled out a pack of bacon from the fridge along with a carton of eggs and butter. Setting the items on the counter he stepped into the pantry. "The green stuff was the best part! All right, all right," he said, coming out with a glass canister of flour. "So, how about we have breakfast for dinner. Pancakes and bacon?" A unanimous cheer went up and all three boys dived off their barstools, attacking Riley's sweat-pant-clad legs. "Okay, okay." He tickled them into submission, then swatted each of them playfully on the rump, sending them out to look for a few ripe tomatoes.

Melvina smiled at the warm picture he made standing in his sister's kitchen in too-tight pink warm-up pants and a white sleep T-shirt with hearts on the front. "Pink's your color." She tried to suppress the giggle unsuccessfully.

Riley did a combo wiggle and turn then plucked at his girly attire. "What? A man can't get in touch with his feminine side?" he asked innocently.

"Those are mine, Riley James Nash, and they are my favorite. So once your clothes are clean and dry, I want them back." Lexi's smile revealed she was joking. She looked at Melvina. "Sorry my big brother dragged you through the fertilizer today. He isn't known for his agility."

Melvina laughed. "Actually, it was my own clumsiness that landed me in your fertilizer." She avoided saying cow poop. "I leaned against the fence and broke it. Sorry about that."

"You don't need to be sorry. That's Riley's fault for not tending the repairs that need to be done in the garden. It was part of the deal about him using the land, huh, big brother?"

Riley whistled cheerfully as he laid strips of bacon in the pan, clearly pretending he hadn't heard Lexi's comment. "Melvina, you want a glass of wine?" he asked as he tossed out the empty plastic package. "Lexi's going to open a nice bottle from my stash that I keep here. Red or white?" His gaze fell on both women.

"If it's breakfast we're eating, shouldn't it be champagne? Or white sangria, maybe," Melvina supplied.

Lexi winked. "Good call, Melvina." She turned to her brother, "I like her, Riley. She's got good taste."

"Melvina is the best baker in all of Texas."

"Even better." Lexi nodded her approval.

Melvina took over the pancake batter while Riley peeled potatoes and fried them up using fresh sea salt and the oregano from his garden. The mingling aromas of sizzling bacon and home fries were heavenly, and she liked that Riley could cook the basics with flare. Breakfast was her favorite meal of the day. She wondered if it was his, too. At first, she was careful not to put too much oil into the pancake mixture. Her diet didn't include Swedish pancakes, but then she tilted the Crisco bottle over the bowl and gave the batter a generous splash. The boys would love them. She found powdered sugar in the pantry and fresh strawberries in the fridge. There was even a tub of mascarpone that Melvina scooped into a crock to top their breakfast dessert. It was fun being in the kitchen with Riley, and she admired the way he kept the kitchen clean as he cooked, making zero work for his sister, who was helping the boys bathe while dinner was prepared.

As the boys returned sporting still-damp hair and colorful pajamas with various comic-book images, Riley set the table and Melvina poured

Sprite in three plastic wine glasses, adding a maraschino cherry in each. For the grownups, she'd set out the mimosas that Riley had whipped up. Lexi joined them a few minutes later and they all sat down to dinner, clinking their glasses more than a few times throughout the meal.

The boys gleefully dug into the dollar-sized pancakes that Melvina had made. She'd shaped them to look like Mickey Mouse, using chocolate chips for eyes and nose and a healthy dose of strawberries and cream for the mouth.

Melvina attempted to eat sparingly, although it was almost impossible with Riley heaping the potatoes and bacon onto her plate.

Lexi chimed in for her. "Riley, quit filling her plate. She said she's full. Stop being so pushy." The sibling banter was obviously an ongoing thing between the two.

Riley looked at Melvina sheepishly. "Sorry, I just love feeding people. I hope you like it."

Melvina smiled, "I love to eat. It's no secret, but I've worked hard the past year to take off a bit of weight. I just don't want to go back to the struggle."

Lexi stood and started to clear the table, asking each of the boys to carry his own plate to the sink. Riley protested that he would do the dishes, but Lexi held her hand up. "It's my kitchen, Riley. Now I appreciate you making dinner and entertaining the boys, but you've held this nice lady hostage long enough. Y'all go have fun and leave the cleaning to me. It gives me something to do after the boys go to sleep."

There wasn't any more discussion. Lexi disappeared with the plates and Riley rose from the table. "I'll go check the dryer. I think we're getting kicked out," he teased.

It was dark when they drove home and Melvina was blissfully content. She hadn't had a night like this in a while. Seeing Riley with his sister reminded her of her own family. Eli teased her relentlessly, but the love was apparent. She couldn't help but wonder about Riley's sister and where the boys' father might be, but she didn't ask. From her own experience and from her volunteer work with Maurice, she understood that not all good families came with perfect parents.

As if reading her thoughts, Riley's voice was soft when he spoke. "Their father was killed in Afghanistan. Damien hadn't even been born yet. It devastated Lexi. They were high school sweethearts and had their lives and dreams all planned out. They were going to make a real ranch out of Grandma and Gramps's place. Jack was a salt-of-the-earth sort of guy. He was golden to my sister and everyone in the family loved him." He swallowed and his voice grew husky. "I wish I could figure out a way to help her move on, but for now, I stop by often to hang out with the boys. So do Ran and Raphe."

Riley made the slow turn into the diner's parking lot. Melvina needed to pick up the catering van so she could drive to work in the morning. "Sounds like it's been rough for her and the boys."

"The oldest can barely remember him. He probably won't in a few more years.... But they spend a lot of time with my parents, and my brothers and I do our best to fill in for their dad."

"That probably helps your sister out a lot. She's lucky to have you all." Melvina's heart ached for the boys, but more for Lexi. Married to the love of her life, only to have him cruelly taken from her. Now she had to raise three boys without him. She attempted to lighten the mood. "Well that explains why you had to wear pink warm-ups."

He turned to her as he pulled up by the catering van. "I like pink. You wait and see. Those will be mine one day when Lexi's not looking."

Melvina laughed at his ornery comment. Riley reached out and pushed a stray lock of her hair back behind her ear. He'd shifted closer to her and then leaned in without warning. His lips brushed hers. She didn't move away, and as if sensing she wanted it but was too timid to engage, Riley put his hand behind her head, bringing her closer.

The kiss was deep, soft, and lingering. She felt too paralyzed to move even after his lips left hers. Riley's heartbeat strong beneath the hand she'd placed on his chest to steady herself. He pulled back, and they gazed at each other for a moment. It was dark but his amber eyes glowed in the moonlight.

He grasped her again with passion. She moaned as his tongue swirled around hers and he sucked at her bottom lip. She could barely breathe from the excitement. It was a totally different kiss than the one she'd shared with Manny, and a different feeling flowed through her. Heart stopping. Breathtaking. She was caught up in the moment and didn't want it to end.

His lips traveled to her neck as his arms slipped around her waist. His mouth grazed her collarbone, then back up to claim her lips once more.

After a few scorching moments, Melvina found her voice. "Riley, we should stop. I don't want someone to walk out the back and see us."

Riley pulled back, a slow smile spread across his face, "Are you ashamed to be seen with me?"

"Of course not, but Eli is working tonight, and no matter how old I am, I'll never be comfortable with my brother catching me making out." As if on cue, Eli opened the back door of the restaurant with a bag of trash and headed for the dumpster. Melvina ducked down a little in the passenger seat.

"Melvina, we aren't kissing any more. You don't have to hide," he chuckled.

Melvina sat up sheepishly, "Sorry."

"It's okay. The windows are tinted anyway."

Melvina frowned as Eli headed straight toward the car. He scrutinized the sedan with a furrowed brow, then walked to the front of the Infiniti. Recognizing Melvina, he waved.

Melvina waved at Eli and then motioned for him to go back inside. "Thanks for the lovely evening, Riley. I'd better get going. I should have known Eli would get suspicious. Your car is too nice to be parked in the back with the employees."

Riley brushed a hand across her cheek. "There's no reason to be embarrassed. We're all adults here."

Melvina nodded. She didn't supply that Mona had probably told half of Magnolia about her date with Manny, and Eli would have surely heard by now. Here she was with another man, just one night after her dinner with Manny. If Mona got wind of it, the gossips would flare up from one end of town to the next.

"Can I see you again? I want to say tomorrow, but there's that meeting to organize for the firemen's—" Riley paused. "What do you call it, a beauty pageant?"

Melvina smiled, thinking about how the firemen would feel if they'd heard Riley's question. "Calendar contest." Her smile faded as she thought of the fire chief and the awkward situation she was putting herself in, but she did want to see Riley again. "I guess I'll see you there. Celia has lit up my phone today, insisting I attend. It's an official Blossoms meeting."

"Great. I'll see you there. Maybe afterward we can pick up where we left off."

His eyes sparked with mischief and Melvina's butterflies did a happy dance somewhere lower than her stomach.

She nodded as she exited the car. Melvina didn't know how things would play out with Manny and Riley in the same room with her, but she couldn't have that talk with herself right now.

Time to go home and take a cold shower!

Chapter 13

It was only seven in the morning, but Melvina could hear the phone ringing as she stood beneath the hot spray of water. She had the rain shower head installed when she'd remodeled the bath last summer. As the phone rang again and again, she cursed her best friend, Mona, and her video chat torture tactics. Damn Eli. Did he have to tell Mona everything she did? Knowing she wouldn't get any peace until she answered the ever-ringing phone, Melvina toweled off and wrapped the soft cotton around her, tucking it in to secure the top.

"Hey, Mona. Don't you work anymore?"

Mona pursed her lips and rolled her eyes. "Of course I still work. It's a clause in my trust fund, as you well know, but I don't have to be there until nine."

"Well, I'm kinda in a hurry this morning. I'm supposed to meet Maurice at the library for a *Spring into Reading* course and then I promised Pop I would help out for a few hours."

"But it's your day off, and I wanted to invite you to lunch." Mona complained as if it was her own freedom at stake.

"The fill-in-girl's sister had her baby and things haven't gone so smoothly. The baby is having some difficulties."

Mona's eyes went soft, "Oh, I'm sorry. Okay then." She waited a beat, her eyes rounded, as if she was waiting for Melvina to say something else. "Melvina Rayanne Banks, if you don't tell me what the whole town is talking about, I'm going to have to unfriend you."

Melvina wanted to laugh at Mona's empty threat. "Mona, I don't know what you've heard, but I guarantee half of it isn't true, and unfriending is something you do on social media. I don't do social media."

"You know what I mean, Mel!" Mona paused, pressing her lips together as she waited.

Melvina didn't budge.

"Well, why don't we get together for dinner and you can tell me what *is* true." Mona pulled out a bright pink makeup pencil to line her almost nonexistent lips, using the phone as her mirror.

Remembering she was pushed for time, Melvina set the phone down and ran a comb through her own hair as she responded. "I can't. I've got a Blossoms meeting tonight." Dabbing moisturizer over her face, Melvina added, "Actually, I really could use your advice because I truly don't know what I'm gonna do. How about we meet for a drink at Bubbles around five. I'll give you the skinny before I go to the meeting at seven."

"Done! We'll catch up then. I've got to tell you about the thing I bought for Jorden. Oh, by the way, there's a package on the way to your house. I ordered it yesterday, so keep an eye out. It should arrive today."

Melvina watched her brow furrow as she stared at her own reflection in the bathroom mirror. "It's not my birthday."

"It will be soon enough, but it's just a little something I saw online that you could use to tend your garden." Melvina glanced down at the phone to see Mona moving a wand of mascara over her eyelashes.

"Okay. Thanks, Mona. You're such a sweetheart."

Maurice and the ten other students who signed up for the spring reading course were a joy to read with. They spent most of the morning going over language drills and a few small quizzes to find out what the students already knew. The kids were different ages, so Melvina divided them into three groups. She put Maurice in charge of the boys at his table to help build his confidence. He had come a long way since she'd first met him at the beginning of the school year, but his father's recent disappearance was affecting his performance. The school year was almost over and there wasn't much time to recuperate.

He'd gotten two Cs and a D on his latest report card and he'd flunked physical education last quarter, alarming Melvina. The boy could run faster than a jackrabbit, so she knew things were off. The mentor program couldn't develop quickly enough in her book. Maurice and the other kids needed positive role models. If there was anything that would keep her involved with the Blossoms, it was heading up the programs that helped their small community. Thinking of Maurice, she tried to tamp down her desire to quit the treasury position over Celia's petty insults.

Melvina drove to Bubbles feeling slightly self-conscious in Pop's catering van. The mechanic had called a couple of days earlier and she was wondering how she would survive until the work was done. Apparently, they were waiting on a part from China.

The elegant lounge was casual enough, but even the trucks in the parking lot were squeaky clean and new. Pop's van had seen better days and was at least a decade old. At least she'd worn nice, fitted jeans that hugged her curves and made her derrière look like she'd done a thousand squats. The silky coral blouse with a wraparound, fluttery fringe complemented her slight tan and made her waist look trim. The red, strappy heels she'd bought at Devil's Diva gave her a boost of confidence. She reminded herself that she couldn't stay more than an hour chatting with the meeting looming over her head.

She didn't know what advice she could expect Mona to come up with, but God knew Mona had tons of experience in this department. She'd juggled more men than a circus clown juggled bowling pins.

The cool air conditioning assailed her as she breezed into the restaurant to find her friend sitting at a plush booth near the front window. It was still early, and the lounge was mostly empty.

Mona smiled, motioning Melvina to join her. Without preamble, Mona jumped right in. "Spill the beans," she blurted.

"What have you heard?" Melvina countered warily.

"Only that you are two-timing Manny Owens with that hot new chef we met the last time we were in this very booth."

Melvina felt her heart race with guilt, but not sure why. She didn't have commitments to either Manny or Riley. "Who told you that?"

"Eli told me he saw you in some fancy black car last night when he was closing up. Jorden and I were at the café for a late-night ice cream after hot-hot sex. Then we went back to my place and did it all over again," Mona giggled. "But that's beside the point. I was talking to Loretta Harrington, who said she'd heard from Manny's sister, Trish, that Manny had called her to get his truck detailed for some reason. And she thought it was for a hot date, and—"

Melvina held her hand up. "Enough, Mona. I can't handle all the gossip. Especially when it's about Manny. I don't want to be a part of it—and I can't believe Eli was the start of this thread. I'll have to talk to him about not talking to you. You're the worst gossip I know!" Melvina tried to sound angry, but it was impossible when Mona's pink lips were pursed with pushy curiosity, waiting for all the juicy details. Melvina complied, indulging her friend with the specifics of her date with Manny at Braised, then how Riley had swung by the next day. She spent more time talking about the garden and Riley's nephews than the two kisses.

"Seriously, that's it? I tell you every detail of my love life, even show you Jorden's assets and all you have to share is some measly kisses without any steamy details." Mona's voice carried, and the two women in the booth across from them turned to look.

Melvina shushed Mona. "And that's exactly why. Would you take it down a notch? I'm working myself into a migraine just thinking about running into both men at the meeting. Riley is catering the event, and Manny—well for obvious reasons—will be there." She rubbed her temples, then took another sip of her wine spritzer. She couldn't afford to be tipsy but needed enough to take the edge off. She silently reminded herself that she had nothing to feel ashamed or guilty of, but her conscience reminded her what a good man Manny was, how she'd been crushing on him for years, and how she'd only just met Riley.

What's wrong with me? Why am I acting like such a ninny?

She chalked it up to her years as the chubby cupcake girl. She wasn't exactly experienced in the relationship department, and even though she was forty years old, it suddenly felt like she was back in high school.

Mona dug in her purse that was shaped like a big daisy. "Migraine? I got just the thing to fix you up."

Melvina waved her off, "Oh no, been there done that and have the chocolate covered shoes to prove it!"

Mona plopped her Pez dispenser next to Melvina's wineglass. "It's just a pain reliever. I know how you work yourself into a frenzy worrying about things. You won't be able to make it through the meeting without it."

"You're probably right. If I take something now, I can probably head off sleeping in the dark tomorrow on my day off." Melvina chased the blue pill with her spritzer. "Is it Aleve?"

Mona shrugged and finished her martini. "I don't know. Probably some generic brand I picked up."

Melvina rolled her eyes and smacked her own forehead with her hand. "You don't even know what you gave me?"

Mona's eyes widened with pretend innocence. "Don't worry, I'm ninety percent sure its generic naproxen." Pausing a moment as she looked up like she was searching for a pair of socks in her brain.

Melvina's mouth dropped. "Ninety percent! What about the other ten?"

Mona grabbed her keys. "I better drive you."

Melvina didn't feel much different than she had at the restaurant. She was a little more relaxed and confident as she entered the hotel. They kept a separate dining room available for such meetings. She circled her menu selection with the small pencil near her place setting and put it to the side for the waiter to pick up. She wasn't hungry after the cocktail with Mona, but she did feel a certain zing of confidence and something else she couldn't name.

Melvina watched as a few of the firemen she knew, along with Manny, filed in through the dining room door. In dark denim jeans that lay snug against his muscular thighs and a light blue button-down casually rolled up at the sleeves, he was the picture of raw masculinity and he was headed her way. Manny wasn't a large man, but his broad shoulders and kind confidence heightened his attractiveness. His country gentleman ways were oh, so appealing. Manny bent down and placed a kiss on her cheek, whispering a breathy hello in Melvina's ear. He took the seat next to her, which momentarily thrilled Melvina, then terrified her as Riley entered through the same door.

Riley moved with ease across the room, brushing off a few of the Blossoms' coos of hello before being waylaid by Celia. His eyes scanned the room, landing on Melvina. His lips pressed together in a stiff line as Celia asked him a question. He pointed toward the other seat next to Melvina, but Celia pressed the matter by holding his bicep and pointing to a chair at her table. Another Blossom joined the conversation, smiling and nodding to him and Celia. He finally shrugged, letting himself be led to the center of the long table.

Melvina felt a moment of regret and then relief as she remembered Manny was sitting right next to her. Both men were too hot for their own good. Riley in his lightweight designer denim that hugged him in all the right places and Manny with his fresh soap and earthy cologne. The excitement was too much for her to concentrate on her own notes as the meeting was called to order.

Celia gave her opening speech, thanking Riley in an elaborate introduction along with Manny and his accompanying firemen. Manny moved to the center of the table where Riley stood. After a few moments of discussing the pageant, there were more than a few giggles and guffaws as the chief elaborated on the firemen practicing their catwalk strut and pole dancing in the firehouse. "I'm told that Robert, or Ro-bear, as we call him now, has perfected the twerk. Don't ask me what that is, because I'm not sure I want to know." Manny's warm Texas drawl sent a jolt of heat through her. She loved his sense of humor and his ability to laugh at himself—or in this case, Ro-bear.

Riley chimed in with a culinary story from the last barbecue he hosted for his fireman brother's friends. "…It was then that Joe and the boys broke into a line dance that looked like it had been choreographed by the Dallas Cheerleaders. That's when I knew this would be an event that I didn't want to miss."

Melvina was glad he hadn't called it a beauty pageant. Riley and the chief seemed to really hit it off. Melvina knew it should be awkward with the two men she was interested in standing side by side, staring straight at her.

Get ahold of yourself, Mel.

The two men were engaging with all the members at the meeting. It was just her gaga brain playing tricks on her. They didn't have eyes only for her. A steady throb started to pulse at the juncture of her thighs, and she was having a hard time concentrating.

It was then that Celia mentioned that Riley should emcee since his brother's model girlfriend had politely bowed out. Manny nodded his agreement, but then added, "You and Melvina would be great!"

Riley turned to Melvina. The throbbing she'd been trying to ignore now zinged. She crossed her legs, trying to quell the steady pulse that sent naughty thoughts racing to her brain. She didn't fear public speaking but couldn't imagine herself on stage, holding a microphone and making funny comments while half-naked men paraded in front of her, especially with Riley standing next to her as Manny looked on. It conjured up an entirely new illicit picture to think about. She shifted in her seat, trying to think of mundane chores she had to do tomorrow to stop her libido from running wild.

What is wrong with me?

You need to get laid, that's what.

Stop it, Melvina. Focus.

Melvina's brain seemed to be playing tennis with itself. Shooting comments around like a wayward tennis ball. Did Manny just volunteer her as emcee? "Um—I'll stick to baking, thank you."

The Blossoms applauded with zeal at the chief's suggestion. She knew she was well liked amongst the ladies who had elected her for three terms in a row.

Riley clapped loudly with them, "Great! Maybe we can pair the competition with a bake-off. We can call the whole thing a Hot Buns Competition."

The peals of laughter and cheers that followed made it hard to resist the challenge. She joined in the chuckles clapping lightly, but her body was on a high of its own. Melvina was gazing at the two men standing in front of the room with more than community appreciation. Her nipples tightened from the silky material of her blouse brushing against her. Remembering Riley's lips on her neck, Melvina's breasts ached to be touched. Manny held up an arm, trying to quell the hoots of appreciation, and Melvina admired his thick biceps, remembering how they'd wrapped around her when they'd kissed.

She'd never been one for fantasies, but the idea of being sandwiched between Riley and Manny was hard to shake from her mind at the moment. She didn't know what was wrong with her, but she was on high alert and the pulse between her legs continued throbbing. She was starting to worry she would leave a wet spot on her chair. She took a sip of water, hoping it would cool her down.

"Melvina," Riley called to her, "What do you say?"

"Sure, I'll take on your buns any day." She was aware of her double-entendre, and the ladies around the room squealed again with delight. Apparently, she wasn't the only one drooling in the room. Manny and Riley were a good-looking pair.

Celia's face was pinched with what Melvina recognized as maximum irritation. The Blossom president liked to be the one coming up with the ideas for promotions, and Celia's red face and narrowed eyes was a reminder to Melvina that Celia did not like sharing the spotlight. Especially when it came to male attention.

Melvina decided to throw Celia a bone. "But I draw the line at baking hot buns. I'll leave the emcee position up to our Blossom president. She's much better at public speaking than I am."

Celia smiled broadly. Riley and Manny nodded at each other with less enthusiasm, but the fate of the contest was sealed. Riley would provide all the smoked brisket and Melvina would make all of the buns, except for the batch Riley would make for the small competition. They would invite a few of the neighboring bakeries to take part and help boost the revenue for the event.

When the coffee and tea was served and the dessert was finished, the ladies gathered around the guests to say goodbye, chatting up a storm. Melvina made good use of the distraction to let herself out of the hotel banquet-meeting room. She made a quick exit to the valet. She texted Mona, but there was no immediate reply.

"Damn it, Mona," she said out loud as she plopped down on the bench near the front door. She crossed her legs in frustration and felt her pants tug against her women's center. She quickly uncrossed them, tugging self-consciously at the fabric over her knees.

"Need a lift?" Riley's rich voice sizzled into the night air, assailing her with a shiver that had nothing to do with the breeze.

Melvina waved her hand at the empty pickup area. "Mona dropped me off and said she would give me a ride home, but I guess she's caught up somewhere. I'm sure she'll remember to come fetch me eventually."

Riley extended his hand to her. "Come with me. Text your friend that you're all taken care of and I'll bring you home."

Melvina couldn't think of an excuse not to and if she hesitated too long, Manny would be out any second and then what?

More complications, that's what.

"Okay."

Chapter 14

Melvina hadn't been this horny since college, and maybe not even then. On the drive home, Riley's sports car hugged the road and a mild vibration of the bumpy areas sent small pulses of excitement through her. Melvina didn't know what was wrong. It was like her body was on some super-sensitive sexual high. The seam of her jeans against her center combined with the smell of Riley's fresh cologne was almost enough to bring her to climax in the soft leather bucket seat.

Melvina had never tried drugs besides the prescription kind Mona doled out to her when she had severe back pain or migraines. Mona had gone a little too far by giving her a Xanax at the party.... Could Mona have given her a hit of ecstasy or some other sexually stimulating drug? As if on cue, Melvina's phone rang with the familiar song she associated with Mona. Melvina tried to ignore it, but the video chat prompt wouldn't stop ringing.

"Aren't you gonna answer it? It could be your friend."

Melvina cringed. "That's exactly why I am not answering it."

Riley laughed. "Well as long as she knows you have a ride."

Melvina tried to stave off the shiver that made its way up her spine as her nipples tightened.

Misjudging her reaction for cold, Riley adjusted the temperature in the car, then turned on her seat heater. As if she wasn't hot enough already. Maybe this was the hormonal push she had been warned about before menopause. Wasn't it widely known that women in their forties were at their sexual peak? How messed up was that? She'd been celibate for so long she'd probably regrown her hymen and now she was itching to get into bed with not one, but two very hot men. Not together, of course, but now that the thought occurred to her, she again imagined being sandwiched between them. Not in the sexy-hot, "I want to be naughty" way, but in the, "I wonder who puts what where?" People talked about threesomes like they were so erotic, but she somehow imagined an awkward scenario of the three of them naked, staring at each other. Melvina tried to shake the thought from her head as Riley pulled into her drive and got out to open the door for her.

Finding her manners, she asked, "Would you like to come in for a drink? All I have is sweet tea, some beer I keep for my brother when he's around and a bottle of wine Mona gave me last Christmas.

"I would love a cold beer. I don't want to drink up your Christmas present. I'll have to remember to bring some champagne with me next time."

"Oh, Mona wouldn't care. I like most wine or champagne, but I can't afford the fancy stuff you buy— yet." Melvina held one finger up and smiled as they climbed the porch and she opened the door. "I'll be famous like you one day, Riley Nash, just you wait and see. That Hot Buns Competition might just give me the leg up I've been looking for."

His tone turned to interest, "Oh really, and which leg would that be— left or right? He glanced down at her legs and stepped closer to her.

Oh Lordy, if he touches me, I'll probably orgasm right here.

Melvina chuckled, stepping away. She led the way to the kitchen and pulled out a Shiner Bock for Riley. She passed him the bottle and the opener she kept in a drawer by the fridge. "I love Pop, but I really want to make my own way. I want to open a small bakery. Bake in the morning and close every day by four or five in the afternoon. Then, I might actually have a normal schedule and a life."

Riley leaned against the opposite counter. "The restaurant business is something you marry. When I'm away too long, everything goes south except for my cost. That goes through the roof. And, because we serve alcohol, it's a major task to keep inventory from walking out the door. If you weren't working at Pop's, I would love for you to come work with me. I could really use someone with your organizational skills, and the baked goods would be all yours. You could choose what you want to make and how it should be made."

Melvina's eyes landed on the package on her counter. Eli must have brought it in. Maybe it was the gift Mona had mentioned. Melvina went to her office alcove between the kitchen and living room to grab the scissors from the cup filled with pens. When she came back, Humphrey was at Riley's feet getting his ears rubbed.

"Who's this?"

"Humphrey. He's my main man. Leo's around here too. Be careful. His claws are sharp."

Riley tilted his head. "I'd be jealous, but I love dogs."

Melvina's heart melted a little more.

"What do you say? Come work for me at Braised?"

"That's a sweet offer, literally." She smiled at him as she sliced through the tape and opened the box. Seeing the colorful string, she pulled it out of the box before realizing exactly what Mona had sent. The cupless bra, thong, and garter belt were a network of silk ribbons and lace with elastic sewn inside. She felt her mouth drop as she gaped at the Fredericks of Hollywood tags that dangled from the three pieces of string. The tags were actually bigger than the sum total of lingerie.

Melvina was speechless, but Riley wasn't. He chuckled, "Not what you were expecting?" He moved toward her, putting his finger through the thong, removing it from her fingers as he looked down at her. "Well, I kinda like it." His humor faded, and his eyes were lit with something she could only define as desire.

"Mona said she was sending me something for my garden." Melvina flushed pink as she realized what she was saying. Riley bit his bottom lip then a chuckle erupted out of him. His nearness robbed her of her breath and the annoying pulse she'd been feeling all night became a throbbing beat.

Do it! Kiss him.

Without hesitating, she snaked an arm around Riley's neck and pulled his lips down to hers. Her kiss was anything but gentle, and though she caught him by surprise, he quickly joined in, pulling her hard against him and hiking one of her legs up against his thigh. They groped, kissed, sucked and moaned for what felt like a lifetime in heaven. Riley lifted her to the counter as if she didn't weigh a thing, relieving her of the blouse she was wearing. Melvina worked at releasing the buttons on his shirt as he kissed his way down her neck, touching her breast, then looking for the clasp to her bra.

Melvina managed to get his shirt unbuttoned and groped lower to find him hard and ready beneath the denim he wore. Riley stood, pulling back from her hand. "We have to slow down," he rasped in a gravelly voice. "At this rate, I won't make it any distance and I want this to last. I've waited too long."

Melvina didn't want to mince words, but they had only known each other a few short weeks at best. "Too long? We just met."

His voice was a soft whisper as he spread her legs and settled between them, wrapping his arms around her lower back to pull her close. "Do you want me to stop?" His erection was pressing against the sweet throb beneath the warm fabric of her jeans and she was sure he could feel her answer. Melvina was devoid of speech. She shook her head no, and his lips came down hard, sucking at her bottom lip, then moving lower. His teeth grazed the bottom of her throat and her head lolled back in uninhibited desire. She knew she was only moments from cresting a wave of pleasure. He hadn't even taken off her pants and she was going to go without him.

As if sensing that taking their time wasn't an option, Riley slid her jeans down and removed her strappy sandals before pulling them all the way off. Stepping back, his eyes met hers and he bent over to tug off his boots. Staring at her with desire, he released the buttons on his jeans. Sliding them down, Riley kicked them to the side and came to her, naked and hard.

As they kissed and caressed, entangling their limbs, Riley's hand slipped beneath the thin fabric of silk separating him from her woman's apex. Melvina lost herself in the first wave of pleasure without much warning to Riley or herself. She couldn't suppress the loud cry that escaped her lips, telling anyone within a hundred yards of her front door that Riley had just found her g-spot.

Melvina clasped tight to his shoulders with both hands and suddenly became aware that her teeth were buried there, too. "Oops, sorry," she said sheepishly.

Riley didn't miss a beat. With a soft chuckle, he cradled her in his arms and started walking down the hall that led to her bedroom. "Which room is yours?"

She pointed to the last door and said a prayer of thanks that it was mostly straightened, and that yesterday was clean sheet day.

"I don't know if I should be flattered or scared. I'm not sure I can keep up with you if that's just the beginning of your performance," he chided softly. The springs gave way on the old mattress of the antique bed as he laid her down and climbed on top of her. Pleasure surged through her once more as she absorbed the heat of his weight. She tried to catch her breath to explain.

"I haven't—I mean, it's been a long time." She heard the rustling of a foil wrapper and then watched Riley as he bit the corner of the package. She thanked heaven that one of them was prepared, and silently chastised herself for *what if.* Would she have done something stupid in the heat of the moment? She'd never experienced passion like this before. He'd ignited a fire in her that she never knew she possessed.

He entered her with a single, slow thrust that had her hands gripping his back hard. Even with the slow tempo, she could tell he was trying to pace them both. It was only moments before she felt the tidal wave of another orgasm washing over her. He tightened up and stopped moving, shushing her as he tried to slow down. Melvina couldn't stop the persistent pleasure. She bucked against him for all she was worth, and he groaned and sped up again. They both climaxed together this time.

They lay spent for a few moments, the weight of Riley's body over hers like a warm, heavy quilt. His heart beat strongly against her chest while his cock continued to pulse inside her. She waited for the throb of her pulse to recede, but it picked up the beat of his organ, and she began to move her hips gently against him, reawakening his member.

"Only for you, sweet lady," he breathed in her ear as he began to move inside her again. "Maybe this time we can slow down and enjoy the scenery." His eyes were lit with desire, and he studied her features as he held himself above her. "You are simply and simultaneously the most beautiful and sexiest woman I have ever been with."

Melvina felt her cheeks heat at his appraisal of her wanton behavior. She could have told him that she had never been so sexual with anyone and had never had the number or intensity of orgasms she was having with him now, but it would have been impossible to speak when she could barely breathe through the moaning. His fingers caressed her skin and his lips glided over the curves of her body, traveling down to the juncture of her thighs, tasting all that she had to offer, bringing her to climax again. It was when he lay spent next to her and she still felt the throbbing desire to be taken again that she silently cursed.

Damn it, Mona, what did you give me?

The infamous Mona ring woke Melvina at just after eight. She sprang up with a start, sending the cat fleeing from the bed. Riley moaned, clasping onto her so she couldn't slide away from him. Not thinking, she quickly answered the phone with a swipe of her finger before The Black Eyed Peas song could blare from the device again.

"Mona," she whispered. "I can't talk right now."

"Are you in bed with him? Which one? Trish told Ali, who told—?"

"Shh!" Melvina looked over her shoulder, then back at the phone. "I'll meet you at Bubbles for lunch."

Mona's lips made a goldfish oh. "Just tilt the phone so I can see!"

"I'm hanging up now," Melvina whispered. It was then that Riley sat up and looked at the phone over her shoulder.

Mona squealed with delight. "I knew it!"

After hitting the end button, Melvina tossed the phone to the foot of the bed and flounced back on the pillows, putting her hands over her face.

Riley chuckled. "What's that all about?"

Melvina couldn't look him in the eye. Last night had been a dream, but this was the cold light of day and her mascara was probably smeared. No telling what he would think seeing her naked in the daylight. "It's only that everybody in town will know by noon that you slept here."

"And that's a problem, why?" His rich voice was like a soft caress as his hand stroked her hair. When she finally looked up at him, he was on one elbow gazing down at her with a smile.

"Because I don't like everyone knowing my business, and this town is horrible for gossip." She let out a sigh.

"Why would your best friend gossip about you?"

"Mona can't help herself. It's not like she wants to hurt me. It's just that she can't keep a secret from my brother, and then Eli will talk to Pop and then Pop will tell anyone who'll listen how his daughter is dating the fancy chef who owns Braised." She shook her head in despair.

"Sounds harmless to me. I mean, it is a small town and that's what small towns are known for, right?" He ran a finger over her cheek, lower to her neck, then down to her hands clutching the sheet. "Are we dating each other?"

His question sent another quick rush of heat to her cheeks. "We haven't even been on any dates." She flung up her hands.

I'm a floozie! I just slept with a man I've never even dated.

"Now that's not true. I took you to my garden and even introduced you to my family." He wiggled the sheets from her grasp and tugged them lower, bringing his lips down to hers. He squashed any further protest as he moved on top of her, kissing away all her fears about who was saying what to whom or what she looked like in the morning light.

Riley Nash, you look delicious!

Her keys jangled between her fingers as she walked into Bubbles. Riley had dropped her off in the parking lot where she'd left Pop's van the night before. She would call Mac today and see if they were done with her car.

Mona sat in what had become their usual booth and Melvina was wondering if this was going to be their one and only meeting place. Mona's brightly painted fuchsia lips were tilted up at the corners in a cat-that-caught-the canary smile before Melvina sat down.

Melvina shook her head. "Don't act like you know anything, Mona, because unless you have a camera hidden in my bedroom, you don't."

"Now that's a thought, since my best friend has excluded telling me anything juicy about her apparently flourishing love life." Mona pulled the olives off her martini stick and popped them in her mouth. Today her lashes had grown triple in length and were twice as thick.

"Mona, did you put on false lashes to meet me for lunch?"

"No, I went to a lash studio and they put them on, and I didn't do it for you. Jorden's ex is in town with their kids. I just know that little slut is trying to get him back."

"Ouch. What makes you think that?"

Mona looked sullen for a moment, peering up over her martini glass. Her lavender irises looked sad beneath her Betty Boop lashes. "He cancelled our date last night because he said he wanted to take his kids for pizza. Eli told me this morning that he was there at the café with the kids *and* his ex."

"Well that doesn't mean she wants him back. It just means she brought the kids to meet their dad for dinner." Melvina ordered a diet soda when the waitress arrived and nodded for Mona to go on.

"I asked Eli which side of the booth she sat on and he said it was Jorden's side. I haven't asked him about it yet."

"And if you know what's best, you won't. You just met Jorden, for heaven's sake. Don't scare him off the first chance you get." Melvina sat back in the booth assessing the room while Mona drained the last of her martini.

"I know, I know. It's just so hard. I really like Jorden. He's been my dream since high school and now he's mine. I don't want to share."

"Well he's got kids, so you're gonna have to share." Melvina patted her friend's hand from across the table. "I know this is hard for you, but trust me, smothering him won't help. Just let him have time with his kids. It's the right thing to do."

Mona nodded and motioned for the waitress to bring her another martini. "You're changing the subject. Tell me about you and Riley." The smile was back on Mona's face.

Melvina told her Riley drove her home and she'd invited him in for a drink. "Hey! That reminds me. Where were you when I texted you for a ride?"

Mona giggled. "I was sitting in the back of the parking lot. I saw Riley talking to you, so I decided to listen to the rest of my audio book. It was at the sex scene part, and I couldn't stop the Audible app." Mona wiggled in her seat for emphasis.

"You sneaky little bitch!" Melvina exclaimed in the way that only a close friend could. "You hung me out to dry."

Mona's eyebrows raised as she stage-whispered, loudly, "You mean I hung you out to get laid! How was the Viagra?"

Melvina sat up straighter in her seat. "You mean that wasn't naproxen?"

Mona shook her head, letting out a tirade of giggles as she fell sideways in the booth.

"You roofied me with Viagra? I knew there was something else in that Pez dispenser. I can't believe you would do that to your best friend! What if I had had a heart attack or some other fatal side effect?"

Mona waved a hand as she tried to quit laughing. "Oh Melvina, no one has ever died of a hard-on. Besides, I didn't do it on purpose. It was Jorden's, though trust me, he doesn't need it. We were foolin' around the other night and he left one on my coffee table next to the bottle of Aleve I had there. I thought it was an Aleve, so I scooped it up and put it in the Pez. I swear to God I didn't know until Jorden asked me on the phone last night to put it on my nightstand for later."

Mona leaned closer. "So how was it? Is it the same for women as it is for men?

"Shelby Dixon told me that Audrey told her that she took some of her husband's and that she looked like she had a small penis. All she could do was rub herself all over the place like a cat in heat. The boys at the garage told Eli that Audrey's husband couldn't walk straight for a week."

Melvina tried to be angry, but it was no use with Mona. She was a lost cause when it came to her Pez dispenser, gossip, and romance. The image

112

of Audrey Harrington rubbing herself like a cat on her portly husband, the chief of police, was enough to make Melvina throw in the towel. It was something she hadn't needed to know but would probably never forget.

"Well, it's not like I needed help to be hot for Riley, it was just a little more intense than I was used to. I'll let you off the hook this time. But Mona," Melvina paused to make sure she had her friend's attention. "Please never offer me pharmaceutical assistance ever again."

"Did you get the package in time?"

"Yes! I can't believe you, Mona. You said it was gardening tools, so I opened it right there in front of Riley."

Mona trilled with laughter, collapsing back into the booth, fanning herself. "I never said gardening tools. I said tools to tend your garden. Well, did you put them on for the occasion?"

Melvina shushed Mona as she waved the waitress over and ordered a martini for herself. Their discussion was causing beads of sweat to form on her brow. "No, I didn't. Humphry was running around with the garter belt in his mouth this morning. I'm sure to find it in my actual garden this weekend." Melvina couldn't help but join Mona as the laughter escalated. "Hush, Mona, before they cut us off! Why ever did you buy me lingerie?"

"Because it was a buy-one-get-one-free sale, and I thought you needed some help getting things started. All you ever wear is Spanks and granny panties."

Melvina snorted, then straightened. "Well, don't do it again. Humphrey has enough toys."

Mona pursed her lips and quirked a brow, "Don't look now, but Miss Stick Up Her Butt is making a bee-line for our table."

Melvina couldn't help but look. Celia looked like the lead baton thrower in the Magnolia High School marching band.

"Melvina Banks! How dare you sic that tax auditor on me?" Celia huffed with her hands on her hips.

Melvina was floored. "Whatever are you talking about Celia? I dropped the papers off with your secretary. Stan ran all the figures again, organized and scanned in every receipt."

Celia's voice rose above the late-lunch crowd. "That's exactly what I'm talking about! You sold me out. Telling the IRS that half of the receipts were my personal expenditures."

"Celia, I did no such thing. I went through the same form we filed for the year. Those spa receipts and shopping excursions were not included in the original batch, and that's why the figures we gave you didn't match what you filed. You added those numbers in yourself. You can't blame me for this." Melvina stood, pulling two bills out of her purse and setting them on the table for Mona to pay the tab. "Sorry, Mona, I gotta go. I'm late for my date."

Celia turned pink with anger. "Date? You can't leave right now. We need to figure this out."

Melvina shook her head and took a last sip of her diet soda. "No Celia, YOU need to figure this out and leave the Blossoms out of this. The Magnolia Blossoms are a charitable organization to help the community, not to stage your house or buy a new wardrobe." Melvina had had enough and wasn't taking Celia's flack anymore. Making her way to the door, she heard Mona's bright cheery voice call out to her. "Say hello to Riley when you go to Braised. He is such a doll."

Melvina didn't have to turn around to know that Celia was probably having a cow. *Damn that Mona.* She giggled.

Chapter 15

Melvina didn't know what to expect. She'd had the day off, but Riley needed to stop by Braised. He told her to come by when she finished her lunch with Mona. Melvina found herself impatient to get there as she drove the six-ten loop into the city. She wasn't big on driving in traffic, so it was rare that she went into Houston, and usually it was Pop or Eli driving.

When she walked into Braised, a young waitress met her at the door, "The restaurant isn't open until five, but you can get drinks at the bar."

Melvina nodded. Before she could find a seat at the bar, Riley came up behind her, pulling her to him in a bear hug and nuzzling her neck.

"Riley," she pleaded, self-conscious of the bar staff and patrons' eyes on her.

He spun her around to face him, kissing her full on the lips. "This is Houston, baby," he said between kisses. "No one gives a damn what we do. Besides, I'm the owner." He laughed at her shocked expression.

"Baby?" She tilted her head, surveying his excitement.

"Sorry. Is it too cheesy, too much too soon?"

"Maybe just a little, but I'll forgive you if you give me a tour of the kitchen," she smiled.

Riley beamed. "Now that's what I'm talkin' about." We'll be back in a minute, Ran," Riley called out over his shoulder. It was only then that Melvina noticed his brother was setting up equipment next to the bar.

"Are the Tomball Cats playin' here tonight?"

He grasped her hand as he led her to the back.

"Yep. It's Friday night. We try to keep live music in the bar on the weekends." Melvina was now embarrassed that someone she knew had witnessed Riley's steamy greeting.

She couldn't help her jaw dropping as she took in the state-of-the-art kitchen. It put Pop's place to shame, not that there was any competition.

Braised was fine dining and Pop's was comfort food. "If I had a grill like that, we would do thick T-bone steaks and ribeye for everybody in town. And I would give my eye tooth for a walk-in cooler like that." Melvina pointed to a sous chef walking out of the cooler door, holding a tub of fresh lettuce leaves.

Riley chuckled, "You could. I mean, I was serious yesterday when I said we had a need for your expertise." He paused and said in a more serious tone. "I know you've been working for your dad all these years, but didn't you tell me you wanted to break free and do your own thing? I would love to see what you could do with our dessert menu and I would give you free run of the kitchen. Just come in and make your magic happen."

Melvina was speechless. She could only dream of working in a kitchen like this, and most aspiring chefs would give anything to work at a restaurant owned by the famous Riley Nash.

"Melvina? It's okay." He took her hands in his. "You don't have to give me an answer right away. I'll show you the rest of the kitchen and you can think about it later."

He led her to the cooling drawers in the pastry area, the massive rotisseries, brick ovens and the private chef's table in the middle of the kitchen. It was a glassed-off room with a white linen-covered table in the center along with eight chairs and a massive, sparkling chandelier. Anyone seated in that room could see every area from prep to serve, and Melvina noted there wasn't one leaf of lettuce on the floor or one smear of sauce on the counter. She spotted a few younger staff members in black uniforms who Riley called The Cleaners. They darted around wiping up any mess as soon as it happened.

Melvina gawked at the entire ensemble. It was a chef's masterpiece, and according to Riley, he had planned it all. "You're a genius. The flow of everything is so impressive. From the tiniest paring knife to the location of the ovens, you have crafted a dream kitchen."

Riley pointed. "The warmers are near the dining area so that everything goes out piping hot to the table."

"I love the fresh herb bins. Who would have thought to add those so that the chef isn't running back and forth to the cooler? You are—" Her words searched for the right praise.

"Stop. You're making my head swell, and all this cooking talk with someone who gets it is making me hard." His eyes danced with excitement as he looked at her.

Melvina slapped at his arm. "You are looking at me like I'm a slab of brisket."

Riley's smile widened as he steered her down another corridor away from the kitchen past some offices, then stopped when no one else was around. He lowered his voice. "You don't even know the half of it. Last night was just a taste of the hunger I have for you. I haven't been able to think of anything else. I have to admit, I've never experienced a woman so full of passion. I wasn't sure at one point if I could keep up. I don't know if that says something great about you or bad about me." He shook his head in wonder as he stroked her hair.

"Riley, about that—"

He put a finger to her lips. "Shh, hold that thought. I want to show you something." He opened the door that led to the dining room and walked with her across the rich carpet to a glass room in the center with wall-to-wall bottles of wine. The room was at least thirty feet, floor-to-ceiling, and had a stark set of stainless-steel stairs that flowed like a corkscrew around the racks of wine. He stopped and pulled a fur coat off a rack. Melvina let him wrap it around her shoulders before feeling its softness.

"Mink?"

Riley nodded. "It's part of the ambiance. It's a little chilly in here and the guests who come in to see the wines like to wear it through the tour."

Melvina made a face. "Poor critters."

"The guests?" Riley shook his head, confused.

"No, the poor little minks that gave their lives to make up this coat." Melvina frowned, feeling self-conscious.

Riley scratched his brow. "If it bothers you, I can get my jacket from my car."

It touched her heart that he would offer. "No, that's all right. I can make it through the tour."

"Good," he nodded.

When they approached the top of the stairs in the wine cellar, Melvina could see the entire restaurant. She hadn't noticed before that the walls didn't go all the way to the ceiling where the kitchen was separated, so from up here she could see the pastry chef icing a cake while the band started playing at the opposite end in the bar. It was a glittering display of candlelit tables, gleaming kitchen, and crystal glasses at every table.

"It's beautiful," Melvina marveled.

"So, what do you think? Will you come here to work?"

Melvina paused as a quick list of pros and cons skimmed through her brain. "I admit it's tempting, and when I first met you, I wanted to ask you to back me in my very own bakery. I've saved a little, but nowhere near the amount I need to land the whole thing. I need an investor, but now—you, me, the whole thing between us. I don't think we should mix business with pleasure. It could ruin everything. Besides, even though this is my dream kitchen, it's not my dream. I don't want to give up on my idea of a boutique bakery that lets me off at five p.m. like the rest of the world. I want to have a life one day."

Riley nodded in comprehension. "I would have backed you and your bakery. I still will if you want. I've got enough money. Hell, I don't even know what to do with half of it."

His eyes assessed her as she shook her head. "It's too late for that now. I was hoping to ask you before we got to know each other."

He crinkled his forehead in thought. "Wait, you mean because I slept with you, I can't invest in your success?"

"I'm saying it would just cause problems down the road. It would be complicated."

He bent toward her and brushed his lips softly over hers. "Well, I don't agree. I don't want to scare you off, but I see a long future for us together. You've got just what I've been looking for. I hope maybe you'll want to share some of those dreams with me."

Why is he saying all this? Surely he could have any woman he wants. Why me?

Melvina felt hypnotized by his husky voice and heartfelt words. She looked down at the restaurant and saw Ran talking to a patron at the bar.

Riley touched his forehead softly against hers, "Okay, enough of the tour for now. Let's go have a drink."

Oh no!

Melvina's heart sank as they approached the bar. Riley's hand curled possessively around her waist. Before she could say or do anything, Manny turned around to greet them.

"Mr. Nash." There was an audible silence as his greeting stopped abruptly, leaving them all in discomfort before picking back up again. "Melvina, I didn't know you were here."

The disappointment in his eyes tore at Melvina's heart. The chief had been nothing but kind, and he'd expressed his interest in her the night he'd taken her to dinner. And she'd shown interest in return.

She hoped Manny didn't feel like she'd been leading him on. Damn, this was awkward. She didn't want this to happen.

Sensing things were strained, Riley nodded to the bartender, "Hey, Luke, why don't you bring the fire chief a cold beer on the house."

Manny waved him off. "Naw, that's all right. I was just stopping in quick to see about the calendar event. Celia is planning two competitions between Harris and Montgomery counties, with a first round here at Braised and a second round at Bubbles, then a final barbecue outside the station when the calendar gets released. She came over to the station insisting I talk to you today. She thought you might say yes if I asked you in person."

Melvina inwardly groaned. *That bitch!* Mona's dig had now landed her in an uncomfortable position. Thoughtless of Manny's feelings, it was proof that Celia only cared about herself. She probably thought she was killing two birds with one stone, systematically showing Manny that Melvina had feelings for Riley and clearing the way for her own hooks to land in Manny's unsuspecting back. Well, maybe not so unsuspecting. He did ask her not to bring Celia to the firehouse. It was possible he would still survive the hunt. Manny deserved a nice partner after all the hard work he did for the community.

"Sure, Chief. Anything to help out. You got a day and time? I can go put it on the books now."

Manny pointed to Melvina. "Melvina here is the planner. I'm just supposed to ask." He smiled, but it didn't quite reach his eyes.

Riley turned to his brother. "You wanna play that evening?"

Ran's smile was mischievous. "Oh, if Raphe is strutting his stuff down the catwalk, I don't think I would miss it."

They all laughed. Manny nodded to the group. "Well, it sounds like my work here is done. I'll let you figure out the details amongst yourselves. I need to get back to the station and check on the boys."

Melvina remembered him mentioning at the meeting that he had today off. "Don't you ever rest, Manny?"

He started backing toward the door as he placed his Rockets ball cap back on his head. "No rest for the weary." He winked. "Y'all take care." And with that, he was gone.

Melvina couldn't help but to feel crestfallen. She had never been in this situation in her life. She had mooned over Manny for years and now here she had blown it on a chance with Riley. Manny was solid, salt of the earth, community oriented, an all-around great guy. What did she know about Riley? He could cook. He was great in bed. He was a city boy now and famous across the nation for his reality cooking show debut. He owned one of the hottest restaurants in the fourth largest city in America.

Melvina was a country girl by all rights. Houston was a forty-five minute drive with no traffic, and she rarely left her cozy little hometown. She was out of her league and she knew it.

Riley had been talking to his brother about the upcoming event and the night's plans. He barked out a few orders to the staff and then interrupted her thoughts. His voice was soft. "Mel, you okay?"

"Don't call me Mel." It was an automatic response. She had been called Mel throughout high school and she hated it. Only Eli, Pop and Mona were allowed to call her Mel, because she knew they only did it with affection. "Sorry, it just brings back bad memories." She placed a hand on his arm to soften her words. Ran had left them and was continuing to tune his instrument. "Riley, I need to go. I'll take a rain check on the drink. You've got things to do, and," she paused. "I need to get back to Magnolia."

Chapter 16

Melvina Rayanne Banks, don't get above your raisin'.

Melvina never understood what Granny meant by those words. Why would any grandmother ever tell her grandchild not to aspire to be something better? Now she got it. Their mother, Rayna, had always wanted more. She wanted to be in the spotlight and a part of the fancy culture that was available in the big city. She left her family for what? Who knew? Rayna must have changed her name or maybe met her end. She wasn't famous and the few times Melvina searched for her on the internet, there wasn't a thread of new information.

Riley would have been the perfect man for Rayna. He was all polished, southern charm. As one of the wealthy elite of the metropolis, he probably got invited to big soirees and sophisticated events. The highlight of her social calendar always involved the name Magnolia Blossoms written in the invitation. Melvina knew she didn't want to leave Magnolia. Pop, Eli and Mona were everything to her. No matter how many times she had dreamed of running off and starting a successful bakery in a bigger town or city, she knew she loved Magnolia. She could still have her dream, but she was sure now it would happen here at home. There was a lot of growth in the surrounding areas, and it was only a matter of time before she could save enough to make it all happen.

Melvina shook off her self-loathing.

I'm a good person and I deserve a good partner. I deserve love and success. I deserve a good life.

The self-help recordings swirled through her brain.

She was letting her imaginary social class separate her from a man she really liked. Riley had shown her nothing but good manners, and he'd even introduced her to his family. He was amazing with children and animals, and though he had seen her with Manny on a date in his restaurant only a few nights before, he was an exemplary model of politeness to Manny. And the best part was, he talked and acted like he wanted a relationship with her.

As for her abilities in the kitchen—well, she was just as good as Riley James Nash, and she was going to prove it. When she won the blue ribbon for the Hot Buns Competition, the media would spread the word. Then maybe she would feel comfortable in his world.

When she pulled into her drive, Humphrey lay on the top step of the porch and his long basset ears hung down like two pigtails touching the step below. Eli sat next to him in his basketball shorts and tennis shoes. He was either on his way to the gym or on his way back. Melvina waved to him as she got out of the car.

Eli and Humphrey both stood. Her brother's long legs were a great contrast to Humphrey's short ones. "Where've you been? I've been here for over an hour."

Melvina looked at him perplexed. "Was I supposed to be here?"

He smiled sheepishly. "No, sorry. I'm just used to you being home on your day off, or not gone for long, and there's nothing to eat."

Melvina couldn't hide her own grin as she looked up at his towering stance. "Sorry, little brother. It appears I have a life."

He raised his eyebrows and pressed his lips together as he blew out a breath.

"I heard." He pulled something from his gym shorts pocket and quirked his head in question as the string of tangled lingerie hung from his index finger. "You want to explain why this is in Humphrey's toy box?"

"Give me those." Melvina grabbed them, scowling up at him as she tried to suppress her laughter. They still had the tags on them, or she knew her brother would have never mentioned the mangled ball of satin and lace.

"You mean there is more than one item here?" he gawked.

Melvina walked through the front door and made a bee-line to the kitchen. She looked in the fridge and pulled out a carton of whole milk. She stepped into the pantry, pulling out all the items needed to make gluten-free pancakes for Eli. She loved feeding people, but her little brother made her feel warm inside with all his praise of her cooking, so it was a joy to bake for him. Cake would take too long, so pancakes would have to do.

"Mona," she said with an exasperated sigh. "She thought it was funny, sending me those strings she calls underwear." Melvina shook her head as Eli laughed.

He watched her as she heated the stove and poured oil in the pan. "I should have known. You need me to help?"

"With the pancakes or Mona?" Melvina smiled, knowing the answer.

"Something in the kitchen. Mona's your friend," he pointed at her as he shook his head, eyes wide in denial.

Melvina looked at him with a sassy tilt of her head. "Oh really? Then why are you two always gossiping about my life?"

Eli ducked his head and studied a magazine on the kitchen island as he rocked back on the barstool. "It's not gossiping when you're talking about family to family. And since you brought it up, what's up with you and the chief, then this other guy?" He looked at her now with pointed interest, shoving the magazine aside as she handed him a glass of chocolate milk.

"It's none of Mona's or your business," she countered, but then thoughtfully confided. "I don't know, Eli. Truth be told, I don't know what's going on. Celia is all over me about the IRS audit, and I know she has the hots for Manny, but now Riley, too, and I haven't done anything, but suddenly both of them asked me out."

Melvina shook her head as she flipped two cakes onto the plate and handed it to Eli. The microwave dinged, indicating the syrup was hot and ready. Eli scooped a chunk of butter on top of his pancakes before dousing them with syrup.

Melvina's mouth opened in shock. "What is that?" She pointed to the glob of butter. "Are you my brother? Is the no-saturated-fat phase over?"

Eli shoved a big bite of pancake into his mouth and moaned, speaking around the bite. "Everyone's got to cheat sometimes, Melvina. Man cannot live on meat and vegetables alone."

Melvina laughed. "Glad to hear it, as long as we're talking about food and diets." The comment brought her thoughts back to Mona, and she wondered how her best friend was getting on with Jorden after the ex-wife's visit. "You seen Mona?"

Eli nodded, then washed down the cakes with the glass of milk, pounding his fist on his chest as the food settled. "She was at Pop's right before I came here. She was meeting her new beau, I guess. When I left, they looked like they were having a serious discussion. However, you are derailing the subject. What's between you and this famous chef guy? The whole town's talking about how you broke the chief's heart."

Melvina shook her head, slapping her dishtowel on the counter. "I don't know, Eli. One day I'm Melvina Banks, Magnolia Blossom treasurer who volunteers at the library, the next I'm a sultry heartbreaker." She heaved a deep sigh. "We both know that no one ever pays attention to me unless they are talking about community work or the café, and now, all of a sudden, I've got two men interested in me. Manny takes me out and I think that it's all great, but I like Riley, too. He picked me up and we spent the day together. There was nothing to it really, but I have this feeling…." She paused. "And then he took me home when Mona hung me out to dry, and well, that's enough of that story." She waved her hand in the air as if to bat her thoughts away. "By the way, if Mona EVER offers you something from a Pez dispenser, for the love of God, don't take it!"

Eli about fell off the kitchen stool as his hands came up to keep the milk he'd just swigged from shooting out of his mouth.

Melvina covered her face with her hands, peeking out at Eli through her fingers. "Oh my God! She told you, didn't she?"

Eli continued laughing as his face turned red.

"I'm going to kill her," Melvina said. "Is nothing sacred in this family?"

After Eli regained his composure, he picked up his gym bag and knelt down to scratch Humphrey behind the ears. "So, who's it going to be? The chief or the chef?"

"It's not that easy, but I think Celia made that choice for me. She sent Manny over to Braised, where he saw me with Riley."

"That doesn't mean anything."

Melvina sighed. "It does after last night." She blew out a breath she'd been holding as she looked down at Humphrey wagging his tail.

"That doesn't mean anything either. It's not like you have a commitment to the chief or Riley. If you still like Manny, there's plenty of time, but it sounds like you haven't made up your mind, yet." He stood.

Wrapping his arms around Melvina, he rested his head on top of hers. She loved Eli's hugs. He always knew just what to say and his reasoning was true. She was single. There shouldn't be this feeling of pressure. Manny was a nice guy. Would he wait for her?

"You're right. I've liked Manny a long time. Now here I have the chance and I can't quit thinking about Riley. I don't even really know him. He just breezed in here and swept me off my feet. He's big-time celebrity chef, and I'm just a small-town baker. I don't know what I was thinking."

"You may live in a small town, but you are not *just* a small-town baker, Mel. You are part of the glue of this community, and no matter who you choose, he will be lucky to have you." Eli backed away, looking her in the eye. "I mean that."

Touching her nose with his index finger, he smiled and headed toward the door. She heard his keys jangle as Humphrey followed him out.

Melvina stroked the big yellow cat who jumped on the counter. She knew her brother was right. She needed to remember his words later when she might forget. Humphrey busted back in through the side doggie door, strings of lace and satin dangling from his mouth as he made his way to his plaid plush bed. Melvina snapped a picture and sent it to Mona captioned *Humphrey loves his new toy.*

Riley wasn't sure what had changed Melvina's mood and made her rush out of Braised, but he knew it had something to do with the Magnolia fire chief showing up. They'd been on a date recently. Hell, he had sent them champagne, but when Melvina obviously showed interest in him last night, he thought her decision was made.

He didn't think she was the kind of girl to take two different men to bed in one week, but who was he to judge if she did? He would be a Neanderthal to think that way, but he couldn't hold back the ache in his stomach, thinking that Melvina might have something more going on with Manny Owens than just a first date and maybe a good night kiss. He didn't have the right to be jealous, but he was. He wouldn't be if Melvina hadn't skated out of there like her tail was on fire. He kicked himself for calling her baby and then Mel. They weren't on that level yet, and he knew he shouldn't be overly familiar, except—damn, she had been almost insatiable in bed. Riley knew she felt something for him more than just the chemistry they shared between the sheets, not that he could forget the way she set him on fire then and now.

Riley held tight to the bar, not moving when the bartender came up with two racks of glasses. "Just set them down and I'll put them away, and can you go offer Ran and the boys a cold beer."

After a few moments of shelving glasses and running a towel over the bar, he went to his office to think. It was his day off, but without being able to see Melvina, he wasn't sure what else he wanted to do, so he threw himself into paperwork.

The following morning, he drove out to Lexi's and made breakfast for her and the boys. He offered to take them to the zoo afterward, but Lexi told them they had other plans. "You're welcome to come along. There's a children's author at the library today and *Naughty Nana* is Damien's favorite book. Nana, the sheepdog, will be there, and the kids can't wait to see her."

The last thing Riley wanted was to go to the library, but he remembered Melvina spent a lot of time teaching kids to read, so he readily agreed to drive them.

Lexi grinned, shaking her head. "I think your sports car wouldn't look cool with a car seat in it. We'll take the van."

He nodded in acceptance. "Okay, I'll follow you over, just in case I need to slide out early."

Lexi gave him a knowing look, rolling her eyes as she ushered the boys out to the car.

"Hey, whatever happened to the pretty lady you brought by last week?"

"Nothing. I saw her yesterday. She's good."

"Well you should bring her around again. The boys really liked her, and I think she's good for you. Maybe she can tame your bachelor ways."

Riley nodded as he got in the car. His eldest nephew ran to the passenger side and jumped in. Riley lowered the window and called out to Lexi, "Is it okay if Gus rides with me?"

Lexi nodded. Riley smiled, giving the other boys a wave. He made a show of peeling out at the end of the drive. He imagined his sister's irritation, but the whooping of his nephew's pleasure was worth the set-down he would get when they arrived safe.

Riley was disappointed when he didn't see Melvina anywhere in the library. He did enjoy seeing Damien so enthused over the story reading, and afterward, when all the kids fawned over the massive sheepdog.

The author, Saralyn Richard, was previously a teacher and had a special way with kids. The boys had recently lost Captain, their Blue Heeler. Actually, the dog had belonged to the boys' dad and had become the family dog after the wedding. Lexi had put off getting another puppy since the loss of Captain had been like losing her husband all over again. It had broken Riley's heart to see his sister and the boys so upset.

He loved dogs but didn't have time to take care of one the past few years or he would have gotten one for the boys to enjoy. Riley would talk to Lexi again. It was time. All young boys needed a furry friend. After purchasing a book for each of his nephews, he darted off to the restroom while they were getting their books signed. He caught a glimpse of a woman with blonde hair in an adjacent study room. She leaned over a long table with the Hispanic kid he had met the other day. When she straightened and looked at him, his heart did a little flip.

"Melvina," he said with pleasure. "I thought maybe you were working today. I mean, you weren't out there."

She smiled as she walked toward him. "And you were?"

He grinned sheepishly. "Lexi and the boys. Damien loves that book," he explained.

"It's a good one. I bet they are all over that dog." Melvina said, smiling as Riley nodded.

"Hey, you want to join us for lunch or the zoo? I'm trying to get the boys to take me to see the elephants."

Melvina looked back over her shoulder at Maurice. "I can't. I kinda got something to finish."

"You guys got much longer? We can wait. The boys really like you, and they would probably love to meet the kid if he wants to come."

"You mean Maurice?" She smiled, hesitating as though mulling over the idea. Finally, she nodded. "Yeah, I think we could use a break. I'll call his mom and tell her I'll drop him at his house afterward."

Riley's spirits soared. Now he just needed to talk Lexi and the boys into the zoo.

Melvina enjoyed seeing Riley's sister and the boys, but seeing Maurice laugh and act his age instead of like an adult was priceless. It was a fun venture for everyone, and Riley feeding the elephants was the highlight of her day. She had a picture of him with the boys all holding bags of peanuts as Maggie, the elephant, laid her trunk over his shoulder and riffled through the bag, giving him a wet smooch after procuring enough of the tasty treats.

Lexi took the boys home after, and Riley insisted on taking Maurice home before dropping her off. Maurice seemed to have had a lot of fun, but in the calm of the aftermath, in the quietness of the car, he seemed to retreat inside himself.

"Did you have a good time?" Riley threw over the driver's seat as he turned into the small trailer park community.

Maurice nodded, but remained silent. Melvina gave Riley a tight smile for his effort. Rome wasn't built in a day. As soon as the car stopped, Maurice raced out and headed toward the door. She asked Riley to wait while she went to meet Maria. After a brief conversation detailing their day, she returned to the car, waving as they drove away.

"What's that all about? I thought he had a good time."

Melvina shrugged her shoulders. "His dad disappeared a few months ago, and since then Maurice has been struggling. I thought today would be good for him, but maybe it reminded him of happier times with his dad."

"Or maybe he has a crush on you and doesn't want to share? I see the way he looks at you. The night I dropped you off at the library and met the little guy, I could tell he had it bad. I used to feel that way about my biology teacher, Mrs. Frasier."

"Are you jealous?" She teased. "I bet you had a lot of crushes, but I don't think Maurice has a crush. He's just vulnerable right now. I've talked to the fire chief about letting him wash some of the trucks with them on Sunday. He really could use a good male role model. That's really why I said yes today. I thought he could use some time around a man who cares about family."

"So is that how you see me? A family guy? What about my famous chef status? You said Pop would be impressed." He joked, smiling at her as his eyes twinkled. As his expression sobered, he concentrated on the road. "Seriously, since you brought up the fire chief, can I ask you a question?"

Uh oh, here we go.

The dreaded question she'd been trying to avoid, especially since she didn't know the answer.

Riley pulled into the library and parked the car next to hers. Most of the cars that had filled the lot earlier were gone, and it was almost closing time. "What's up with you and Manny Owens? I mean, I know that it's technically none of my business, but I like you and I want to know what kind of chance I have before I put myself out there." He put his hand on hers, rubbing a finger over the sensitive area at her wrist.

Melvina gulped. It was the moment of truth. "Honestly, I don't know. I mean, he just showed up and asked me out and took me to Braised, and I had just seen you kissing Celia, so I said yes."

"I knew it. I knew you were upset by that kiss, but Melvina, you didn't let me explain. Celia kissed *me*. I didn't want it. I got out of there as quick as I could. I saw you, tried to catch you. Damn near got a speeding ticket over it."

Melvina put her other hand over his, forming a sandwich. It was time to come clean. "Riley, I didn't go out with Manny because you kissed Celia. I've really liked him for a long time. It's just that he was married, and then widowed, and I felt so guilty for even liking him that way, and he never seemed to notice me until you showed up. Then, suddenly—" she sighed with exasperation.

"When it rains, it pours," he finished for her. He leaned back in his seat, a crease between his brows. "You still want to be with him?"

Melvina stared ahead, looking at the spray of gold, orange, red and blue of the setting sun. "I really like you Riley, but I hardly know you. We just met. You live in Houston and I live here. Your life is Braised and celebrity chef shows. My life is small town Magnolia, cupcakes, and working at Pop's."

"And the fire chief is Magnolia, too. Is that it?"

Silence engulfed her, then she found her voice.

"If you need an answer right now, Riley, I can't give you one. If I asked you what the future held for you, could you honestly tell me that I'm in it?"

Riley paused in thought. "I'd like you to be, but I hear what you're saying. I'm a patient man, Melvina. I can wait, but don't keep me in the cooler too long. I've got my pride."

Chapter 17

I'm scared.

She could admit it to herself. Melvina lay in bed staring into the darkness with Humphrey at her feet and Leo at her head. She thought about Riley's words. They'd had a great day and she really enjoyed her time with him. On the other hand, she'd liked Manny for so long....

She recalled when she was a teen, a friend of Pop's said women are like monkeys because they couldn't let go of one man until they had a hold of another.

At the time it had made her so mad....

Isn't that exactly what I'm doing?

She was holding onto both men until she'd worked out her own feelings. Riley was handsome, sexy and dynamic and yet he was also loving and caring about his family. But all the excitement he'd brought to her life was overwhelming. Then there was Manny—good looking, grounded, salt-of-the-earth. She'd pined after him for years. She'd known him forever and knew where the future would take her. Manny was everything she'd ever wanted in a man—until Riley snuck into her life.

What am I going to do?

Melvina tossed and turned for hours until Humphrey finally got off the bed with a huff. She slept in patches until five a.m. and got up to make tea and take a shower before work. She needed to bake rolls today and make sure she brought her A game on Sunday night. The contest was just a week away and Melvina was determined to nail it. The Magnolias were putting up a prize, but since she was a Blossom, technically she couldn't win cash. She would designate a charity to receive the money, which would be split between the library and the mentor program she wanted to develop.

She also needed to carve out some time to see Stanley. She needed an affidavit from him stating that the documents she submitted to the IRS for the Blossoms were the same ones that she'd checked figures for and that anything filed after that was added by a third party and didn't reflect on her accounting or the Magnolia Blossoms. She also wanted him to look over her own account figures and see what he thought about her investment portfolio. She had been putting ten percent of her checks away for twenty years. She never touched it and acted as if it didn't exist. It must have amounted to something by now. She should look at her quarterly statements, but she usually tossed them in a cubbyhole in her desk and forgot about them. If it was enough for a down payment, maybe he could help her draft a business plan for a bakery.

Pop was in his office when she arrived. "Early morning for you, Melvina."

She sat across from her father's desk in the tattered chair with its peeling upholstery around the arms. "I couldn't sleep, and I wanted to put some bread in the oven early. We'll have a bunch of rolls today, so you may want to tell Darcey to add it to the specials."

He lowered his reading glasses, looking at her with concern. "What's got you up at night? Is your back still hurting you?"

Melvina thought about it. "Actually no, I've never felt better. Maybe that pill Mona gave me did the trick." Melvina tried not to smile as she thought of the other pill Mona had given her, leading to the hot night she shared with Riley.

Pop nodded. "Good. Glad to hear it. Well, the customers will be happy today. The whole town loves your fresh dinner rolls. Does this have anything to do with that Hot Buns Competition?"

Melvina couldn't suppress a grin. She put her hands up. "That was not my idea. That was all Celia's, or wait, maybe it was Riley's. Celia wanted to do the calendar, but I think it was Riley Nash who challenged me to a bake-off. The buns part seemed like a perfect fit for the contest."

"Naturally." Pop grinned, holding his chin between his thumb and index finger.

Melvina waved a hand at him as she got up from the chair. "I don't have time to play *Tease Melvina*," she said in an airy voice. "I've got work to do."

Her father's chuckle followed her down the hall on her way to the kitchen. She stepped into the cooler to grab the necessary ingredients: butter, yeast culture, milk, eggs. The live culture needed to be fed and then come to room temperature. She loved its beer-like smell. It was her secret ingredient. Her homegrown yeast had been fermenting more than fifteen years.

As the second batch of rolls came out at lunchtime, Melvina put the five trays in the warmers except for two dozen rolls that she placed in breadbaskets and carted out to the guests. With a pair of metal tongs, she placed a free roll on every plate that wanted one. Everyone wanted one. She saw some of the guys from the fire station and walked over to say hello.

"Do any of you men want hot dinner rolls?" She smiled at the eager pleas that ensued.

"Melvina, you are going to wipe the floor with that fancy city-boy chef," one called out after taking a big bite of the butter-laden roll.

"I might take offense to that," a voice said behind her. Melvina's heart did a flip-flop as she recognized the smooth baritone of the fancy city-boy chef himself. A zing of excitement played with her emotions as she turned to see Riley's smiling face.

"You guys know my brother is a fireman, right? I'm a supporter of the cause, so go easy now. I love the pretty lady's baked goods as much as the next patron, but let's just have a taste and see."

Melvina held out the tongs and dropped a roll in his proffered hand.

Riley moaned with pleasure. "Well, gentleman, I clearly have my work cut out for me, but don't count me out just yet. My great-great-grandma's recipe has been passed down for generations and I have a secret ingredient in mine that I bet Melvina doesn't."

Guffaws and different renditions of no-way and not-gonna-happen flew up from the table of firefighters.

Melvina laughed. "I love you guys. Feed hungry men every day and they will always have your back."

Riley chuckled. "Well I can't argue with that. I'm a bit the same. There's nothing I wouldn't do for a good woman who's beautiful and cooks like an angel." His comments were followed by a lot of "that's right," and "Amen." Riley shook a few hands, did a high five and one fist bump to the youngest guy at the table.

Melvina's cheeks flamed with all the praise. "Why, thank you. I guess I better get on to serving the rest of these rolls before they get cold. She laid one basket in the center of the table for the firemen before making a round of the remaining tables. Riley took a seat at the counter. Melvina grabbed the coffeepot and a pitcher of sweet tea, making her way to where he sat.

Darcey was busy taking orders at the other end of the restaurant, and the new girl was on break.

Melvina held up the carafe. "Coffee, tea?"

"You're missing the *or me* in that sentence." Darcey returned, swinging behind the counter and bumping Melvina with her hip. The saucy waitress bent over, looking for a pack of straws to fill her apron pocket. Darcey winked at Melvina as she stood, then spun around before Melvina could chastise her.

Riley choked back a chuckle. "Don't be mad at her. I was thinking it, but too afraid to ask, but since she brought it up." He motioned to Darcey making her way to retrieve orders at the window. "I didn't come for lunch. I want to take you out."

"Say yes!" Darcey called back before Melvina could find her voice.

Melvina rolled her eyes at the constant interruptions, whispering low. "I swear one day I will fire her big mouth." Turning her attention back to Riley's expectant expression, she said, "You mean now?"

Riley smiled. "Whenever you are ready, willing, and able. I can help bus tables if it gets you out of here sooner."

Melvina looked around at the full restaurant and shook her head. "There's no way I can get out of here. The new girl isn't ready yet and I've got rolls in the oven."

"I can help with that too. What do you want me to do?"

Melvina sighed with exasperation. "You know, if I didn't know any better, I would think you were trying to steal my secret roll recipe. There is no way I'm letting you into my kitchen," she teased, smacking a towel down on the counter to wipe an empty space for the next guest.

Riley made a mock face of shock. "What? I showed you mine, and now you refuse to show me yours." The patrons in the near vicinity chortled.

Melvina wondered how to get him out of her hair so she could get back to work. She couldn't think straight when she was in his too-handsome presence.

"Oh, for the love of God, show him yours, before I show him mine," Darcey hooted as she saddled up beside Melvina, putting her elbows on the counter, which pushed her cleavage up in the deep V of her uniform top. The cheeky waitress smiled at Riley with a bold wink. Looking up at Melvina from her bent position with an innocent bat of her lashes, she added, "We got it here. Ginny is doing great and the guys love her North Carolina accent. What are you waiting for, Melvina, a marriage proposal? Take this man to the kitchen or better yet, bed."

Melvina stared daggers at Darcey for the scene she was causing. Untying her apron, Melvina threw it under the counter. "I'm taking an hour break, but when I get back, this place better be runnin' tiptop or I'm making you work Friday and Saturday night, ya hear?" As she came out from around the counter, she motioned for Riley to follow her out. A grand cheer went up from the restaurant.

For a moment, he thought stopping by Pop's was a lost cause. He hadn't really wanted to see the kitchen. He had worked in dozens of cafés like Pop's growing up. He just couldn't quit thinking about Melvina. Though he knew he should step away and let her decide who she wanted, there was a part of him that saw a great thing and didn't want to lose it.

He picked up his pace, rushing to hold the door open for Melvina as they exited Pop's. He always held the door for ladies, even the ones who bristled about it.

"Where to?" Melvina sounded matter of fact as he led her to his black Infiniti parked behind the café.

"Do we really only have an hour?" he asked, closing the passenger door for her.

She looked thoughtful, then asked. "That depends. Are we going some-place fun?"

He nodded with sage authority as he slipped into the driver's seat. "Oh yeah, It's more than fun. It's soulful, and if you don't like it, well then I have obviously picked the wrong woman."

Melvina laughed. "Then drive on, Mr. Nash. I am dying to see what you call soulful, but I've got to warn you. I've never considered church fun."

"Who said anything about church?"

He hit the gas as they sped out of the lot and made their way to the two-forty-nine. Riley activated the GPS on his phone and then they exited, turning toward Austin on the backroads.

"Somehow, I think I'll be calling Eli to go check on the girls. This seems like it might be a long way. Should I have brought my overnight bag?"

"Naw, we're almost there, but what a great idea. Ran's band plays up in Austin a lot. We could make a night of it and stay at the Driskill, grab dinner at the Salty Sow." He grinned at her, hoping to entice her to say yes.

Melvina scrutinized his profile, trying to see if he was teasing. "Is that really a restaurant?"

"Hell yeah, best duck fat French fries ever. I love that place. White table-cloths, champagne, braised pork belly, and they make the best chocolate cake you've ever had outside of my momma's Christmas recipe."

She held her hands to her ears. "Stop, you're making me drool."

"Don't worry. If you like, I'll take you there one night."

"Well, you haven't told me what *this* is. Will I survive it? You aren't taking me out in the middle of nowhere to leave my dead body in a shallow grave, are you? Seems like we've come a long way."

He reached over and patted her knee. "Almost there, I promise."

They pulled down a gravel drive and through a massive iron gate that stood open. The bronc horse over the entrance boasted Remington Ranch. Melvina looked out the window and her expression was one of pure joy. Riley thought of her reaction when she saw all his horses. He knew she loved animals. He had met Humphrey and Leo. Riley remembered Humphrey carrying around the lingerie in his mouth and smiled. He really liked that dog.

He stopped the car in the large circular drive, and a woman about his grandmother's age stepped onto the porch. She was dressed in country casual, but the press of her clothes said dry clean only rather than barn work worthy. It was a working ranch, but at her age, someone else was doing most of the work.

Riley moved around to open Melvina's door when a slew of basset hound puppies poured out of the front door along with a boy of about nine or ten. Melvina's breath caught in audible surprise and it was just the reaction Riley had hoped for. She squealed a little bit as she bent down to rub all of their downy heads. They clamored around her, a few nipping at her feet and the tail of her shirt.

"Oh my, they are beautiful! Can I hold one?" She looked up at the boy standing over the litter.

The freckle-faced imp nodded with an irresistible grin. "You can take 'em all home if you want. They're tearing up everything 'round here. Except this one. He held up the smallest pup. "He's gonna stay with me. He's the littlest like my baby brother, Todd, and my dad says we little guys got to watch out for each other."

Riley's heart tripped as he watched Melvina smile at the boy with warmth and understanding.

Melvina held the fattest female in her arms, kissing its head and cooing. She looked up at Riley with pretend anger. He knew it was fake, because she couldn't quit smiling. "Riley, you don't fight fair. I don't need another dog. Humphrey will be jealous."

He bent down next to her, petting the lemon-colored female pup she was holding. "Well, see, I talked to Humphrey the other day and he told me he wanted a friend. Someone he could dress up in those strings you got from your pal, Mona," he chuckled.

Melvina shook her head. "Oh no, then we would have puppies!" she exclaimed.

Riley smiled at her use of *we*. "Well, what if I'd like to share a house full of basset hound puppies with you?"

Oh lordy! What do I say to that?

The woman on the porch hollered for the little boy to come inside and then called out to them, "We'll be inside filling out the papers, so you guys come on in once you've picked the ones you want."

"Ones?" Melvina looked at Riley, wide eyed.

"Yeah, I figured Humphrey would like a buddy, but I wanted you to agree first and then I also wanted to pick one out for the boys. Though if my sister raises hell over it, I might just take the puppy myself, but I don't think it'll happen. Those boys need a dog. It's been two years since their old Blue Heeler passed, and it's time they had a pup."

Melvina smiled, holding the sleeping pup to her chest. "Well, I've picked mine, so I guess you need to pick out one for the boys. You truly are a wonderful uncle. I hope Lexi doesn't tan your hide." She shook her head with doubt.

He nodded, stood and walked over to a grassy area where the other pups had scrambled to play and roll around. Bending down, he scooped up a mostly black with a touch of white male and held him up for inspection. "Buddy, you are one lucky pup. Those kids are gonna love you to pieces. Lexi, too."

Melvina held one puppy on her lap while the other snoozed on a blanket in the box at her feet. They drove out to deliver the male pup to Lexi and the boys together. She was touched Riley wanted to include her in this moment with his family, but worried she was intruding. Her heart did a flip-flop when they pulled up to the house and the boys tumbled out the door. Riley had called ahead to warn his sister they were coming and that he had a gift for the boys, but that's all he divulged.

Melvina laughed as the boys swung the passenger side door open, squealing with delight. The poor puppy she had named Lulu squealed a little herself, afraid of all the excitement. The male Riley had picked shot out of the box, and the boys were rolling in the grass with him instantly. Melvina calmed Lulu with soothing endearments then set her down on the grass. She chuckled as she watched the pup lope toward her littermate.

"Riley James Nash, you didn't!" Lexi stood at the door in her favorite pink sweats, one hand on her hips and the other waving a wooden spoon.

Melvina made an O with her mouth, looking at Riley to gauge his response. "Looks like you're in trouble now," she whispered.

"I know. She's armed for battle, and trust me, I've been on the receiving end of that spoon before."

Melvina whistled and shook her head as she envisioned Lexi tearing after him.

Riley scratched his brow, looking like he was planning his defense. "Lexi, you know it's past time, and if I waited for you to say yes, these kids would never get a dog."

"That's not true, Riley. Who's going to potty train this dog, feed it, pick up after it? I've got my hands full enough as it is, and you know how hard it was losing—" Lexi's words broke off as she watched the boys play. She looked like she was going to cry, but Melvina wasn't sure if it was over the memory of their dog, Captain, that died, her deceased husband, Jack, or the look of pure joy on her children's faces. Maybe it was all three.

Riley used the moment to drive his point home. "Look at them. They need a dog. It will teach them responsibility, kindness for animals and they're big enough to help. I'll stay on them if they don't. Ain't that right, boys?"

They all clamored around their mother, holding up the puppies to show her.

Little Damien wrung his hands. "Please, Momma!" he whined while Gus and Bert rambled on that one of the pups was for Melvina and they would only keep the other one.

Lexi's shoulders slumped and she shook her head in defeat. "Now that there's no way to say no, you get to come in and finish dinner and bathe the boys. I'm going to go take a hot bath and try to ease the migraine you've given me. I hope you brought puppy chow and lots of newspapers!"

Lexi waved them into the house before leaving them all in the kitchen. Melvina looked at Riley, "Is she okay?"

Riley blew out a breath, "She will be. I didn't think she would get this emotional about it, but I know Lexi. She'll come 'round." Looking at the boys he said, "Y'all get in the bath and get washed up. I'll be around to check on you in a minute. Then I'll see if there's something good in the cupboard for dessert!"

Gus looked at Riley, crestfallen, "What about the puppy, Uncle Riley? We haven't even named him yet."

Riley leaned against the counter. "There'll be time enough for namin' later. Bath time first, then dinner. Trust me." He bent down to scratch the black and white male behind the ears. "This puppy's gonna be 'round for a long time. So take time coming up with the best name you can."

That got the troops moving. All three heads bobbed as they made their way down the hallway spouting out names as if it were a game they could win. Both pups sat staring up at Melvina as Riley herded the boys into the bathroom and got the water running.

"Don't look at me. I named you already," she said to the lemon-colored female, then looked at the dark male. "You better hope those kids are past the Sponge Bob phase, or you might end up being named after a pet snail." The small basset made a timely whimper, prompting Melvina to scoop him up. "Oh, now don't you fret, I'm sure they will give you an honorable basset name."

Riley made a batch of fresh chicken tenders and homemade French fries that Melvina had helped peel. The boys gathered around the table in their pajamas and Melvina began to worry when Lexi didn't re-surface. Eventually, she joined them for dessert.

Lexi's pale, drawn face looked like she'd cried buckets in the bath while Riley's eyes exuded both sorrow and guilt. Without waiting for an awkward silence, he cleared his throat. "Why don't you boys take your sundaes into the TV room and watch a little boob tube until bed."

The boys squealed, "Boob tube," in unison as they skedaddled with their desserts.

The chocolate brownies topped with vanilla ice cream and chocolate syrup tempted Melvina, but she'd declined a bowl. The fried food she'd indulged in was enough to put her in the doghouse with her conscience for quite a while.

What am I going to do about this sexy man who loves puppies, family and cooking?

Riley made her heart melt, her loins flame, and her willpower nonexistent. Admittedly, not the best combination for a woman who counted calories. The man was downright dangerous to her peace of mind.

Lexi was silent as she placed a few cold fries on a plate and squeezed ketchup over the top.

"I'm sorry, Lexi," Riley said softly. "I should have asked you first. Can you forgive me?"

Lexi stared at her plate for a few moments longer, then blowing out a breath, she looked up at her brother. "You were right to get the boys a dog. They've been asking forever, and I probably would have never done it on my own. It's not realistic never to get a dog again because the last one passed away. They need to learn about those kinds of things—birth, life, death, loss—because it's gonna happen…." A tear slid down her cheek. Riley reached across the table and put his hand over his sister's.

"I'm okay, really, I am. But next time, please talk to me first. I needed to be prepared." She turned her attention to Melvina. "I'm sorry for all the drama. I hope this hasn't dampened the excitement of getting your own puppy."

Melvina shook her head. "No, Lexi, I understand. I was just as surprised as you, but Humphrey could use a friend. I'd been thinking about it for a while but hadn't acted on it because of all the hours at work. I'm due some vacation time and I had thought about going to a spa, but now maybe I'll just stay home and play with Lulu." She smiled at Lexi, who nodded.

"This has been a great dinner," Melvina said. "I loved seeing the boys with their new family addition, but it's time for me to get Lulu settled. Can you drive me home, Riley?"

Riley nodded, stood and grabbed his car key from his pocket, handing it to Melvina. "I'll meet you in the car."

Melvina offered to clear the table, but Lexi wouldn't hear of it. There were murmured apologies from all parties, and the boys called out goodbye from the living room as Melvina gathered Lulu from the laundry room. She waited outside, letting Lulu tinkle and then praised her. Riley was only a few minutes behind.

They drove in silence back to her place, and Humphrey bolted out onto the porch with a long bay. Melvina felt the tension rolling off Riley in waves. He'd said very little on the drive back, and she wondered what he'd talked about with his sister after Melvina had gone outside with Lulu.

Melvina reached for the car door and looked at Riley. "Do you want to come in and see the introduction?"

He suddenly smiled and seemed like his usual self. "I wouldn't miss it for the world."

As she exited the car, Eli and Mona walked out on the porch. Mona's face was tear-stained and her drawn-on lips were smeared.

Melvina turned to Riley.

He seemed to feel her thoughts. "Maybe now's not the best time. Should I take a rain check?"

Melvina nodded and said her goodbyes to Riley, then made her way to her brother and best friend. As she approached Mona and Eli, another fresh round of wails began, and Eli took the puppy from her as she wrapped Mona in her arms. She heard Eli gushing over the puppy and Humphrey baying with excitement as she took Mona into the house.

"What happened?" Melvina waited for a response, but Mona's mouth made an O then pressed into a frown before releasing another loud wail. Melvina patted her shaking shoulders. "Is it Jorden?"

Mona nodded, wiping her nose with the paper towel that Eli handed her. "He, he—" she hiccupped her way into another crying jag.

Melvina looked at Eli, who murmured, "He went back to his ex-wife."

Melvina winced. "Oh honey, I'm so sorry. I know that must suck, but you didn't know him that long. I thought he was just a bootie call. Were you in love?"

Mona blew her nose hard, then winced at the rough paper towel. "Don't you have any Kleenex?"

"Eli, go get the box from my bathroom." She looked at her friend, taking Mona's hand that was free of paper towels. "Now tell me all about it."

"You're right, I wasn't in love with him, but he sure was a good time. I was lonely before I ran into him. We did everything together these last few weeks, and then he went to see his kids...and I knew it was all over. He hated being separated from his boys." Mona snuffled, then dried her eyes. It looked like the waterworks might be over. "What am I gonna do for fun now?"

Melvina chose her words carefully. "Mona, if you weren't in love with him, and he missed his kids, don't you think that it's really best he go back with his ex to make amends? You can hang out with me. I am your best friend."

Mona snorted. "No offense, but I can't do the things with you that I did with Jorden."

Melvina shook her head. "There are more things to life than sex, Mona."

Her lifelong friend looked at her with a deadpan expression. "Like what? I mean, it's all downhill after forty. My ovaries are drying up and I've had two hot flashes this week!"

Eli dropped the tissue box on the kitchen bar between them and headed for the TV room, his hands in the air. "I'm out of this one."

Melvina laughed. "He never could handle too much girl talk. Remember that time you got your period at that volunteer job you had, and I didn't answer the phone, so you had to call Eli to go buy tampons?"

Mona nodded, then snorted with laughter again before reaching out to Melvina. "You're right as usual. Jorden was just another notch in my bedpost, and he needs to be with his kids. Besides, if you're all hot and bothered by Riley, then I'm setting my sights on the chief. There is no way I'll let that skinny bitch, Celia, have him."

Melvina's eyes widened in surprise. "Are you teasing me, Mona? Really?"

Mona looked at her with a serious expression. "If you still want him, of course I wouldn't dare, but you look like you have your eye elsewhere. You didn't sleep with the chief, did you?" Her brows rose in question.

Melvina shook her head, baffled. "No, I didn't, but I didn't even know you liked Manny."

Mona chortled, "Hell, every woman who has a pulse in Montgomery County lusts after Manny Owens. I was just giving you the room you needed to tag and bag 'im. Now that you've moved on, I think he's fair game. At least, that's if you give me the go-ahead."

Melvina nodded. What else could she say? Mona was right. She'd had the choice to sleep with Manny and she didn't. She'd chosen Riley. Despite her long-time crush on the chief, her feelings for Riley had packed a wallop.

Now that Manny had started dating seriously, he wouldn't be on the market long, and who better to have Manny than her best friend, Mona? Melvina nodded with sincerity. "Sure, you have my blessing."

Mona's energy seemed renewed as they shared a cup of tea and played with Humphrey and Lulu. Eli made a bed on the foldout couch and they all three lay propped up on pillows watching a comedy to lighten the mood. They'd watched movies that way since grade school.

Melvina found it hard to concentrate while she picked through the events of her day and filed away her emotions.

When Mona stood after the movie, making her way to the front door, Melvina stopped her with a light touch to her shoulder. "You have my blessing, Mona, but please don't use Manny as another notch in your bedpost." She emphasized Mona's earlier expression. "Don't be afraid to give your heart this time. Manny's worth it, and he will be lucky to have all of you. You hear me? You Are Worth It!" She tugged on Mona's arm for emphasis.

"You and your motivational crap." Mona made a funny face, sticking her tongue out while tilting her head.

Melvina scowled at her playfully, balling up her fist.

Mona sobered and hugged Melvina. "Thanks for everything." With a quiet goodnight, she clattered down the wooden steps in her four-inch pink stilettoes.

"Hey Mona," Melvina called across the yard to the driveway where Mona stood by her car. "If you give him one of your pills, make sure he knows beforehand. You might give him a heart attack."

Chapter 18

Braised was packed to the gills and the woman-to-man ratio was ten to one. The preliminary contest between the Harris and Montgomery county firemen had arrived. They would choose the top twelve tonight for the calendar and the winner for the calendar cover would be selected at Bubbles the following weekend. The Hot Buns competition would take place tonight since it was the overall theme. All the firemen competing strutted around in their tightest pair of denim cut-offs.

Melvina worked her way through the crowd to the kitchen. The rolls she'd kneaded in the mixer a few hours earlier had now turned golden brown in the oven. Melvina was competitive when it came to baking. She'd be lying if she said the contest was all in fun and for a good cause. She wanted to win. Just like she'd wanted to win every other contest she'd entered before.

Riley worked on the other side of the prep area, but she felt his eyes on her as she put another baking sheet of rolls in the oven.

Smiling, he approached her with a pan of his own. His rolls had fluffed up three times the size of hers. She deflated with worry. "Wow," was all she could say.

"Nervous?" he teased.

"It's not about the size. It's the taste," she reminded him.

"Sounds like something I've heard my brother's crew swear on barbecue Sunday." He slid past her, purposely brushing his backside against her as he passed to the oven. He turned, looking over her shoulder with a brazen look, "Mind if I join mine with yours?"

Melvina rolled her eyes but couldn't help smiling at him. "It's your oven."

Riley put the rolls in and set a separate timer. He came back, putting his hands on either side of her, coming in close to brush his lips softly against hers.

"So, what will you do if you win?" he asked.

Melvina shook her head. "I can't keep the money because I'm a Blossom, so I'm supposed to pick a charity. I've already selected the library and the mentor program, though we haven't come up with an official name yet. What about you?"

Riley nodded at her charitable answer. "I'm gonna buy a new Harley."

Melvina slapped him on the side with her dishtowel. "You are not. For one, a thousand dollars wouldn't even buy you a moped, and two, you run this place, so it wouldn't look good to keep the winnings."

He laughed, standing straighter. "I guess you're right. I'm not much on old, dusty books, but my nephews really seem to like that library. Maybe I'll donate my prize money there."

Melvina nodded her approval. "That's nice of you—*if* you win."

He grabbed her to him, leaning them back against the opposite counter in the galley. "We've got twenty-five minutes. You wanna go to my office and make out?"

Melvina felt the heat of his body through the kitchen frock she wore over her nice jeans and blouse. She smiled at his devilish grin. "I don't think this is the time or the place. Though I appreciate the offer." She backed away from him, looking around the almost empty kitchen. Her eyes locked with a newcomer at the set of stainless-steel kitchen doors.

A lanky busboy pointed the chief in their direction. Manny didn't move toward them, but instead turned and followed the busboy out.

"Manny, wait," Melvina called out as she tried to catch up with him. She glanced back at Riley, who gave her a nod to go.

Clutching a swinging door with one hand, she scanned the restaurant and spied the chief headed toward the bar. When she caught up with him, he was talking to Ran. She put her hand on his forearm. "Can I talk with you for a moment?"

She could see by the look in his eyes that he didn't want to talk to her, but Manny was always a gentleman. He turned to Ran, who excused himself on a pretend errand.

"I've been meaning to talk to you for a while now, but our paths haven't crossed in a proper manner." The heat raced to her cheeks as she tried to explain her hesitation.

Manny shook his head to stop her. "Melvina, you don't have to explain to me. It's clear that you have feelings for Riley, and I'm not the kind of guy to stand in the way." His eyes crinkled at the edges as he smiled at her with kindness and what looked like regret.

Her heart lurched with sadness. She hated hurting him and knew she was letting a good man go. But, how could she be with Manny when her heart had already embraced Riley?

Her breath caught at the sudden realization.

I love Riley!

She clutched the apron just over her heart.

"Melvina, you okay?"

She stared up at the chief, losing all the words she'd wanted to say to him. "Yes—I mean no. This wasn't what I'd planned."

Manny touched her shoulder. "Life rarely ever is." His sage words were like a balm to her guilt. "It's okay, Melvina. You're a wonderful gal, and Riley is a lucky man. I hope this won't keep you from coming 'round to the station with those blessed cupcakes. After all, your friendship is something I would truly miss."

Melvina smiled. "You can always count on my cupcakes and my friendship," she said in a loyal tone. Manny's big heart and down-to-earth personality was what she loved most about him. He was offering them both a way out of any discomfort and giving her his blessing to find love. What a rare man. There was a clattering of heels on the wooden floor and both of them turned to see who was rapidly approaching the bar.

"I need a double martini with Tito's Vodka and four olives." Waiting a beat, Mona flung her hand up dramatically. "Hold on," she called out and the bartender spun on his heel. "Make it a dirty martini—really dirty," Mona drawled out as she sidled up to them on a barstool, swinging her legs around to face them. Her buoyant smile appeared as she stared at their silent greeting. "What? Did I interrupt something?"

Melvina smiled, remembering Mona's earlier proclamation. "Manny and I were just talking through the festivities for the evening and he was just saying he needed a drink." Melvina motioned to the bartender. "Buzz, get the chief a beer and put their drinks on my tab." She waved and made her way back to the kitchen, leaving Manny in Mona's capable hands. Even if Mona wasn't his type, the chief was sure to have a good time in her company tonight.

The evening was a fun-filled affair with live music and bare-chested firemen in tight denim jeans. The smell of fried food, braised meat, and fresh yeast rolls wafted through the air. It was an even pick of men for the calendar. Six hot men from Montgomery County and six from Harris.

With so much hooting and hollering, Melvina thought she might permanently lose her voice and her hearing. It warmed her to see Mona half stand on her barstool, holding onto the chief as she whistled like a sailor. The chief laughed heartily, catching her as she almost toppled off. Melvina hoped Mona would go easy on the martinis so that she wasn't a sloppy mess before the end of the night.

The baskets filled with hot rolls for the tasting were empty and the ballot boxes were taken away for the counting. Melvina felt anxious excitement when Celia took the stage, interrupting the band for the contest announcement. Melvina had successfully avoided Celia over the past few weeks, doing all their correspondences and organization for the contest through e-mail and third parties.

She didn't know what had ever become of the tax problem Celia had created for herself, but she knew that all the figures that she'd gone over with Stan were straight as an arrow, and she had copies to prove it. If Celia were having any difficulties, you couldn't tell it by her face. The woman was sporting a smile that could grace the cover of Vogue.

"I would like to again congratulate the winners of the Hot Buns Calendar Contest tonight. The Blossoms give each one of them a special thanks from everyone in the counties for their daily selfless service to the community as well as their goodwill for taking part in this event. As everyone knows, the money for this calendar will go toward building the new fire station and helping the community launch a program for children in need of strong role models. This is the time to step up and help them in their young lives. An excellent idea fostered by the chief himself."

Loud applause went up, and Manny's eyes met Melvina's, a blanched look on his face. He held up his hand in protest and opened his mouth, but Melvina shook her head and gave him a wink, silently telling him not to bother. What did it matter who'd thought of the idea? It only mattered that the community was behind helping young kids like Maurice. The applause ebbed, and someone brought a piece of paper to Celia, who cleared her throat. "The totals are in and the best buns belong to…." She waited for The Tomball Cats' drumroll. "Riley James Nash!"

A roar went up and the band started to play. Melvina's heart sank a bit with disappointment, but she clapped loudly for Riley. She'd tasted his rolls and they were amazing. She had high hopes that the crowd would like hers better, but the money was for charity, and the community benefited either way.

Riley took the stage, and Celia threw her arms around him in a tight embrace, leaving a huge lipstick stain on his cheek. Melvina didn't want to be a spoilsport, but she managed to avoid running into Celia all night and now that the contest was over, she could quietly make her way out. She had put her baking stuff in Eli's car earlier. As if on cue, her brother spotted her and headed her way.

He put his arms around her and gave her a hug. "His rolls had too much butter in them. Yours were way better."

Melvina made a snort as she laughed. "Too much butter, huh? And that's a bad thing?"

Eli stood straight, looking down at her with his warm brown eyes. "Yeah, don't listen to Honey Boo Boo, she doesn't know anything about cooking."

"*More butter, more better,*" Melvina laughed as she quoted the former child star. "Eli, you should be ashamed that you know that," she teased.

"Look who's talking," he zapped back. They both rolled with laughter. "I caught Humphrey watching it, and it was such a train wreck I couldn't look away."

Melvina jabbed him in the middle with her finger. "Don't blame your bad taste in reality TV on my dog."

"Well, you better talk to him, because I bet he has Skin-a-max on right now, teaching Lulu things that young pups shouldn't know about." Eli took a swig of his beer as Pop joined them.

Pop scratched his head and looked at them both. "Are you two bickering again?" It reminded her of when they were growing up and her dad had caught them arguing over who could use the phone. Eli had scads of girlfriends early on, and Melvina had teased him mercilessly.

"Naw, Pop. I was just trying to cheer Mel up," Eli confided.

Pop hugged her, and she hugged him back, appreciating his warmth. "They were delicious rolls. I'm proud of you no matter what."

Melvina knew his words were sincere and it brought a small tear to her eye.

Pop cleared his throat. It was hard to hear over the ruckus around the bar. "I know you want your own bakery, Mel, but Pop's wouldn't be the same

149

without you. You know the place is as much yours and Eli's as it is mine. If it's the money for the contest you're upset about, I can give you the money."

Melvina smiled at her father, who meant well. "I couldn't have kept the money anyway, Pop. I talked to Stan the other night about my investments. I was hoping to have more saved by now, but it looks like a lot of my investments tanked in the last downturn in the market. I chose riskier stocks that had potential to earn more. It looks like you're stuck with me for now."

Her father rubbed her shoulder as she heard Riley's voice chime in behind them. "Stuck where? You need a ride Melvina?"

"Congratulations, Riley." She gave him a quick hug with a pat on the shoulder. "I have all my stuff in Eli's car. I'm just going to catch a ride with him and Pop." She tried not to sound as beaten as she felt.

Why are you acting like such a frump? It's only a baking contest. Get over it, woman.

"I'd really like to take you. Give me a moment to speak to the staff, and I'll drive you home." Riley held a finger up as he backed through the crowd toward the packed bar. Melvina tried to stop him, but her voice was lost in the racket.

"Just go, Mel. I'll leave your baking pans at the café when I drop Pop off. Go have some fun and forget about the bake-off. At least you took second place to someone who obviously cares about you, rather than Celia."

At the mere mention of the name, Melvina remembered why she was ready to get out of there. With a last glance at the bar, she saw Mona wrapped in Manny's arms. The chief looked like he was holding her dear friend up on her dangerously high heels rather than a romantic embrace, but it could be the beginning of something to soothe both their hearts. Melvina followed Eli and Pop out, and waved goodbye as they drove off.

Riley joined her only moments later. "You're not sore at me, are you? "He wrapped her in his arms and brushed his lips across the top of her head. Melvina felt liquid heat race down her spine.

"I would be a pretty sore loser if I was."

Riley squeezed her to him. "Good. Because I personally thought your rolls were better."

Melvina laughed. "Yeah, Eli said that your rolls were way too buttery."

Riley pulled back enough to look down at her in mock surprise. "What?"

Melvina laughed. "I know, like there is such a thing."

Riley shrugged his shoulders. "Well, it all benefited the community either way, so it doesn't really matter does it?"

"I don't know, how would you feel if your butter rolls had taken a back seat to mine?"

Riley's mischievous grin said it all. "Enough talk about hot dinner rolls. At the risk of sounding brazen, let's go to my place so I can show you what's in my pantry."

Melvina laughed. "You already showed me what's in your pantry and I have Humphrey and Lulu to care for. I better get home."

Riley scratched his forehead with a look that said he wasn't giving up. "How about we go grab the pups and we can all bunk down at my ranch tonight?"

Melvina's eyes lit up. "Ranch? I picked you as a city boy. I was sure you lived in some fancy high-rise overlooking downtown or the Galleria."

He chuckled warmly, "I do, but I also like to get out of town every chance I get and relax. It's not too far from Magnolia. Let me take you there."

His eyes were smoky with desire and Melvina forgot her earlier disappointment and Stanley's bad financial news. Melvina nodded. "Sure. I'd like that."

Humphrey gave Melvina a forlorn look as she opened the door. He sat with his head hung low as he glanced back at the living room. The doggy gate was lying in the floor half chewed and the trash bag's contents were strewn as far as the eye could see. Riley came in behind her, resting his hands on her shoulders. "Uh-oh."

Melvina sighed, "It's okay, Humphrey. I know you didn't instigate this."

Lulu came tearing around the corner into the kitchen when she heard Melvina's voice. Her front paw was imprisoned in a mini Rice Krispies box as she jumped on Riley to say hello.

Riley laughed as he stooped to help remove the evidence. "Oh lord, Lulu, Humphrey has got to teach you how to look at least a little ashamed."

Humphrey flopped down on the scuffed wood planks of the kitchen floor and let out a deep sigh.

Riley helped pick up the trash while Melvina gathered up the few things they would need for their overnight stay. It wasn't long before they were back in Riley's car headed for his ranch. Melvina couldn't discern much about where they were in the pitch dark as they drove to get there, but as promised, it wasn't far from her home.

As they got out of the car and she clipped the leash on Lulu, Riley told her not to bother. "Cows are out to pasture and horses are in the barn. The only thing they could get into trouble with is a porcupine, and hopefully God wouldn't be that cruel to poor Humphrey tonight."

Melvina's eyes slowly adjusted to the dark and she could make out the simple ranch house that sat behind the many trees growing around the drive. Looking up at the sky, she picked out a few of the constellations she knew and was happy to see the Milky Way sparkling like gold dust in the night.

"I've never seen the Milky Way like this. It's so bright out here."

Riley held Melvina's overnight bag in one hand and Lulu's puppy bed in the other. Melvina clutched Humphrey's bed to her chest as she looked at Riley's handsome outline in the dark.

When they reached the porch, floodlights illuminated the area and Melvina could see more of her immediate surroundings. While Riley unlocked the door, Melvina reached down to pet the black and white cat she saw beneath the bush by the entrance.

"Riley, you never mentioned you like cats."

"I like all animals, but I don't have a cat." Riley paused, turning. "Wait! Melvina, don't touch that!" His words were drowned out by the dogs barking and the shock of the warm, putrid spray.

Melvina shot up from her knees to a standing position, pulling her t-shirt up to wipe her face. "Oh my God, Riley. It's a skunk!" She couldn't stop the obvious observation from parting her lips.

Riley disappeared inside and returned with a fresh towel and a bottle of water. Melvina doused her face and wiped it with the soft cotton towel. He then helped her with her things and led her inside to his bathroom. As she shut the bathroom door and began to disrobe, she heard him call out for Humphrey and Lulu. Hopefully he would find them before they tracked down the critter that sprayed her.

Melvina stood beneath the massive rain shower as six other jets streamed water all around and over her tired body. She'd hoped this would be another sexy evening with Riley so she could see if the passion they shared was the same as it had been when Mona had given her the Viagra. It wasn't likely to happen now. She probably wouldn't be able to stand to sleep with herself, let alone Riley. She heard the door latch click and Riley's warm voice. "Can I come in?"

Melvina sniffed at her hands and frowned. She could still smell the skunk on her scoured flesh and moaned with dissatisfaction. "Enter at your own risk. I don't think you'll want to be within a mile of me now. Maybe you should just drive me home when I get out of here." Melvina heard a soft popping noise and a few moments later, another and then another. She poked her head around the tile enclosure and saw industrial-sized cans of what looked like crushed tomatoes. "Riley, what in the world are you up to?"

He smiled at her as he opened the fourth can. "My brothers and I got skunked one time when we were kids and I remember my maw-maw putting us in a tub with tomato juice. I don't remember if it worked entirely, but we sure had fun and made a big mess."

Melvina looked at him doubtfully. "Riley, I don't think I want to douse myself in crushed tomatoes or whatever that is."

He gave her a wicked smile. "Oh, you're not. I am." With those last words, he shrugged out of his clothes, getting into the shower with a large can. Melvina squealed as he doused her with the first cold contents without ceremony. The freezing tomato puree poured over her body like a silken salve. The hot spray of the water made the steam smell like spaghetti and they both laughed. By the fourth can, Riley was rubbing her all over, and slipping around in the shower under the hot spray, washing the bits and pieces of tomato from her naked form.

They lathered in multiple layers of shampoo, body wash, and conditioner. Though Melvina could still smell the skunk, she was entranced by the feel of Riley's own naked body touching her everywhere beneath the warm jets. The steam button had been activated. The shower vent crackled and popped before releasing a billow of hot steam into the tiled stall. Bits of crushed tomato swirled around the large silver drain. She hoped the tomato pulp wouldn't clog Riley's plumbing.

He reached out and grabbed a couple of thick towels from a teakwood table and made a bed on the built-in shower bench that lined the long wall. He pushed Melvina back onto the towels and ran his hands through her long, wet hair. She sat in the cloud of steam facing his taut middle, silently wondering how a chef as famous as Riley could be in such great shape. She reached a finger up to run it down his abs, then looked up at his parted lips. His erection bobbed at her touch and she wanted to move her hand lower, but Riley caught her wrist and kneeled before her. Without words, he leaned into her, taking her lips in a hot kiss that left her breathless as his attention slid lower down her neck and to her breast.

Melvina could only smell the lavender shampoo they had used and the eucalyptus billowing up through the steam. Riley took one erect nipple into his mouth and suckled her as her head tilted back in ecstasy. Her hands grabbed at his shoulders and head restlessly as she felt her woman's pulse throbbing in demand. As if sensing the call of her body, his warm mouth slid down, slurping at the wet skin until he spread her legs and kissed the sensitive flesh of her thighs just above her knees. Sliding his warm tongue up to the juncture between her legs, Riley moaned with satisfaction. Melvina tried to hold back the gasp of pleasure as he lifted her hips higher to meet his hungry kiss. As his tongue delved inside her, darting in and out in a rhythm she could barely stand, she wrapped her legs around his shoulders and cried out in wild abandonment.

Sliding his body over hers, he gently cupped her breasts, kissing each nipple with tender care. Melvina pulled at his shoulders, beckoning him to enter her. She wrapped her legs around him, welcoming him when his manhood poised at the apex of her woman's entrance. Sliding his hand behind the shampoo bottle, he retrieved the small item he'd stashed without her noticing earlier. With a quick tear of the foil wrapper, he was ready. Sliding inside her with ease, he filled her with the fullness she had been craving.

He slid his erection in and out, building a pressure inside them both that ached for release. Melvina cried out first as the intensity of their dance overwhelmed her senses. Riley's tense frame followed suit as he groaned with deep satisfaction. There wasn't enough room on the bench to roll to the side, so he wedged his hip between her legs, stroking the length of her slippery wet skin. Melvina couldn't find the energy to rise in the aftermath of their lovemaking and the suddenly too-hot steam.

Staring up at the beautiful etched grey tiles that covered the walls and ceiling, she confessed, "Riley, I think I'm going to faint."

Chapter 19

Melvina had never been a small woman and even though she boasted a healthy normal weight for her five-four frame, she wasn't the kind of gal men just swung up into their arms to carry places. She tried to protest as Riley lifted her and walked to what she supposed was his bedroom.

The light gray walls, white trim and soft tan curtains reminded her of a five-star hotel room. The sleek modern bed and minimalist decor was exactly what she expected of Riley. What she didn't expect was Humphrey and Lulu in the middle of his bed, snoring belly-up like a couple of old men who'd had too much beer and were sleeping one off. Their dog beds were at the foot of Riley's bed with fresh towels folded over each. She began to apologize for the pups being on the furniture as he turned and left the master bedroom.

Riley chuckled. "I forgot I'd put them there. That's okay, we can use the guest room for now. Let them sleep."

There was a loud squeak and Riley stumbled, then chuckled as he braced himself against the wall, grasping her tighter in his arms.

"What was that?" Melvina clung to him.

"I think Humphrey brought luggage. Don't worry, it's just a toy. We're almost there."

They entered the guest room with a queen-size bed. It wasn't the opulent king that Humphrey and Lulu were sleeping on, but it was perfect for what she had in mind. As Riley lay her on the blankets, she rolled to her side, shaking her head as he grabbed for her. "Not this time. It's time for me to pleasure you."

Riley didn't try to dissuade her, but instead pulled the covers back so they both could feel the soft cotton sheets beneath them. Melvina looked at him beneath the gleaming light filtering in from the hallway. His tan skin and the crisp brown hair that covered his chest and legs had a hint of gold that highlighted his naked body. His hands were strong, and the cords in his neck flexed as she touched him.

First, she explored his torso, dipping her head to his chest, swirling her tongue around each nipple and delving lower to trail across the taut stomach she adored. His masculine need bobbed beneath the weight of her middle as she positioned herself between his thighs and let her hair cover the view of where she longed to kiss him. He sucked in air then let out a tight groan of pleasure as her hair tickled him. She grazed her lips over his hard tip, then allowed her mouth to encompass the top few inches. His moan of pleasure sent a thrill of confidence to her loins. She slid her tongue down his masculine flesh and then sucked his length in until she couldn't hold any more of him.

His breathing came in short gasps as he tried to stop her. She was curious what he would taste like past the juices of his initial excitement. A hunger grew inside her to taste all of him, but Riley quickly lifted her and pulled her beneath him. She heard the rustling of foil and then he pushed himself inside her with a strong, satisfying thrust. He built a rhythm between them that sent her spilling her own juices over his hard flesh and she wondered if she might die from the endless pulses that raptured through her. She gripped his torso and sank her teeth into his shoulder to muffle the loud moan. He groaned with her, holding her in a tight embrace. Their release was simultaneous and they both lay spent in the aftermath.

Melvina awoke to sun shining in through the large bedroom windows and Humphrey curled into her middle. She felt a definite hardness from Riley's nakedness at her back and a soft snoring of Lulu somewhere around her head. Turning slowly so as not to disturb Riley, she saw he was already awake petting Lulu with one hand as his other rested on Melvina's waist.

"You're awake," she yawned.

Riley smiled as his member flexed against her leg. "I've just been enjoying the view."

"Do you have to work today?" Melvina asked

Lord in Heaven, will I ever get used to this gorgeous man looking at me like that?

Riley's eyebrows furrowed. "No, do you? I should have asked, but with all the excitement last night...." He wiggled his eyebrows, making her giggle.

"No, I'm off today, but I thought I might drop by the café later to pick up my baking pans."

"I need to check on the foreman here at the ranch and make sure everything's runnin' smooth, but after that, I'm all yours." He ran a foot up her calf.

"If you have a ranch, why do you need to grow your herbs at Lexi's place?"

"Because I only bought this place two months back and the decorator has just finished the interior. I haven't had time to hire a landscaper, and I like to use the garden as an excuse to keep an eye on my sister and the boys. I will branch out and do some organic farming next year for the restaurant if things progress. We'll need more fresh produce anyway."

Melvina nodded and Lulu wiggled, rolling over to get Riley to rub her belly. He looked like he was wearing a basset sombrero.

Melvina laughed. "Shameless hussy."

Riley nodded. "I think I'm gonna have my hands full with you gals."

Melvina blushed, remembering her own shameless behavior the evening before. "At least I know now it wasn't all due to the Viagra."

Riley threw his head back and whooped with laughter. Melvina had been embarrassed when she confided in Riley about the Mona-Viagra mishap, but he'd found it funny and sexy. She felt his hard shaft flex again at the reminder.

"What do you say we go check out that shower again?"

Melvina still smelled the faint aroma of skunk beneath the soap they used in the shower, so she'd slathered herself in lotion afterward to cover the lingering odor. She hadn't smelled it when they'd visited the cows in the pasture or petted the horses and goats in the barn, but now in the tight space of the sporty coupe, she felt self-conscious of the odor.

As they drove down the winding backroads that eventually led them to Pop's, Melvina wondered if he could smell her too. He'd been quiet most of the drive and she was wondering what he was thinking about.

Riley turned into an open lot with a rundown house sitting in the center. It had been vacant for years and the overflow from the café often parked there. "Oh, it's the next turn in," Melvina corrected.

Riley pulled up in front of the building and put the car in park. "Oh, I think it's the right one."

Melvina was confused. She pointed next door to Pop's, but Riley shook his head. "You said you've been wanting to open your own bakery ever since I met you. I want you to come work for me, but somehow, I haven't been able to twist your arm. I heard you tell your dad last night that the money you invested hadn't done as well as you'd hoped, so I have a proposition."

Riley paused as his words sank in. Melvina's thoughts churned from no to yes and back to no again. "You turkey. You pretended you hadn't heard."

He stared out at the lot with weeds growing through the cracks. "It would have been rude to have said otherwise."

"Riley, I can't afford it. Pop tried to buy this place years ago, but the owner wouldn't sell. And even if the owner did sell, I don't have the money for the renovations." Her heart clenched with doubt, uncertainty, and then crashed to disappointment.

Riley put a finger to her lips, then slid closer to cover them with his. "One thing I got plenty of is money." Melvina started to protest, but he kissed her again. When she settled from the onslaught of his lips, he pulled away and continued.

"It's not a gift. It's an investment. You're the best baker in town, and you want a shop to call your own. I want to buy into your talent. Pop will need you to continue baking all of the items you do now for the café, or believe me, things won't continue to go so well for Pop's. If we buy the place next door, Pop can buy your baked goods, of course at a discounted family rate, and I can buy the bread I need for Braised. Throw in some of the local hotels, restaurants, and other coffee shops, and you will be booming in no time. Hell, the way I see it, you'll be able to buy me out in a year if you want to."

He paused, running a finger down her forehead to her cheek.

Melvina sniffed back tears as his kind words poured over her.

"Melvina, what's wrong? I'll help you get the place running. I've got the experience to help you."

Her lips trembled as the tears spilled over and she turned away from him.

"Melvina, look at me." He touched her chin and turned her back to face him. He gently wiped her tears with his fingers, his hands moving down to massage her shoulders. "I believe in your talent. I believe in *you*."

He believes in me….

She let out a deep, shuddery breath as his whiskey colored eyes stared into hers. Melvina studied the amber flecks that made the color so unique.

He wanted to help her and he liked her just the way she was, even if she smelled a little skunky. Everything he said held promise, but as she looked at the whole picture, she realized he would be holding all of her dreams in his hands.

It was overwhelming to put so much of her heart into one place. What if he broke it? "I don't know, Riley. I'm scared," she admitted.

"What's there to be scared of? We'll sign papers, make it legal, and for the most part, it will all be yours. You can do what you want. I'll just be around if you need help."

Melvina looked ahead. She watched as Pop came out, looking in their direction. She waved, but he squinted from the glare on the windshield. He was looking older these days. If she opened her own place and then his health should take a turn, who would run the café?

As if reading her thoughts, Riley spoke gently, "Melvina, you can't live your life wondering what if. You have a chance here to do what you want, something for yourself, and you need to think hard before you pass up this opportunity."

She nodded, still staring at the café. "I'll think about it."

Chapter 20

The Black Eyed Peas' song blared a few times before she swiped the screen to accept the video chat.

Melvina had just tied her apron around her waist. She was pressed to start the morning baking to have all the pies and cakes ready before lunch.

"What's up Mona? Pretty busy this morning." Melvina didn't like the lines she saw around her own eyes as she looked at the screen.

Mona's lips pursed in an O shape as she licked the lipstick off her teeth. "Um-um-um, girl. Do you know what Sara Lynn heard from Janie Patterson, who'd heard it from Wanda Mann at the Kroger?"

Melvina couldn't stop her eyes from rolling. Eli turned the corner with a dish tub full of glasses, almost colliding with Melvina as she made her way to the kitchen door. Several days had passed since her talk with Riley about opening her own place, and now Pop was out with a stomach virus. She was thinking hard about the offer, but the reality of *what if* was staring her right in the face.

"Mona, I hate to rush you, but people are coming in and I need to split my time between the register and the ovens today."

"This'll only take a minute," Mona whined.

Melvina tried not to blanch as she saw a naked Manny Owens coming out of Mona's bathroom and darting to the side of the screen. "So, Celia told Sara that you had actually won the Hot Buns contest, but it wouldn't be polite for one of the Blossoms to take home the trophy since Riley had been gracious enough to host the event. Can you believe it?"

Melvina wasn't sure what she was more shocked over—Manny and Mona's sex romp or Celia's latest antics to woo Riley.

Melvina wouldn't tell Riley. That would just be rude, and it didn't matter who really won anyway. They both made good rolls and the whole thing was for charity, for goodness' sake. It was Celia's meddling that always made things a sticky mess. What if word got around and he found out the truth? She supposed she would just have to take him to bed and make him forget about it. Melvina smiled at the memory of how he cheered her up after she'd lost the competition.

"Mona, please don't tell anyone else about this. I don't think the information is helpful, and it hasn't slowed down our business at the café."

Her friend nodded and winked at her. "I agree, but I just thought you should know Celia is letting the cat out of the bag. No doubt because of Riley's interest in you."

"Looks like Celia hasn't decided who she wants to play revenge with most. Me for not covering her wild shopping expenditures that she tried to write off through the Magnolia Blossoms' non-profit status with the IRS, or her failed attempt at snagging Riley." Melvina shook her head in dismay. "I guess I'll need to warn Riley before someone waylays him with Celia's story."

Mona nodded in agreement and Melvina said goodbye. She leaned against the wall for a moment's reprieve from the stress.

Eli passed by her and sniffed with exaggeration. "Do you smell that?"

"Yeah, it's your upper lip. Not funny Eli. I know the skunk odor is gone by now."

"Melvina, your entourage is here!" Roberta called out through the cook's order window. Melvina peeked through the wide slot, seeing the chief walking in the front door with Riley coming up the steps behind him.

She stepped through the swinging doors to the front counter, glaring at Roberta as she went to the register to ring up her orders. She smiled and waved at the chief as he took a seat with some of the firemen. Riley stood waiting for her to finish taking care of the checks.

When the customers had left, Riley approached with a broad smile. "I haven't heard from you since the other day. Everything okay? Don't tell me Lulu has tied you up in string and left Humphrey in the doghouse."

Melvina grabbed the coffeepot and a menu to seat the incoming guest. "You want to sit down? I'm sorry, I don't have much time to chat. Pop is out sick and Eli, Roberta, and I are swamped. I do need to talk to you, though."

Riley nodded, taking a menu from the counter next to the register. "Go ahead and do what you need to do. I'll be at the counter when you've got time."

It was another twenty minutes or more before Melvina returned. She swiped a wet towel over a blob of ketchup that had dripped off a plate and onto her apron. "I'm sorry, Riley. Today's not a good day to chat."

Riley surveyed the café, frowning. "Yeah, I see that. Let me treat you to dinner tonight. I'd love to take you out on a real date. Candlelight, champagne, maybe a little dancing?" His smile was tempting. There was nothing Melvina would like more than to see Riley tonight, but she needed to check on Pop. Eli and she would be closing the diner on their own since half of the staff was out sick as well.

"I'm sorry, I can't tonight, Riley. All I'll have the energy for when this is over is a hot bath and bed."

Riley's eyes twinkled, and Melvina could almost predict what he was about to say next, but his lips twitched and he just nodded. Pulling out his wallet, he left a twenty on the counter and stood to leave. Leaning over the counter, he brushed his lips across hers before she could move away. Melvina wasn't one for public displays of affection, and the middle of the café was about as public as it got.

She self-consciously looked around, gauging how many tongues would be wagging all over Magnolia tonight. She pressed her lips together, trying to play it casual. She would have to have a talk with Riley later and explain that he couldn't be kissing her in the middle of Pop's.

"Okay then. Call me when you're ready to have some fun." The invitation was innocent enough, but a whistle went up and a few catcalls ensued as Riley turned and exited the café. Melvina couldn't help staring at his tight jeans and broad shoulders. He was one tall order of fun and he was just waiting for her to join him. If it wasn't too late, she would call him when she got home, and she would definitely be thinking about him during her hot shower. She tried to put Riley from her thoughts and get back to work. Damn, she sure hoped Pop felt better soon.

Riley didn't seem frazzled when Melvina broke the news to him about Celia's latest gossip. In fact, he was smiling from ear to ear.

"What? What's got you smiling like you just ate the canary?" Melvina asked.

Riley bowed his head, shaking it back and forth as he made a tsking sound. "Here I was worried about you. Ran told me that Raphe told him that the chief mentioned to one of the guys that Celia was saying that you said that the contest wasn't fair. She said that you were accusing her of throwing the ballots." His eyebrows raised as he blew out a soft whistle. "Clearly Celia is crazy. I know you wouldn't do such a thing, but now tongues are wagging, and I suppose we need to do something to satisfy the masses."

Melvina felt her brows knit together with anger. "That bitch!" She couldn't stop her fist from balling. "Of all the low-down, dirty things to say. I congratulated you. Hell, I slept with you! I didn't accuse anyone of anything. It was a charitable cause for Christ's sake!"

Riley leaned an elbow on the bar. Bubbles was slow for the moment, but happy hour would pick up soon and they would be surrounded by thirsty Magnolia patrons. "I hope you're still talking about the contest," his sly grin was infectious.

Melvina couldn't help but smile as heat flushed over her body. Memories of how he had comforted her after the contest made her heat with desire.

"Screw Celia. She can go jump in the lake for all I care. I've already sent my resignation as the treasurer for the Blossoms and I am done with anything she is involved in."

Riley rested a protective hand on Melvina's hip. "Hey, Melvina, don't let her get to you and please don't let her take away something you enjoy. People love your charitable causes and kids like Maurice depend on you. How is he, by the way?"

"The chief set him up with the crew to wash trucks again today and then they were going to take him on a call to collect Miss Kitty from a tree. He seems to be doing much better with his schoolwork, and I think this mentor program will really help him until his dad comes back. *If* his dad comes back." Melvina frowned.

"There isn't enough work in Magnolia for Hispanic men who don't speak English. I think that's why Maurice's dad disappeared. If I could get more adults to come in for the language classes, it could really help some of the families. There's a ton of construction work about to be started down the exits of that new tollway."

Riley nodded. "See, that's what I'm saying. The Blossoms champion the community by developing these programs or at least putting them in front of the people who live here. That's what you're good at and you shouldn't let Celia's ill intentions ruin it for everyone."

Melvina's heart soared. It felt good to have someone support her. Even if she didn't take him up on investing in her bakery dream, she still radiated from his belief in her. She'd never had this before with any man. Mona, Eli and Pop had always cheered her on, but for once, she was hearing encouragement from another soul who got what she was all about and wanted to share the journey with her.

Riley was someone she had lain with, wrapped in cotton sheets, and shared her thoughts, hopes and dreams. He'd confided in her as well, and that only added to her feelings. She was seriously considering letting him invest in the lot next to the café.

She had Stan run a few preliminary numbers for costs. It might take five years before she could turn enough profit to be independent, but she had read that most starting businesses took the same amount of time. The question was, would Riley be around in five years to help her see it through? They weren't married. Hell, they hadn't even discussed the depth of their relationship. But they did spend almost every night together and most of their free time. That had to mean something.

Mona approached, interrupting Melvina's thoughts. "Hey, y'all. Mind if Manny and I join you?" Melvina looked around, but there wasn't any sign of the chief. As if reading her mind, Mona informed them, "He's parking the truck."

Riley stood, holding out his barstool for Mona, and she gladly hopped up, swiveling her hips where Riley had sat. Turning to Melvina, she asked, "How's Pop? Any better?"

Melvina nodded. "Yeah, he'll live. Eli's holding down the fort tonight, but I told him to close up early. Pop said he'll be coming in tomorrow, so we can both get a day off. Most of the staff is back to work and only Darcey is off sick now."

"Poor dear. Her boyfriend ain't the type to bring chicken soup. Is she okay at home alone?" Mona sounded truly concerned.

Melvina smiled. "She broke up with him. As a matter of fact, I think Riley's brother is taking her soup tonight."

Mona pursed her lips, playfully smacking Melvina on the shoulder. "Good for her! That last baboon she dated wasn't good enough to lick her red stilettoes."

The chief walked up with his natural swagger. He looked quite at home when Mona draped an arm around his waist. His larger bicep rested around her petite shoulders, dwarfing her slight frame. They looked happy and Melvina was relieved. Her time with the chief was all but forgotten.

"So, what do you think about doing a hot chili cookoff for the grand finale tomorrow night?" The chief threw them all for a loop with his sudden suggestion. The three of them looked at Manny as the chief waited for Melvina to answer.

"It's a contest to pick out the hottest of the twelve men chosen for the calendar to do the cover. I think a five-alarm chili cook off sounds perfect, but who will judge?" Melvina rolled her eyes, knowing the drama that would ensue at Bubbles a short twenty-four hours away.

The chief smiled. "Don't you worry, I fired Celia. Mona's going to do the emceeing for the evening and the boys from the firehouse that are not up for the calendar will do the judging. We will have good ol' fashion grease pens and mini eraser boards, and they will put a number on them at the time of the tasting. It will be a blind taste test, so no room for skewed votes."

Melvina smiled and all three of them nodded with approval. "I gotta ask. How did you get Celia to step down?"

Manny pressed his lips together and then blew out a loud sigh. "I told her that we would withdraw from the calendar event altogether if she didn't sit this one out. She is also going to make a formal apology to you both sometime this week if she wants to keep her position with the Magnolia Blossoms. I heard Lindsey say they're just about ready to vote her out. Word has it, you may be the new president."

"President," Melvina gasped. "I just put in my resignation as treasurer!"

"Well, I might hold off quitting. If push comes to shove, those ladies will back you over Celia any day, and you are the best person I know for the job." There was a twinkle in his eye that had nothing to do with their former attraction and everything to do with Mona's hand in his back pocket.

Melvina thought about what it would mean for the Blossoms. She did love the work at the library and all the things they did for charity, but with the café taking up her working hours and Riley taking up her free time, it didn't leave a lot left for planning a new bakery.

"I don't know, Chief. I don't think I want to be president. I just like helping out. It's been so busy lately and I can't imagine more responsibility on my plate."

The chief sighed and then squeezed her shoulder. "Mona told me about you possibly buying the land next to the café for your bakery. I think it's a great idea. Don't let this new fiasco push you into any responsibility you don't want."

Melvina smiled, nodding her thanks.

"Maybe *I'll* run for president," Mona announced.

Melvina's mouth dropped in shock. "Mona, you aren't even a Blossom."

Mona waved a hand in the air as if it were no real issue. "That's just a formality. Those ladies need a real leader."

Melvina looked at her friend skeptically, trying to discern if this was all just hot air. "And you think the person for the job is you?"

"I may not be the biggest community busy-bee in the county, but I do care about what happens around here. I think this might be good for the Blossoms and me."

Melvina could see there was more at stake here than Mona was telling. The blush in Mona's cheeks told another story. Her best friend was smitten over the fire chief and it would look good on paper to marry a charitable sort of gal. If Manny ever ran for office, Mona would do well to be immersed in bettering the community.

The chief put an arm around Mona, pulling her into his side. "I think it's a wonderful idea. You'd be great at it."

"Perfect, how about a round of drinks to celebrate?" It was a rhetorical question. Riley waved the waitress over to fill their order and it wasn't long before they were laughing and having a great time. With all the details of the chili cookoff sorted out and a new prospect for the Blossoms president, Melvina could take a breather and just enjoy the good company for the evening.

Chapter 21

What if things don't work out between us?

Taking Riley up on his offer would be easy at first, but would it be easy in the end? She pushed away her panicky feelings at the possibility that they might break up down the road. Heartbreak and business trouble at the same time? Melvina blew out a breath as she sorted out her thoughts. She'd been called in to cover for the new waitress, who hadn't shown up. The lunch rush was almost over, and Darcey was back, taking the main brunt of the work.

The bell on the door pinged as Stan walked into the café. "Good afternoon, Stan." Melvina waved him over to her booth in the corner. She'd arranged to meet with Stan again to review some of the figures before her meeting at the bank. She hadn't made a decision yet, but part of making that decision was knowing what she could afford and how much of a loan she could get. She would see what the bank had to offer before making any decisions about Riley.

She had a busy day ahead of her—in addition to meeting with Stan and heading to the bank—she had plans to pop into the library and check on the progress of the registration for the next class.

If she launched her own bakery, she might not have as much time to teach the classes in the evening as she used to, at least, not starting out.

Her brain hurt from all the *what ifs*. Sometimes the decision-making process was worse than the actual ramifications of the decision.

Melvina had been sorting the morning checks and adding totals for the shift. She moved some of the paperwork aside to make room for Stan to sit. She motioned to Darcey to bring coffee for her guest.

"Hello, Melvina. I've got the papers from your taxes, and it looks like you will have a bit of those risky stocks to cash in if you need a down payment. All totaling about twenty thousand. I hope that helps."

Melvina sighed. "I had hoped to put down more, but it is what it is."

Sticking a pen behind her ear, she stood, excusing herself for a moment. She returned with a full glass of diet soda, an energy bar for her, and one of the morning's cinnamon rolls for Stan.

Stan wore a broad smile. "Thank you. I skipped breakfast this morning, knowing I would be visiting you today. I didn't want to ruin my appetite for whatever you might have. I see you are still dieting?"

Melvina nodded as she unwrapped the bar.

"It's gotta be tough working here, with the way you bake and all." Stan moaned with pleasure as he took his first bite of the roll. Sugar-rich icing dripped off one side of his mustache.

"It is, but I have to stay on top of things. I don't want to let myself go again. It's not about trying to be what society tells women we're supposed to look like. It's about feeling better than I have in a long time. I have more energy and my doctor tells me my bloodwork is perfect. I would like to dodge things like diabetes and heart disease if I can."

"Well, good for you. You're a strong gal, Melvina, and the best damn baker around. I personally hope that you get that loan. I'll never stop coming to Pop's, but you bet your bottom dollar that I'll be a regular patron at your new place as well." He took another bite, followed by another moan and then a napkin wipe.

Melvina smiled with pride. "Thanks, Stan. I appreciate the vote of confidence. By the way, how did things turn out for the Blossom tax situation?"

Stan raised his eyebrows and shook his head in exasperation. "That Celia almost got the Blossoms in a mess of trouble. There were so many receipts, it was hard to tell which were her own financial responsibility and which were purchases for the Blossoms' operating costs. In the end, the IRS slapped us both with a fine. We had to settle or things would have gotten messy. They should have gone after Celia, but I think even the IRS is scared of her, or maybe her daddy stepped in to minimize the damage. Rumor has it the Blossoms will be voting her out on grounds of mismanagement of funds."

Melvina frowned. "I'm sorry about this whole mess, Stan."

He patted her hand. "It's all water under the bridge now. No need to rehash it."

"I guess the Blossoms will vote me out too, since I was the treasurer. But I had no idea she was altering the tax forms after I turned them in to her."

"It's all right, everyone knows you were on the up-and-up. I was able to verify that the forms had been amended *after* my filing. Ultimately, it was my responsibility because I'm the accountant for the Blossoms. If I had known what she was doing, I would have reported her myself." Stan's voice rose with indignation.

Melvina patted his hand. "Well, it's over now. The chief has removed her from emceeing the pageant tonight, and the whole town is talking about the shenanigans she started with the last contest. I think Celia's britches have grown too big for this small town, but maybe she's learned a lesson. Anyway, I already put in my resignation for the treasury position, so it doesn't really matter."

"Sorry to hear it, Melvina. The ladies won't be happy."

Melvina gathered the papers Stan had brought her and cleared the table of the tickets she had finished. "I guess I better go see what the bank has to say about the loan and then I need to get ready for tonight. Thanks for your help, Stan."

Stan tipped his imaginary hat, "Any time, Melvina."

The library parking lot was mostly empty. Melvina supposed most of Magnolia would be at Bubbles for the final contest tonight. She should be home getting ready herself. Her pot of chili had been slow cooking at the café all morning and she needed to swing back and pick it up before heading to the lounge.

Melvina took a few minutes to chat with the librarian about the last fundraiser, and how Riley had generously donated to the literacy program on her behalf.

"I don't know what we would do without your help, Melvina. The class is on an overflow list, and we are trying to find another volunteer. Five adult students from the last class have found work, and I think they have told their friends. Now it's brimming with immigrants who need to learn English fast to get jobs."

It was a familiar story—one she'd heard before—and it pleased her that the little class had helped both young and adult students. Unfortunately, the library needed more help than she would be able to give. Maybe she needed to campaign with the school for some after-hour space and recruit a few local teachers. She would bring it up at the next Blossom meeting. It was just another reminder of how much the women's organization helped Magnolia's families. She knew she couldn't give up that part of her life.

The community she lived in included everyone, and raising awareness as well as funds to tackle those obstacles was as important as breathing. Melvina wanted their town to grow and all the families who lived in it to prosper. She signed the papers for the class and looked over the names of the prospective students. She recognized the name Jose Salas and wondered if there was any relationship to Maurice's family. Since his father had left, maybe there was an extended family member who traveled in to help the young mother. She sure could use the help. Maurice and his little sister were good kids, but Melvina wondered how the Spanish-speaking woman managed to pay the rent and keep food on the table.

As she headed for her car, Melvina heard a familiar voice behind her. She turned just in time to catch Maurice in a hug before he toppled them both over with his excitement.

"He's back! He's back!" Maurice exclaimed.

"Slow down, Maurice. Who's back? What's all the excitement for?" Melvina caught the shy gaze of a Hispanic man standing in the distance. He barely looked twenty with his tight cotton t-shirt, pressed jeans and Nike shoes. He was handsome and bore a striking resemblance to Maurice. An uncle perhaps?

"Miss Melvina, that's my dad," Maurice gushed with pride.

Melvina was surprised. The man looked barely out of high school and Maurice was half-grown. "That's...." Melvina paused, looking from the boy to his father. "That's great."

"He came home to sign up for your class. He wants to learn English."

Melvina smiled. "Wonderful. I'm so excited for you both. How's your mom?"

Maurice didn't miss a beat. "She's so happy. We all are. We're going to be a family again, and when dad learns to speak English, like me, he will get the best job ever and we'll be rich."

Melvina chuckled at his exuberance. "I hope so, but first things first." She waved to the man, who still stood a few car lengths away, waiting for his boy. "Tell your dad I'll see him in class. I gotta run. Chili cookoff's tonight." She squeezed Maurice's shoulder before ducking into her car. The sound of the sports car engine revving was music to her ears. The guys at the shop had the Mustang running like a top. It seemed there was plenty of good news for today. Now it was time to win that cookoff.

Melvina was glad the finals for the calendar contest were being held at Bubbles. It had become her favorite watering hole. Celia was nowhere in sight, a welcome relief that put Melvina more at ease. The hot pots of chili were being set out on the tables with the grease pens and eraser boards as the chief had promised. Mona had volunteered to emcee. The flare of the orange and pink sequins she wore sparkled like a live flame as Mona twirled across the makeshift stage announcing the selected firemen.

Happiness washed over Melvina in a great wave of relief. Mona looked fabulous and the chief's beaming smile boasted pride in the woman he'd arrived with. There very well could be wedding bells in Mona's future. Melvina hadn't seen Mona this keyed up over a guy since Bran Wilson in high school, and that had only lasted a week. Mona and the chief were becoming an item, and Melvina was truly ecstatic for both of her friends. They deserved to find love.

Two strong masculine hands snaked around her waist, and she wasn't surprised to be pulled back into Riley's hard body. His warm breath on her ear made her knees weak. "Penny for your thoughts."

Melvina turned in his arms, snaking her own around his trim middle. "Oh, they're worth a lot more than a penny, Riley James Nash."

His mouth opened in mock surprise. "I love it when you use my full name. Turns me on." He growled softly. "I think I got enough to pay. 'Fess up."

Melvina laughed, batting him on the chest playfully. "Shameless. Don't you know that the best things in life are free, or that money can't buy every-thing? I really need to have a sit-down with your momma." Her eyes sparkled with her teasing words.

"Don't bring my momma into this. It's not her fault that I've fallen for the most beautiful gal in town or that you keep me in bed most of my free hours in the day. Come to think about it, my momma may just want to give you a dressing down. She's still upset we missed the last family dinner."

"That's not fair. I had to work that night, and I missed it because of *your* dressing down."

Riley kissed her softly, stealing any other words of complaint from her. "Now about those thoughts."

Melvina opened her eyes slowly, half hypnotized from his sultry gaze. Her voice was husky as her words slowly dripped from her cherry painted lips. "I was thinking of how you were going to feel when you lose tonight, and if I could console your wounded pride the way you massaged mine."

Riley groaned. "Oh God, Melvina. You make me want to lose in the worst way."

Melvina's pulse raced as she envisioned what they would be doing later that night. Her head turned as Mona's voice boomed across the speakers and the microphone squealed in protest. She was calling them to the center table where the chili was set up and ready to be tasted. Spinning her around, Riley gave her a sexy smack on her backside and urged her forward. "May the best chef win."

Mona called names from randomly selected tickets in a bowl. People congregated around the table and each were given two small bowls of chili and a grease pen with an eraser board. Mona made a show of talking to each judge and getting their responses over the mic. Obviously, she'd seen too many episodes of *Dancing with the Stars*. Melvina almost expected a commercial break in-between and was not surprised when Mona asked the finalists of the calendar contest to do another walk-through to get the audience riled up for the cookoff finale. Cheers from both men and women went up as the hometown firemen passed through. The women put in the extra efforts to catcall, clap, and make high-pitched wolf-whistles.

Riley's brother hit the catwalk with dance moves from a male review. He set the bar high for the men who followed. Mona dubbed him Five Alarm, followed by Pants on Fire, Pole Slider and Engine Revver. One heavyset fireman wearing nothing but his skivvies and a pair of suspenders was dubbed Fastest In and Out. The chief took over the microphone before Mona could explain why to the ladies.

Shrugging her shoulders, Mona followed the firemen until they lined up on the other side of the chili table. Taking center stage, she raised one arm motioning to the chief to bring back the microphone with the other. She held the mic to her mouth and in a sultry, very Mona-like way, she called out to the judges. "Okay, let's see those chili scores!"

The crowd hooted and hollered. The judges turned over the dry-erase boards and the totals were nearly the same. Only one judge had used decimal points, giving one of the bowls a nine point five and the other a ten. One of the bowls had won by a half a point. The name would be revealed by lifting the bowl and looking on the bottom for hers or Riley's initials. Mona walked over to the bowl with the perfect ten and lifted it skyward to see. The chief hurried behind her to steady the bowl so that Mona didn't add chili to her flame-colored ensemble.

"And the winner is MB, Melvina Banks!" Mona set the bowl down with a thump, sloshing the chili over the rim of the bowl and onto the judge that had favored Melvina's chili. "Woo-hoo!" Mona called out, piercing the room with her cheer. Melvina hopped up and down as she turned around to hug Riley with delight. His lighthearted laugh and heartfelt squeeze told her that he didn't mind the loss. The consolation prize would give them both a night to remember.

Mona handed Melvina a large, golden trophy that boasted a bowl and a spoon on top. It read, "Magnolia's finest bowl of chili, first prize."

Riley laughed. "What's second prize?"

The chief took the microphone from Mona as she leaned over to embrace Melvina, trophy and all. "Second place gets the back page of the calendar, of course, and a free copy once it's published." The chief winked at Riley with a light chuckle.

"Hey, I think this is rigged. That sounds like something for the first-place winner, not the second." Laughter rumbled through the audience.

"I think the ladies of Magnolia will be more inclined to buy the calendar if you're on it. It's a win-win. Great advertising for Braised and the fire department."

Melvina smiled at him with mischief. "You can't argue with that kind of publicity, besides, my chili won by half a point because I used the brisket from your restaurant."

Riley looked at her, beaming with pride. "You did?"

"It's the best brisket anywhere to be found and my recipe calls for the best."

He handed the trophy to the nearest fireman and scooped her up in his arms, spinning her around. "You're the best, Melvina. Best thing that ever happened to me." Setting her down, he got down on one knee and pulled a small box from his pocket. The crowd immediately hushed.

Melvina covered her mouth with both hands. "Oh my God, Riley. What are you doing?" She guessed she could throw that talk about public displays of affection out the window.

Was he really going to propose? Here? Now? Over chili?

He gazed up at her, his eyes reflecting all the love that filled her own heart. "Melvina Banks, I know we've only known each other a short time, but I've never met a woman like you. I want to spend every day of my life cooking great food with you, laughing with you and loving you." Riley flipped the ring box open with a snap. The overhead stage lights caught the facets of the perfect, emerald-cut diamond. "Melvina, will you be my wife and make me the happiest man in the world?"

The wave of emotion hit her full-force, stopping any word she was about to utter. In fear of bursting into tears from immense happiness, her hand clutched at her throat as she choked back the emotions threatening to spill over in front of the massive crowd.

"Say yes!" she felt Mona smack her in the rear with her evening bag. Looking up, she saw Pop and Eli give her the thumbs up.

Riley shifted in discomfort from the hardwood floor beneath his knee.

Melvina finally found her voice. "Yes. It would make me the happiest woman in the world."

Riley stood and kissed her, pulling her against him. His body vibrated with emotion. She snuggled even closer to him, but something hard jabbed her in the chest.

Melvina leaned back, pointing at the lump in his shirt pocket. "Ouch, what's that?"

Riley pulled out another box and offered it to her. "It's also for you. Consider it a wedding present."

Melvina looked at him with elated surprise. "Don't you think the ring was enough?" She lifted her hand, wiggling her fingers. The light danced across the diamond in its platinum setting. "Riley, all I really want is you."

He smiled as he placed the box on her palm and folded her fingers over it, giving her hand a warm squeeze. "I think you might like this gift just as much."

Melvina opened the box with care, looking at the papers rolled up inside with confusion. Before she could ask, Riley supplied, "It's the deed to the lot next to Pop's. It's yours to do whatever you want with. If you want your own bakery, Melvina, it's yours. If you want to stay at Pop's and use it as a parking lot, it doesn't matter. Whatever you want to do, I'll be there to help. It's yours—I'm yours."

"But the bank gave me the loan."

"Give it back. Once we're married, you won't need to worry about finances or anything else, sweetheart. Everything I have is yours. I want us to be a team. I want to wake up knowing that every day of my life will be filled with loving you. 'Til death do us part."

Epilogue

Two years later

The café was buzzing with patrons, and there wasn't an empty seat anywhere to be found. Hiring the extra help had been the best idea Melvina had ever had. With the passing of time, Melvina had trained Maurice's mom, Maria, to bake, and his dad, Jose, to help run the front end of the store.

Jose was working the register while Maria ran food for Roberta and Darcey. Maurice's mom was taking the second language class at the high school at nights and helping out on the morning shifts. It wouldn't make them rich like Maurice had hoped for his family, but Melvina could see the many changes that benefited them. The Salas' now had a chance to make a better future for themselves.

Melvina passed by the newly remodeled office and spotted Pop with a cup of coffee and his feet on the desk. They may have remodeled the old café and expanded by adding the bakeshop inside, but some things would never change.

"Melvina, you're needed at the bakery counter," Roberta called through the cook's slot.

Melvina hurried out front to find Riley leaning over the baked goods glass. One section was full of cinnamon rolls, bear claws, and every kind of cake and pie imaginable. The other side was filled entirely with cupcakes.

Even though Pop's Café had been renamed The Cupcake Diner and Dive, it still had the flavor of Pop's homestyle food, but with a wide array of Melvina's baked goods. The idea to use the extra land and double the restaurant space to add an in-house bakery had been Riley's idea. When he'd proposed, he put the image into Melvina's mind, and she'd been thrilled with the vision. She realized she could have her dream without leaving Pop's

Pop, Eli and Riley were all family now, and a good family stayed together.

The remodeled café had quickly turned into a gold mine, which meant putting off their honeymoon. A minor disappointment, as they were well on their way to building their dreams together and there was nothing to stand in their way.

Now that a year had passed since their wedding and the grand opening of their joint restaurant, they were finally leaving for that much-needed honeymoon. Which brought her mind back to the beautiful specimen of a man staring back at her from across the bake counter.

"Mrs. Nash, are you going to let your entrusted family and employees take over, or am I going to have to hop over this counter and carry you out of here?"

Melvina's eyes sparkled as she leaned over to kiss him. "They're *our* employees, remember? You helped build this place."

"It was my wedding gift to you," he reminded her. "I'm just here to support you along the way, as promised. Besides, I've got my own employee issues at Braised, but I think my manager has it under control until we get back." He took her hand and looked down at the ring he'd given her the night of the chili cookoff. "Now, how about that honeymoon?"

"You mean you taking me away to an island to lie in the sand with you, drink fruity cocktails on the beach and have unmentionable sex in a super air-conditioned plush hotel room with no one around to bother us?"

"That's exactly what I'm talking about!" His white teeth flashed as he bit his bottom lip with anticipation.

She grew serious for a moment as her eyes roved over his masculine frame, handsome face and dark tinted sunglasses. She couldn't believe they'd met just over two years ago, and now they lived on a beautiful ranch with Humphrey, Lulu and Leo. She had fulfilled all of her dreams. She had her cupcake bakery and the best man she could have ever wished for.

"Penny for your thoughts?"

Melvina remembered Riley saying that the night he proposed. She smiled lovingly at him and put a hand to his cheek. "I was just thinking that you're the best thing that ever happened to me, Riley James Nash. Now kiss me and take me to paradise."

Five Alarm Kisses

Hot in Magnolia Book 2

SNEAK PEEK

Chapter 1

Raphe Nash squatted on the pavement and patted the lemon-colored Basset hound. Lulu gave him a doe-eyed look of innocence. "Your momma says I'm supposed to ask the new librarian to the fireman's ball. See, I don't know if that's a good idea, since she's probably not gonna be my type, and we'll probably not have anything to talk about, but let's face it, if I don't man up and take one for the Nash family team, my brother is gonna kick my ass."

Lulu stared at him with her big brown eyes and barked.

"Yeah, that's what I thought. But, since he's on his belated honeymoon with your momma, I can't argue with him. So here goes nothing." Raphe pushed open the library door and waltzed in with Lulu trotting by his side. Her bluebonnet colored bikini bottoms had white polka dots and a cute ruffle around the top like a tutu. He didn't believe in dressing dogs in costumes, but after Lulu stained the comforter on his bed, he understood why his sister-in-law, Melvina, had left a stack of dog diapers.

Raphe strolled up to the information desk and said hello to a stern-faced heavy-set woman with Coke-bottle eyeglasses sorting books on a trolley. "Um," Raphe stalled in asking his question, but finally asked, "Bonnie Bush?"

The grim woman looked up at him with narrowed eyes. "Whom should I say is calling?"

Relief poured over Raphe. At least this battle-axe wasn't Bonnie. "Raphe Nash, I'm Melvina Nash's brother in-law."

The information desk lady's terse harrumph followed her to the back of the library.

Raphe wanted to bolt. "Does she look pissed to you?" He murmured to a whining Lulu. As if agreeing, the hound flopped down. A moment later the librarian returned with a much younger and slimmer version of herself with matching horn-rimmed glasses.

Simultaneously, both women's jaws dropped, the younger one covered her mouth to suppress a gasp. The older lady cried out in horror and pointed at the dog.

Raphe looked down just as Lulu was making a massive puddle around her not-so-absorbent diaper. "Dang, Lulu!" He stepped sideways to prevent the river from touching his new boots. Thank goodness the library had upgraded from real wood flooring to tile. Raphe bent down and scooped Lulu up in mid-stream, carrying her out the front door as he threw an apology over his shoulder.

"No animals allowed in the library young man," the info desk lady shouted after him, "unless they are trained service dogs!"

Raphe sat Lulu down on a patch of grass near the flagpole so she could finish her business. He straightened and glanced down at the dribble decorating his new shirt.

Pulling the wet material away from his chest, he frowned. "Great, just great."

Lulu let out a whine of apology, or maybe she just wanted that silly polka dot bottom taken off. Leaning down he pulled the Velcro and tossed the outfit with its soaked pad in the nearest trash can. Melvina could fuss all she wanted later, but there was no way he was putting that soiled diaper in his new truck.

Raphe had moved to Magnolia six months ago. He was familiar with the small, bustling town, since his big brother Riley married the cupcake queen, Melvina Banks, and settled there officially last year.

Raphe had never dreamed of moving away from Houston, but recent events made him re-assess his life's purpose. Right now, that purpose was to find unsoiled clothes and maybe grab some grub at The Cupcake Diner and Dive. Even with the owners—Melvina and Riley—out of town, the coffee should still be good. Besides, Maria Salas, the new cook, had been trained by the best—the best being Melvina—so the pancakes were probably as heavenly as usual.

Raphe left his truck in the library's visitor parking area and decided to walk to the firehouse just down the road. He was new to town, but he wasn't new to fire stations. Raphe had been a firefighter all his adult years. And he'd recently started a new job at Magnolia's local firehouse. He was immediately greeted by Mona Calhoun, Melvina's best friend, scurrying out the front door while she pulled at the hem of her black mini-skirt.

She whistled at him. "Hey, sexy. Are you and Lulu trollin' for trouble?"

"Naw, we already did that. Got kicked out of the library." He pointed at his shirt and down at Lulu who was regarding them with a floppy-eared tilt of her head.

Mona chuckled. "I'm sure Manny has an extra t-shirt somewhere, though you may want to give him a minute to put his shirt back on before knocking on his office door."

Raphe took in Mona's rumpled chestnut colored hair and smeared pink lipstick and grinned. Was that a pair of underwear hanging out of the side pocket of her purse? "Okay then. Will do." He glanced at the bay doors, noticing they were all open and the trucks were gone. "Where is everybody? Did half of Magnolia catch on fire?"

"Miss Kitty drill," Mona threw out as she opened her car door. Her skirt hiked up as she slipped into the sporty coupe.

Raphe cleared his throat and looked away. Mona was an attractive woman, but not his type and clearly hooked up with the chief, Manny Owens.

Revving the engine, she backed up too quick and slammed the breaks. The window of the Lexus glided down. "Are you taking Bonnie Bush to the ball?" She called out loud enough for the whole town to hear.

Raphe shrugged his shoulders, trying not to grimace. "I tried to ask her, but that's when Lulu got us kicked out."

Mona laughed, throwing her head back as she pushed the gas. "Better luck next time."

Raphe shook his head, looking down at Lulu. "If there *is* a next time. Bonnie throwing us out of the library is a solid *no* if you ask me."

Lulu gave him a droopy-eyed look and whined.

"All right, Lulu girl, let's go find me a clean shirt."

He would put Lulu in the locker room where she would be safe until the men came back. Most of the station was tile, but Mona had hired a swanky interior designer to do up the chief's office and Raphe didn't want to take a chance of Lulu soiling any of the fancy furniture. Melvina said the dog was potty trained, but clearly Raphe hadn't figured out Lulu's signals.

Raphe grabbed a cup of coffee in the break room while Lulu checked out Jake's bed. Jake wasn't a typical firehouse dog—he was a rescue from one of the fires the men put out several years back. His blocky head said Labrador parents, but his red coloring was all Coon dog. There must have been something else in the mix, because of his shorter height. Unlike most larger breeds, Jake was only about fifty pounds. All the firehouse dogs before him had been purebred Dalmatians, but times were changing, and the community liked that Jake was a rescue amongst rescuers. No one knew his age, but Raphe supposed he was getting up in years now. The older dog still went on a few runs, like the Miss Kitty drill, but he usually moseyed around the station when the real calls came in.

Lulu scratched at the plaid pillow with its matching tartan blanket. After a few moments of doing a rendition of the moonwalk, she made a small huff and nuzzled her nose between her front paws.

Raphe grinned. "Lulu you are some kinda cute." Truth be told, he hadn't wanted to dog-sit. He'd missed two chances at a weekend getaway. Roxanne, one of the gals he was on and off with, had invited him to her Biloxi beach condo. Then, some of the guys from his old firehouse had flown to Vegas.

He could use a little R&R right now. He didn't want to admit to himself how the massive five-alarm fire a few months ago in Houston still haunted him, but then moving to Magnolia was an admission in and of itself.

His move to the small town had surprised everyone back in Houston, even though he'd come up with good reasons. He told his old firehouse that he needed to help his big brother, Riley, manage the ranch and he needed to be closer to home for his sister, Lexi, and her boys. But deep in his heart lay the truth. He'd saved a woman and her three kids from their flame engulfed high-rise apartment. When he went back inside to collect their new puppy, a huge metal beam gave way and pinned him to the floor. His men dragged him and the puppy out just in time, before the top five floors of the building were completely ablaze. When he came to his senses thirty-minutes later, he realized he'd come close to dying. He loved his job and especially saving lives, but as he thought about being trapped inside that fiery building, he admitted dead was dead. He couldn't get the *what if* out of his head. Afterward Raphe worried his work anxiety might get the best of him and get someone killed.

Lulu whimpered and he drained the last of his coffee. "I'm goin', I'm goin'. You wait here and don't leave any presents for the boys. Jake will be back soon, so I need to get you outta here." He rose and made his way to find the chief. Plenty of time had passed since Mona had left. Manny surely had reorganized his office and his clothes. Raphe knocked on the door and waited for an invitation to enter.

"Come in," the chief bellowed.

"Hey, Chief."

The chief cleared his voice, looking a little caught out. "Hey there, Raphe."

184

Maybe Raphe hadn't given him quite enough time. That Mona was one sassy firecracker—perfect for mild-mannered Manny. Chief Owens was respected by everyone in Magnolia, but he wasn't exactly a player. Mona had definitely added some much-needed sizzle to his life. Raphe didn't like barging in to ask for favors on his day off. He probably should have driven home. "Sorry to bother you, Chief, but I'm lookin' for a t-shirt." Raphe pointed to Lulu's dribble and the chief raised an eyebrow in question. "I'm watching Melvina and Riley's dog, Lulu, while they're on their honeymoon."

"I thought Eli was Melvina's backup. He takes those dogs everywhere." The chief stood and rifled through a large closet by his desk.

"Lulu's in heat and Humphrey's got it bad. Melvina means to fix the poor girl, but the timing's just been off. She's gonna do it when she gets back."

"Timing is everything isn't it?" The chief nodded.

Two years ago, Manny had his eye on Melvina, but she fell head over heels for Riley. But time can change anything. Now, Manny was hot and heavy with Mona. "This should do ya." The chief tossed a Hot Buns t-shirt to Raphe, who couldn't help but chuckle. He'd been in the Hot Buns calendar contest two years ago and had even graced the calendar. They dubbed him Five-Alarm for his fancy dance moves.

Melvina and Riley, both amazing cooks, had gone toe to toe in a bake-off to see who could bake the best dinner rolls in the county. Riley had won by a smidge, but then Melvina took home the best five-alarm chili prize. They were both equally good in the kitchen as far as Raphe was concerned, and he didn't care who won what as long as they both still fed him when he went to the diner. His stomach rumbled at the thought. That's exactly where he needed to be.

"Thanks, Chief." He gave a small salute and turned to leave. He heard the rumble of the fire engines as the guys rolled into the station from their weekly Miss Kitty Rescue. The loud ruckus of the returning men and the new recruits made Raphe smile. He jaw-jacked with a few of the men and then said his good-byes. Halfway across the parking lot he remembered Lulu and did an about face, almost running to the break room.

"Lulu!" He called out, but he was greeted with only blank faces. "Have you seen Lulu, Melvina's Basset Hound?"

The men shook their heads, looking around the breakroom.

Raphe's pulse leapt. "Jake? Where's Jake!" He rushed into the locker room, but there weren't any canine shenanigans going on in there. "Lulu? Come here honey. I got a treat," he called out in desperation.

185

One of the new recruits snapped a towel at him. "Did you lose your girlfriend, Five-Alarm?"

Raphe pressed his lips together, recalling the words that threatened to tumble out. It may be bad timing, but the kid was just joking. He called out for Lulu as he searched every corner of the firehouse. He went full circle to the chief's office, but the chief wasn't there. However, Lulu and Jake were.

"Lord have mercy, Lulu." *Melvina's gonna kill me.*

Raphe ordered a coffee and deposited Lulu in Pop's office at The Cupcake Diner and Dive, deciding not to mention the firehouse incident to Melvina's dad. Sitting at the counter, he took a sip of his coffee and sighed. It was cold. "Why me?" He ran a hand through his tousled hair.

A waitress came to refill his cup with one hand on her hip. "What's wrong? You don't like?" Her accent gave away her Latin American heritage, but that was nothing new to the area and especially at the café. Melvina taught English as a second language at the library in her free time and two of her students worked at the café. This gal was new, and if he wasn't so depressed over how his day was going, he might have appreciated the fact that she was the best eye candy he'd ever seen in Magnolia.

He'd dated one of Melvina's waitresses before and it hadn't worked out. When they broke up, Melvina lost a waitress and he lost the right to date the diner's staff. It became a strict family rule. If Raphe dated an employee, he couldn't step foot in the diner. He was a single bachelor who hadn't a clue how to cook, and he knew which side his bread was buttered on. Besides, this was Texas. As far as Raphe was concerned, the state offered a smorgasbord of beautiful women. His eyes roamed over her dark hair, thick eyelashes, and body to die for. The beautiful lady was just another punch to his gut for the day.

Oh, man. Hands off for you buddy.

He looked at his coffee. "Ah, it's cold." He lifted his cup to her.

The pretty waitress huffed. "Well, *cabron*, if you drink when I pour…." She filled a new cup and sat it in front of him before she spun around on her pretty petite-sneakered feet. Raphe couldn't help but follow her curve-hugging jeans with his gaze as she sashayed away.

Lord help me. What did I promise Melvina? Surely Riley would take pity on me. That woman should be in the movies.

She reminded him of a young Salma Hayek. Raphe had a weakness for beautiful women and he certainly had dated his share, but lately, the revolving door routine was getting old. He'd turned Roxanne Remington down for the weekend and Gail Hartley the weekend before. He had no regrets, except for the Lulu fiasco at the fire station. He surely regretted that, and Melvina was going to be none too happy when she found out about it. How many days did a dog pregnancy last? Maybe he could move to Tahiti or somewhere before then. Maybe the hook-up hadn't taken. He was sure that not every mating session ended up with puppies. Maybe Jake was too old and was shooting blanks? Raphe could only hope, but it seemed rude to wish impotence on an old feller like Jake, not to mention bad karma for his own mojo.

The beautiful waitress bent over, searching under the counter between cups, lids and straws. Her derriere swayed as she reshuffled the arrangement. Raphe took a gulp of his coffee and yelped.

She swung around, staring at him in alarm.

Raphe choked a bit, while grasping a napkin to wipe the spill from his t-shirt. "Damn."

"It's not *bueno*?"

Raphe tried not to look at her cleavage as she stretched both arms out on the counter, leaned toward him and gave him a challenging stare. He coughed a little and tried to look in her eyes. That was a mistake. They were sherry brown with glints of amber flashing in the center. The woman was blazing hot and had a fiery temper.

"The coffee was too hot." Too late, he realized he should have explained that he wasn't paying attention and scalded his tongue, but now the waitress was about to throw a tizzy.

"It's too cold. It's too hot. Okay, Goldilocks, you want some cream to cool it off so it can be *just* right?" She slammed down a silver carafe—it tilted precariously on its side, wiggled, and then settled into place.

Raphe's jaw dropped. Was this little spitfire mocking him? Raphe Nash, firefighter, community fundraiser, family supporter, hard worker, champion to all women, children and pets of any kind. "Look here, Miss ah…?"

"Salas." She put a hand on her hip that jutted out to one side. Her head was tilted at a challenging angle and she smiled as if she'd enjoy tearing his napkin into pieces.

"Okay, Miss Salas. I wasn't complaining about the coffee. I just drank it too fast. My mind was…" He touched a finger to his head and then let it go skyward. He decided then it was time to go home. He'd get some chips and beer from Wag-A-Bag and call it a day. Standing up, he put a twenty on the counter and turned to leave. He heard the lady speaking in rapid Spanish through the cook's window. A few moments later he felt a hand on his shoulder as he reached the door. Maybe his luck was changing. Imagining the sexy waitress, he turned around with a wide grin. Maria's worried face greeted him.

"Mr. Nash, is everything ok? Please take back your money. Nina doesn't deserve it. She's a terrible waitress, but Roberta called in sick and I didn't know who else to call. Please don't complain to Melvina. She deserves to enjoy her honeymoon. I'll make Nina apologize. She'll do better. I promise." Maria's English was slow and carefully enunciated, but much better than when she'd first started at the café. The job had been a great help for her language-building and for her family.

Raphe assured Maria he wouldn't say anything to Melvina or Riley.

"Nina Salas." She didn't look like Maria past the long dark hair and tan complexion, but the last name was the same. "She's your sister?"

"Jose's third cousin." The look Maria gave him said it all. She wasn't overly fond of her husband's cousin, and apparently, Nina wasn't fond of helping at the café.

He nodded with understanding then squeezed Maria's shoulder. "Keep the tip Maria. Your secret's safe with me."

End of Sneak Peek

Like what you've read so far? You can buy *Five Alarm Kisses* on Amazon. Or visit minettelauren.com to find out more.

About the Author

As soon as Minette was old enough to write, she composed a play in one act called *The Love of Seth and Beth* inspired by the movie, *Gone with the Wind*. Undeterred by the play's questionable success, she's been in love with writing ever since. Growing up in a small town outside of New Orleans, Louisiana, has fueled a lot of Minette's creative endeavors. She travels often and takes advantage of anyplace with a view that inspires her to write. Minette now resides in Texas, where she loves to write outdoors by her pool, with her five furry writing muses. Besides her menagerie of tail-wagging pooches, she also has a loving husband, three turtles and a Macaw to keep her company. Together, they make all of her dreams come true.

Sign up for Minette Lauren's newsletter on her website: minettelauren. com. Follow Minette on Amazon, BookBub, and Goodreads. You can email Minette at info@minettelauren.com.

Made in the USA
Coppell, TX
02 December 2019